A Summer in Limousin

Patrick R. Faure

PublishAmerica
Baltimore

© 2007 by Patrick R. Faure.
All rights reserved. No part of this book may be reproduced, stored in a retrieval system or transmitted in any form or by any means without the prior written permission of the publishers, except by a reviewer who may quote brief passages in a review to be printed in a newspaper, magazine or journal.

First printing

At the specific preference of the author, PublishAmerica allowed this work to remain exactly as the author intended, verbatim, without editorial input.

ISBN: 1-4241-7143-1
PUBLISHED BY PUBLISHAMERICA, LLLP
www.publishamerica.com
Baltimore

Printed in the United States of America

*To Le Père Marzet
and Torpille*

INTRODUCTION

I decided to write this book so that I could share my experience of spending my summers in Limousin as I was growing up. Limousin is a not so well-known province of France, and is sometimes seen as a backwards and non-progressive place. Yet, in all my sojourns there, I only got to meet decent hard-working people. I wanted to preserve the memory of so many of these people who were anything but kind to me over these few summers months from 1959 until 1967 when I was part of their life and they accepted me as a surrogate member of their families. In this short time I spent with them, I discovered a new world so completely different from the one I knew in my native Monaco, that it opened my mind, modeled who I became, and made me an overall much better person.

It also allowed me to form a lifelong friendship with an amazing person, a man the rich people in Monaco would simply have dismissed as a poor peasant unworthy of consideration. He was a humble man whose values and humanity would always guide my life. This simple man, Robert Marzet, known as the Père Marzet, was a veteran of World War One, a man who had served France during four years of carnage, a man who had killed enemy soldiers, and then had gone back home, to mind his own business, his farm and his animals, and raise a family. This is a man the Delphi Oracle would certainly have labeled as the wisest man in Limousin, as she had with Socrates in Greece. It is he who taught me how to take care of cattle, how and where to collect mushrooms, how to plan and grow a garden, how to hunt, how to remain true to myself at all times, and most importantly how to be a decent human being.

All of the anecdotes, events, and tragedies related in the book actually took place, and all of the people and places exist or have existed. Some names have been changed, and some locations modified both intentionally and unintentionally, and some events may not necessarily be in the correct chronologic order. This is unimportant. The book reflects how my Limousin family lived when I first met them in 1959, and how hard life was for them, compared to what I knew in Monaco. None of the facts about cooking on the fireplace, doing the laundry, or caring for animals were altered for the purpose of making more interesting reading, and I relate these as I remember them from memory or long ago discussions, with the help of too few photographs.

You will find that there are many characters in this book, and that's because I had a big family in Limousin. You will also find that my parents have a very minor role in this part of my life. This is because as soon as the sun rose, I was out of the house, and I did not come back until dinner. Thus I had very little to do with my parents during the days I spent in Limousin.

Finally, I could not introduce this book without talking about Aline Lemaunier who was my companion for so many years and whose life was cut short so tragically.

Fairport, NY

October 5, 2006

http://www.asummerinlimousin.com/

CHAPTER 1
I Learn About Limousin

Limousin. The first time I heard this word, I must have been about six, which would have made it 1959. Although I cannot recall the exact date, I remember the exact context of the event. I was playing with cars and trucks on the living-room tile floor, trying to solve a serious traffic jam situation created by a flipped over dump truck on the narrower tiles running around the room, when I heard my father trying to convince my mother that they should buy a car. In this manner, "we could all go on holiday in Limousin." Upon hearing these words, my interest in taking the truck driver to the hospital with my army ambulance suddenly vanished. I stopped worrying about towing the dump truck to the nearest garage, and listened more intently to the conversation. At that time we lived in Monaco and my universe was limited to the big city of Nice, about twelve miles away to the West, and to the French city of Menton and its sister city of Ventimiglia in Italy to the East. I had no more concept of what Limousin was than I had of Saskatchewan (I did not learn until I was fourteen years old that Saskatchewan was actually a place in Canada, and not an invented word to use as tongue twister for French speakers). In any case, this Limousin thing seemed to be somewhat nonsense. Here we were, a family of three, my mother, my father and myself, living in a perfect world in Monaco, a place people paid thousands of dollars to come on vacation to, and my father was talking about leaving, and going on holiday to some Limousin place.

Limousin is indeed a place, a place most Americans, like me on that fateful 1959 day, don't even know exist. And they are in good company.

Microsoft Word does not know it exists still today: as soon as I typed it on my computer, it insisted I had made a mistake, and corrected it to limousine, which of course has nothing to do with a place since it is a car named after Limousin, and is now simply referred to as a limo. In the United States, the most likely people to know about Limousin are farmers since the cattle from Limousin, known as Limousin cows, is widely raised on American farms. But I know from experience that although they may know the cows, they also have no idea where or what Limousin is. And contrarily to me in 1959, they plain don't care. In my first experience with the word, I could only assume that it was some type of very fancy place, because my mother answered to my father that going there would be "very expensive". Again, I wondered how it could be. I lived in Monaco, the land of Rolls-Royces, Ferraris and Mercedes, and my mother was saying that Limousin was even more expensive? It could not possibly be.

Well, that day, on top of learning a new word, I also learned that we had family there, and a house. My universe was at once shattered. It was as if the Big Bang, which did not exist then, had just taken place in my small head. Here we were in Monaco, living in an apartment, and we had a house in this fancy Limousin! How could it be? And a family as well? I could not understand how it was possible. I only had one family outside of my parents. It consisted of my maternal grandparents, my aunt, my grandmother's two brothers, my great-grandfather, and that was it! And, now at the ripe old age of six, I suddenly discovered that I had another family! I could not get an explanation from my parents, as they were intent on sorting out this car thing. And by the way, what was this story about a car? Did I hear right, that my father wanted to buy a car? Well, this would have been a front page story, had it not been for the Limousin issue. My personal internal editor had put this Limousin story on the front page. Forget about the car.

Well, not exactly. At that time, in France, there were six manufacturers: Peugeot, Citroën, Renault, Panhard, and Simca. I was wondering whether we would get a fancy Peugeot 203, like our friends the Deschamps or a beautiful Citroën Traction Avant, or whether we could even get a Panhard like my uncle Adrien. That was "a freaking car" as he often said. As I listened further, I was hoping to hear these magical words, Peugeot, or Citroën. But it seemed that besides completely ruling out the

Panhard, my father had already decided that Renault would be the car he would buy. I was not exactly pleased with this decision—I loved the pointy hood of the Peugeot 203, and even had a Peugeot 203 police car, which had been on the way to the accident scene—but could not voice my opinion, as the debate between my father and my mother entered this phase of intense discussion, that I knew I would be best advised not to interrupt. On top of this, I had much higher priorities to handle, like finding out about Limousin.

It turned out that Limousin is a province of France. If you want to get there from Paris, it is very easy—getting anywhere in France from Paris is always very easy. At that time, 1959, you would simply take the second most famous road in France, Nationale 20, simply known as N20, and you would drive about six hours in the a southwesterly direction, toward Bordeaux, and bingo, you would be in Limoges (that's another city Microsoft Word has never heard of), the capital of Limousin, and you would be there. The thing that is interesting about Limousin is that it is still today a very remote place. In the past, it was used by the French government to exile its dissidents, somewhat in the same manner the Russians use Siberia. There is a French word "limoger" that has its roots in the city of Limoges, and means to exile, to remove from favor. Needless to say, I did not know that in 1959, when I thought that Limousin had to be a fancier place than even Monaco. We had a house there, a family, and my father was ready to buy a car to go there! It must be a sight!

What I also did not know about Limousin is that people don't necessarily speak French there. You see, Limousin is technically in Southern France (although the climate would clearly indicate it belongs to Northern France), and people there speak a dialect of what is known as the Langue d'Oc. Langue d'Oc is the language of Southern France, and is much closer to Latin and Spanish than French. Langue d'Oc is a bona fide romance language that the successive kings and presidents of France have been trying to eradicate since the fourteenth century. They haven't been very successful at it, since when I arrived in Limousin in 1959, my "other" family still spoke the Langue d'Oc fluently and preferred its use to that of French—and almost fifty years later, they still speak it. In any case, I soon learned that Limousin was not even the correct name of my future vacation home, and that the right way to write it and say was "Lemosin".

This was getting even stranger as I decided to go upstairs to my grandmother's apartment, which was directly above ours, and seek an explanation about Limousin and the strange things I had heard.

Mémé Lainey as I called her was the nicest person I ever met in my life. She had patience beyond belief, and she spoke so softly that I never heard her once raise her voice at anyone. She always had Alsacienne brand madeleines ready for me, and made tea in which she poured evaporated milk, which I loved so much, but was a big no-no in my house (my father did not like its taste). Her apartment was always absolutely spotless and she and I spoke in a different language. I did not realize until I was older, at least eight, that she and I had been speaking Italian all of these years. I knew we spoke a secret language between the two of us, that neither my parents, nor my aunt, or even less my grandfather could understand, but I had not realized it was Italian, until one day, after my father got the car, when we went to Italy, and he was stopped for speeding by the Polizia Stradale. Unable to understand what the officer was saying, he turned to me to translate. That day three things happened: first, the officer was so impressed by my Italian, and so bemused that my father could not speak it and had to rely on me, that he did not give my father a ticket; second, I realized that my grandmother's and my secret language were spoken by fifty million people besides the two of us; and third, I found out what being an interpreter was all about, and beginning that day my mother decided that it would be the career I should pursue.

Well, coming back to the topic of Limousin, I was absolutely amazed, but my grandmother did not know anything about it either. She could only tell me that it was next to Auvergne (another French province Microsoft people have never heard of), where there were volcanoes. This did not sit well with me. Not only was I no more informed about Limousin than when I had gone upstairs to my grandmother's but she had added another unknown element: the volcanoes. And when she described them, she did so using terms that could only trigger the most anxiety laden nightmares. Exploding mountains spewing fire and molten rock that destroyed entire towns, and buried people alive! Forget Limousin, this volcano thing is front page news. I immediately felt the urge to figure out whether, one there were volcanoes in Monaco, and two if the volcanoes of Auvergne, like long-range ballistic missiles, could reach Monaco and burry it under their unbelievable destructive powers. Was Monaco at risk? How did we escape? This was now a lot more urgent than finding out about Limousin. My life was at stake! And at a crucial moment in my short life, my grandmother was failing to provide correct up-to-date information!

Fortunately, my aunt was home. Tata Dédée as I called her was still in high school, and she came to the rescue. She was well informed about volcanoes. The volcanoes of Auvergne were extinct. That had to mean something good—I had no idea what extinct meant. And they could not have reached Monaco because they were so far away. That was even better news. But that also meant that Limousin which was far away, and worse, right next to Auvergne, was probably within volcanic range! And my father wanted to take me and my mother there? I had to delay these questions to a later conversation, because the only thing I cared about was the imminent destruction of Monaco by a volcano. And no, my grandmother said, there were no volcanoes in Monaco. Unfortunately, my aunt wanting to show how much she was learning in school, vehemently disagreed, and before my grandmother could stop her, she uttered these horrific words "there is a volcano at the Pointe des Douaniers". I knew too damn well where the Pointe des Douaniers was. My grandfather and I sometimes walked there from the house! Although it took us the better part of an hour and a half to get there, I knew it wasn't that far, and this stupid volcano was there, waiting to lay ruin to the city, and even kill me. Thirty minutes earlier I had been concerned about Limousin, and now, I was literally fighting for my life. And from the look on my grandmother's face, seeing how upset she was, it had to be true: I and everyone I loved were in constant danger of perishing in an eruption. We'd better move out.

The Pointe des Douaniers is indeed the remnants of a volcano whose crater is about two miles off-shore, under the Mediterranean Sea. In fact, the entire rock promontory, we know as Pointe des Douaniers, is the result of the catastrophic eruption of an unnamed underwater volcano. Such revelations could only create more panic in my world. Especially when I found out, again through the help of Tata Dédée, that there was a volcano named Vesuvius that was the closest danger to us, and it had erupted fifteen years earlier. I was doomed. For sure, I would die in one these eruptions. By this time, after all of these revelations, I could not even focus on Limousin any longer: I had to warn my parents, and possibly save their lives from the crutches of the Pointe des Douaniers volcano. It was only the tea and the Alsacienne madeleines that my grandmother had prepared that prevented me from rushing back downstairs. Food has a way to temper my sense of panic. If my grandmother thought there was time to have tea and madeleines, certainly this was not as big an emergency as I first thought. The key word I had missed in my aunt's explanation was "that the volcano had erupted twohundred million years ago". Of course I knew what a million was back then. A million francs were needed to buy a Rolls-Royce. This is how I measured millions. And I knew how to count—I had been in school at the Sisters of Saint-Maur for over two years, and I knew how to count and how to read. So, I figured that I would need enough millions to buy two hundred Rolls-Royces before this volcano could erupt again, and since nobody had enough money to buy two hundred Rolls-Royces, the volcano could not possibly erupt again. Which brought me back to cars. Which brought me back to Renault. Which brought me back to informing my grandmother that "my father is going to buy a Renault". Oops!

I should not have said that. My grandmother reacted with more alarm to this piece of news, which by now was a single column three liner in my internal newspaper, than I had to the news of the impeding destruction of Monaco by the Pointe des Douaniers volcano. The only thing I remember her doing was her exclaiming with a sound of complete despair "non è possibile!" (it is not possible) as she let herself drop on the chair behind her. Whoa! That was powerful news. Maybe, it should go back to the front page. No. Limousin and the volcanoes were definitely more important. A car was fun. I used to go to the Monaco Grand-Prix, and watch the cars race around the track, in the streets we used every day: Cooper, Maserati, and Ferrari! That was exciting. And some of my friends' parents had cars—I had ridden in them, and when the cars were parked, my friends and would get in them and we would take turns pretending to drive, and that was really fun. We would make engine noises, including the revving of the engine as we changed gears, swear at imaginary drivers who cut us off, and argue about when to use the blinker or not. And one day we broke the blinker hand, the one that used to stick out of the car rather than lighting a lamp, on my friend René's father's Peugeot 203, and boy were we in trouble! We tried to fix it with Scotch tape we stole from his mother's kitchen, but it did not work. I could not go back to his house for a full month as a punishment. And he could not ride in his father's car for a full month as well. I certainly did not consider a car as a major source of concern, and could not comprehend how my grandmother could be so upset about it, and summarily disregard the danger of real life volcanoes.

This is when my grandfather got home. It must have been between four and five in the afternoon. My grandfather was a police officer in Monaco, and he kept schedules that were incomprehensible to me. In any case, before he had finished kissing me, and before I could ask him about Limousin, my grandmother had already told him that my father had ordered a car. His words were to the point: "he has gone mad". At that time, my grandfather Lainey (who was my mother's father) and my father were not exactly in the best of terms. This went back to the previous summer events, when we had had guests at our house. I was not exactly sure who everybody there had been. I knew only that my other grandfather, Léon, and my other grandmother, Louise, who had come from Paris, were having lunch with us. Anyway, we were at the dinner table with a whole bunch of other people (I found out since, they were my grandmother Louise's brothers Pierre and his wife, and Adrien and his companion), and the conversation grew more and more animated. For what reason? I have no idea, and I did not care. I had a much more important task I was focusing on, which was to test drive the Maserati Formula 1 miniature car which my grandfather had given me before lunch. This car was the sure way that would allow me to beat my father in the car races we conducted every evening around the apartment. He always picked the Ferrari, and I could not ever beat him. My grandfather Léon had assured me that this car would do the trick, and I was impatient to verify his affirmations.

Suddenly, the conversation went from animated to furious, to angry, to vociferation, to the point when my mother sent me to my room so that I would not be exposed to the violence of the exchange, but more importantly to the expletives being thrown about the room. One of the last clear sentences I heard was my grandmother's brother Adrien, who was about six feet and two hundred fifty pounds tell my grandfather Léon "I am going to kick your ass!" I quickly figured that this would be pretty ugly, since my grandfather was about ten years older, about five feet seven, and must have weighed hundred and fifty pounds. As if this peaceful family dinner did not have enough excitement, while my mother was taking me to my room—and I was rather disappointed because I had now become clearly more interested in the potential spectacle of a pugilistic event than in testing my new Maserati—my grandfather Lainey suddenly showed up at the apartment door, in full police uniform, followed by a French policeman. Because my grandfather was a Monaco police officer and our apartment was in France, he had no jurisdiction, and he had fetched a neighbor who was a French police officer to assist him in pacifying the Faure family Sunday lunch. My mother suddenly shifted from taking care of me to opening the door to the dining room. Things got very ugly from that point on. Hiding behind our dining-room heavy buffet so that I could be protected from eventual projectiles—I had experience from other such dinners—I watched as my uncle Adrien decided that he would rather kick a policeman's ass than my grandfather Léon's. He rushed forward as the French cop pleaded for him to stop, as he was in no way of a size or physical form to stop Adrien. Adrien bulldozed into him like nothing I had ever seen, knocking out a chair and rushing forward like a Dallas Cowboys linebacker. Today, I can only compare it to the determination of the bulls in Professional Riding Bull events, when the bull charges into the horse and rider trying to subdue him. In any event the cop went flying, and was laid out cold, after which Adrien turned to his girlfriend and gallantly took her hand to get out of there. That was a mistake since it gave my grandfather the time to quickly handcuff him from behind, an action that did not subdue the fighting Adrien who turned around and charged again, only to be tripped by my grandfather. He fell forward, hitting his head on the corner of the dining-room table and opening a gash on his forehead, while stumbling over a couple of chairs, including the one he had previously knocked over, smashing it into a useless pile of splintered wood in the process. This is when my father tried to intervene, thereby interfering in police operations, and experienced the threat of arrest yelled out by the French police officer who, while still dazed, had recovered enough to fulfill his duties. That stopped him dead in his tracks. The whole sorry disaster ended up with the participants leaving as well as they could, my uncle Adrien being arrested and taken to the hospital for the customary stitches and my grandmother Louise telling my mother that her father was nothing but a bully who had spoiled a fine Sunday dinner. "After all we were only having a family discussion", she added.

My grandfather, the same one who had brutalized my uncle Adrien, was now on his way downstairs to explain to my father that he should not purchase a car, which according to my grandmother Lainey he had already ordered, but which my father was in fact trying to convince my mother they should buy. And I was the one who had told of the car to my grandmother! I enjoyed the tea and madeleines nevertheless still wondering about how I could find out about Limousin.

CHAPTER 2
The Renault Dauphine

The car was eventually ordered and delivered by the Renault dealer. It was a light blue Dauphine Renault. Now, there have been poor designs in cars over the years, but the Renault Dauphine must have been one of the worst designs ever made. Basically, the car was a Volkswagen Beatle with four doors, except it did not have the shape of the Beatle. It was all curves in the sense it did not have a single square line in it. The engine was in the rear of the car. For me, sentenced to years of back seat riding, this was a torment, since I was privileged to hear the noise of the engine first hand, and a blessing, since I could always pretend not to hear what my parents were telling me from the front seat. The car also had the trunk in the front. It was a big trunk, which gave it the less than enviable quality of having no weight on the front wheels, which in turn gave it a distinct instability, no protection in case of a head-on collision, and improved aquaplaning qualities in case of rain. It was a car that I had not even judged worthy of adding to my car collection: who would want a Renault Dauphine? When my father had first talked about Renault, I thought he intended to buy a Quatre Chevaux, the official French carbon copy of the Beatle. This at least was respectable. I had even gotten one as a reward for being so brave during my last diphtheria vaccine shot. But a Dauphine? It was supposed to take me where? To Limousin? No way!

As if the car had a mind-reading capability, it seemed to know I did not like it. And from the first day on, we never really got along. The day my father got it, he decided he would drive to the Beausoleil market. Despite my disdain for the Renault Dauphine, I still was excited to ride in the car, and I agreed to accompany my father to the market. The market was a magical place. Food would appear there on fantastic displays in the middle of the street four times a week, and be gone by two in the afternoon. At that time in my life, I still had a challenge understanding where vegetables came from since in Monaco there were no farmers and the farmers I had visited between Ventimiglia and Nice only grew flowers. When I went with my grandmother Lainey, every day the market was open, we would not talk about where food came from. We did not have time. My grandmother knew everyone in town, and we spent the entire trip either avoiding such and such, so we would not be delayed, or hiding from a specific merchant so that he would not be upset at seeing us buying oranges someplace else, or trying to find a way to cut down on gossip time. My grandmother and I used to strategize. If she gave me the signal while she was talking with someone, I had to squeeze my legs and pretend great discomfort, as someone ready to pee in his pants. This allowed my grandmother to say "Oh, I am sorry, I have to go. My grandson needs to go to the bathroom", and turning to me, she would say in a reprimanding tone "I told you to go before we left the house, but you never listen!" In return for my acting, my grandmother would then stop at the boulangerie and get me one of the Fougasses Monégasques, the ones with the pine nuts, and the red and white sugar grains, which I liked so much. Sometimes, we would stop at the candy store, and she would get me some of the sugar candies, the ones that are either blue and white or red and white, and as she shopped, I would play with them, making the blue, white and red of the French flag in the palm of my hand with them.

As is clearly obvious, we did not have time to talk about where food came from. With my father, it was a completely different story. Especially now that the Dauphine had opened the road to Limousin. According to my father, every food item came from there, and if it did not come from there, it was better there than any place else. I came to see Limousin as this huge farm where all of the food in the world was made, and I kept wondering how I had been able to survive before I had known about Limousin. And I also could not reconcile how a place that was more expensive than Monaco could have so many farms. I had been to the carnation farm above Monaco, and I knew that it was not a clean place, and that before the flowers filled the air with their perfume the farmer had to use cow poop on the fields to make sure the flowers would grow. How could a place full of cow poop be better than Monaco? And my father constantly showed me how the food from Italy was not as good as the food produced in France. If it was spring, the Italians only had yellow peaches, which were not as good as the white ones produced in France; if it was summer, the tomatoes in Italy did not have enough water and tasted too "tomaty"; if it was fall, the Italian grapes had a tough skin that was impossible to swallow, not like the French Chasselas grapes; and if it was winter, the Italian chestnuts were full of worms, not like the ones from Limousin. One day, later in the year, we had received chestnuts from Limousin. My father told me it was from his aunt who was part of his family in Limousin. He had given me the honor of opening the parcel which had arrived via the French mail. I untied the coarse string around the package, ripped the brown paper apart, to the horror of my mother who stated she could have used it later, and opened the box. My father was pretty upset when I told him the Italian chestnuts were better than the Limousin ones. The box of Limousin chestnuts was filled with a mixture of multiple species of fungi. Worms were crawling all over the chestnuts and the entire package could only be thrown out. My father immediately blamed the French postal service, which was responsible for the spoilage. If we had been in Limousin now, my father would have shown me how much better those chestnuts were.

Anyway, that day as we were making our way back home, we put our purchases in the trunk and sat in the car. I was in the front passenger seat, next to my father. Cars in these days did not have seat belts. And my father in these days was not exactly Mario Andretti, since he had received his driving license the day after the car had showed up (I found out since then that car dealers usually don't deliver the car to their customers, unless of course, their customers don't have their license). And now, on this beautiful Saturday morning, at around eleven, he was blocked in his parking spot by two cars, which had arrived while we were shopping. Unlike my father, I was very experienced in the maneuvers required to get out of tight parallel parking spots. I practiced them everyday with my cars either on the kitchen floor or on the living-room floor. It required patience, and as I had seen on the streets of Monaco, no hesitation to bump both the car in front and the car in back. I especially like the big Chrysler to do it with, since it would easily push the more puny French cars. As I was giving these highly technical explanations to my father, who told be to keep my mouth shut while he was getting used to the grinding of the reverse gear, he popped the clutch too hard into first gear, causing the car to lunge forward, hit the car in front of us, stall, and causing me to very unexpectedly fly forward and smash my face into the glove compartment which was made of steel. Thank you Renault! My upper lip was split, and blood starting pouring onto the glove compartment, the new floor mats, and my clothes, while I started screaming, my father swearing and telling me to take a handkerchief from my pocket to stop the bleeding. That's when the owner of the smashed car in front of us showed up.

Frankly, I could not understand how my father could have smashed two cars, my face, and be concerned about me dropping blood on the floor mats. To make matters worse, he started yelling at me for distracting him during the maneuver. I could not answer because I was too busy crying, feeling pain, and more interestingly watching the owner of the other car inspect the damage. While I finally extricated myself out of the car, the owner of the other car started the proceedings by telling my father he was an idiot, not for smashing his car, but for letting a child ride in the front seat and smashing his face into the windshield. I can still hear the man responding to my father's "mind your own f...ing business", with a "one has to be a real cretin to drive like a moron and almost kill his own son, and I'll mind your business if I want to!" By this time, a crowd had assembled around the car and the event, since this promised to be quite interesting. Not surprisingly, nobody cared that I was literally bleeding to death, and not surprisingly as well, a policeman appeared out of thin air. And while my father was trying to regain a semblance of dignity, to make matters really worse, who should show up but my grandfather Lainey in his Monaco police officer uniform? Unbeknownst to me at the time, my grandfather had actually helped my father acquire the Dauphine, by advancing the money to pay for it. So, technically the car was not my father's but my grandfather's. Upon seeing his investment's front end turned into an accordion, my face bleeding, the other car damaged, a French cop, and the owner of the other car ready to assault my father, my grandfather only had four words "what a freaking idiot". Of course, the owner of the other car, not knowing the family relationship, promptly reassured my grandfather that he was correct in his judgment, and had just shared the same idea with my father a few moments before. To which my grandfather quickly responded "you shut up, or I'll get you arrested for illegally parking your car". Indeed, the force of the impact had pushed the right-front wheel of the other car onto the sidewalk, a clearly illegal parking practice. The outcome was much less in my father's favor however, because he had to pay for his car's repairs, the repairs to the other car, and had to wait almost three weeks before the Dauphine was fixed. I would never be allowed to ride in the front again, and I really did not like the Dauphine at all.

The Dauphine was the first car any member of the Faure family ever owned, and it was an object of wonder, as family members subsequently assumed that my father made a lot of money. It was a means to increase the radius of our activities, and we were now able to go to the mountains above Monaco during the weekend. This is when this stupid car really got back at me for not liking it that much. It took advantage of its hard back seats, noisy engine, and limited visibility, and striking a deal with my father's constant smoking, this car regularly made me sick during our weekend trips. After about twenty hairpin turns in the mountains over Monaco, I would get nauseated. Regardless whether I ate, did not eat, looked at a fixed point on the horizon, thought of something else, closed my eyes, or did none of the above, it was automatic. I would ask my father to stop the car, I would run out, and barf my head out. There was no cure for this. And it angered my father to no end that every time we went out I was sick. My dislike for this car increased even more the day my mother caught my finger in the door as I was climbing in the back seat, and she slammed the door shut without looking. This car was a destructive machine that had claimed my upper lip, two of my right hand fingers, and made me sick on every single trip. And I was supposed to travel to Limousin in it? I did not believe this to be possible. When I shared with my father that he should switch to a Peugeot, as I had never been sick in our friends' Peugeot, he did not think I was serious. And the Peugeot had never hurt me. My father did not listen to me, and over the years he has owned many Renault cars: Renault 12, Renault 16, Renault Safrane, and he has now purchased yet another new Renault. Of course, he gloats about Renault winning the Formula One championship.

So it is that I never really solved the mystery of how food appeared on the market, and why it was better in Limousin than in Monaco. The fundamental problem here was that my father is not from Monaco. He was born in Paris. As a Parisian, it is his right and his duty, to be condescending to the people from any other city, region, or place in France, especially if they are from the South, which Monaco happens to be. But born a Parisian, my father has to contend with the fact that his family came from Limousin since, like everybody living in Paris, he is not really from Paris, but rather from someplace else in France, where his family made such meager living that they had no choice but to move out and join the crowd of people seeking a better life in Paris. You see, Parisians are bipolar creatures. They have to love Paris beyond reason, criticize anything not Parisian, and at the same time they must deal with the fact that they are from somewhere else. What made my father's case worse is that during the war, he went and lived in Limousin, and went to school there, establishing further roots that no Parisian really wants to claim. What made my father suddenly love Limousin better than Paris was and remains a mystery to me. My father never spoke of his years in Paris, but always told stories about Limousin. For me, it was a lot simpler, I was born and raised in Monaco, and nothing really existed beyond the realm of the Principality. But with my father's driving improving on a daily basis, the unavoidable fact that sooner or later I would be deported to French Siberia became a nightmare. I would have to spend summer away from Monaco. This was indeed the work of a mad man.

CHAPTER 3
The Trip to Limousin

Little by little, I received education about Limousin. My father explained that driving there would take two days. This was due to the fact that every road in France leads to Paris. If you try to not go to Paris, then, you have to find your own way on a mixture of second rate Nationales and barely maintained Départementales roads, the latter being no more than two lanes with minimal traffic signage. There were no big Nationales like N20 to go from Monaco to Limousin. There was no famous N7, the Nationale to the South that was then the main road linking Paris to Marseille and the summer vacation beaches of the French Riviera. Instead, like a military campaign commander, my father poured over tens of regional maps of France, figuring out the shortest way to the fabled destination of Card. You will not find Card (pronounced like car, and not like card) on any map of France. It is way too small to even get an italic name. Therefore, my father was planning the best way to reach Ambazac, the closest village to the house we owned in Limousin. He had to avoid as many as possible of the notorious "points noirs", a French euphemism for deathtrap used to designate flawed intersections where people died needlessly because of poor road engineering. And we had to avoid the traffic congestion of the big cities. And find good places to eat, and a good hotel to stay in, because there was no way we could drive there without overnighting. I started being taken by the excitement, even as my grandfather warned my father about the dangers of such a trip.

It was as if we were embarking on a crusade, with enemy cars waiting at every corner to attack and smash into us, and truck drivers drunk from too much wine during lunch who would surely squish us between their trucks like flies, and other drivers who had too many cognacs after lunch and would sway into our lane for a head-on. I grew more scared with every danger my grandfather uncovered. I felt like we were allied aviators flying on a bombing mission over Germany in World War II with little chance of coming back from the quasi-suicidal trip. Obviously every French driver was determined to keep us from arriving and finally seeing Limousin. My grandfather knew best, since he was a policeman. The truth is that French roads in 1959 were in dismal shape, with no safety measures such as guard rails, and the macabre and famous French plane trees bordering every road never swerved for cars, and always won the confrontation between them and the car occupants. There were no speed limits, no seatbelts, and Belgian drivers did not even need a license to drive. As far as alcohol was concerned, there were no rules that prevented you from drinking an entire bottle of wine, jump in your car and drive. And then there were the fences running along the railroads in a futile attempt to separate roads and railroads. They were made of steel, and their top bar was right at neck level when you sat as a passenger in a car. Hadn't this lady just died when her husband had rammed the car into the side of the road, and the railroad fence had perforated her neck, cutting the carotid artery, and causing her to bleed to death?

Yes, this trip was going to be worse than any war. During this time my father had established a precise itinerary, as if he were to drive across the Sahara, with each road listed, each city and the time at which we should get there, the places where he was going to fill up, those where we would eat, and the place where we would sleep. That was great planning, the likes of which I had never seen. It would have made a German army general proud. And it really worked well. For about the first seven miles of the trip. On the day we left, July 1, 1959, at eight in the morning, we took the direction of Nice, and that was no big deal. We had been there tens of times. My father had taken the middle road to get there, rather than the lower one by the sea, which was so much nicer. We knew there were massive road works going on to make the road safer. As we approached the construction site, there was a long line of cars, not usually a good sign, and traffic was stopped. I could have told my father from my experience with dump trucks that they overturn easily, and that they were unlikely to use the road by the sea. He would not have listened. Actually, my father never listened. Well, he wished he had when we got there, and there had been an accident at the work site, as the suspension of an overloaded truck failed while it was turning, flipping it on the side, and spilling tons of rocks on the road. After waiting almost half an hour, my father turned around, and went to Nice via the road by the sea. The schedule was off already, and nobody dared say anything in the car, as we got to Nice almost an hour behind schedule.

The day before we left, we had had a big dinner at my grandparents. We would be gone for a full month, and I had never been away from Monaco or from them for more than a day. This was like a ceremonial dinner to wish good luck to the soldiers going to war, straight out of a Gounod opera. The atmosphere was solemn, full of recommendations about what to do and what not to do, about the dangers of the road—my grandfather warned that a loaded car would not accelerate as fast as an empty car. That was not news to me since I had never really noticed any acceleration in that car. Not like the cars racing in the streets of Monaco during the Grand Prix. We were stuck with a dog of car that would have even less acceleration on this critical trip. This new worry and the excitement of the trip made it hard to sleep that night. I wished my father had a real car, a Maserati. That was a car worth going to Limousin in. And it was blood red. A machine made for racing. Which brought me back to my own Maserati. My grandfather Léon was no expert in cars. The car he had given me was no Ferrari beater, and I barely could keep it on the road. I had not won a single race against my father, and I was now using it more as an obstacle to block the road for my father when we raced. I was mostly concerned with which ones of my cars I should take to this fabulous Limousin. Upon my father's recommendation I took a couple of Berliet dump trucks and an army Jeep which he said would do well there. Apparently Limousin was not designed for Grand Prix racing.

Our first day of travel was indeed exciting. About a hundred miles into our trip, my father decided that the left-rear wheel did not sound like it should, and required an immediate pit stop. He pulled off to the side of the road, looked at the wheel, and crawled under the car—now this was serious. I had seen the race car mechanics crawl under the cars in Monaco, and when they did that it meant the race was over for the car. I did not dare ask if it was the same for the Renault Dauphine, because I knew that in times like that the drivers were never very happy. I had seen them throw their gloves and helmets on the ground in disgust with the piece of crap they had been given to drive. Since my father had no gloves and no helmet, I wondered what he could throw on the ground instead. To my dismay, at this point in time he was not ready to throw anything, it was more like when the car stops, something is wrong, but the driver bravely continues, oblivious to the risk he is exposing himself to, should a critical mechanical failure take place. This pit stop was more like Le Mans: look at it, be perplexed, decide to wait until it really breaks, and continue. But as soon as we arrived in the town of Le Muy, my father parked the car in front of the first garage he saw, which I noticed was conveniently located across the street from a bar, and asked the mechanic to look at it. Since it would take sometime, he sent my mother and me across the street, and we settled outside on the terrace bordering the road with a glass of pineapple juice each, watching the proceedings. The problem with situations like these is that the driver hears a noise, the mechanic looks at the wheel, sees nothing wrong, takes the wheel off, then the brake housing, and still sees nothing wrong, repacks the bearings, replaces the wheel, and then he has to drive the car, to ensure everything is back together. Still nothing is wrong, and the customer, my father, does not agree. He heard something, he is sure of it. So, the mechanic takes the car for another spin, and the customer, my father, crosses the street to enjoy a well deserve cold beverage. And this is when his wife, my mother, asks "where is he going with the car"? "To test drive it" answered my father, who could not possibly understand why my mother was asking such a question. He was soon enlightened when my mother said: "with all of our suitcases in it, you gave the car and our stuff to the first stranger you saw, without even asking him his name"? Needless to say, the next few moments were rather tense. If the car did not come back, we were stuck in Le Muy, and my two dump trucks and my army Jeep were gone for ever. It was with an immense sigh of relief that I saw the Dauphine come back. I was the first one to spot it, and identify it by reading the license plate: 573 FB 06.

In France, which is roughly the size of Texas, some bureaucrats decided that the region each car is from should be readily identifiable from the license plate. So France was divided into ninety-five départements, roughly each the size of an American county, and the same bureaucrats decided to use the last two digits of the license plate to identify the département. In the case of the Dauphine the last two digits "06" indicated we were from the Alpes-Maritimes. This rather innocuous piece of information was not as benign as it seemed, because now that we were in the département with number "83", everyone knew we were outsiders, and that we were not from their town. As we moved forward on our trip, this proved more and more a problem, as some people still unaccustomed to car travel, tourism and the movement of people, proved openly hostile when they saw our "06" number. As we arrived in département "30" we were six hours away from home, and somehow, these people really had a grudge against us zero-sixers. To the point that one gas station pretended to be out of gas, while my father was not pretending to be almost out of gas with the Dauphine. The crisis was averted when my father declared he was going to call the cops. Reluctantly the attendant filled up the tank, but not without issuing warnings that next time, we should get gas someplace else. But this worked both ways as the people from Paris, with their distinctive "75" were despised by all, me included, as my father has taught me to be. We even have a song in France making fun of Parisians: "Parisiens, têtes de chiens, Parigots têtes de veaux" (Parisians, dog heads, Parisians, calf heads).

Fortunately, the mechanic in Le Muy did not have such a grudge against zero-sixers. He simply thought my father was nuts. There was absolutely nothing wrong with the car, he emphatically stated. Just keep driving and leave him alone. He took payment for his services, and as he walked away shaking his head from side to side (another one who thought my father to be crazy), we were on our way. Now, mind you, we were way off-schedule, and my father held a war council to decide where we would sleep that night. The planned stop in Rodez was simply out of the question. My grandfather had been right: driving to Limousin was not a simple matter. And from what I could tell my father was not fully qualified to do it. Now we would have to sleep in a place called Saint-Afrique. Saint Africa? Now we were going to Africa? Nobody would ever hear from us again, I would die before seeing Monaco again, and I would never see my toy car collection again. This was the tragedy my grandfather had warned us against, and it was unfolding in front of my very eyes. I had heard all types of nasty things about Africa. My friend Daniel had been shipped back to France from his home in the Ivory Coast in Africa because of the diseases he had caught there, and he had warned me never to go there least I would die. He was not doing so well himself. He had some type of brain disease and he could not keep up with his reading at the Sisters of Saint-Maur. From the back seat I blurted "I don't want to go to Africa! I am scared"! Of course my parents burst out laughing, and my father explained that the village was in France, and that Saint-Afrique was a saint who had gone to Africa and given his name to the village. Well, it may have been so, but I did not like this Saint-Afrique place.

And I was right. The place was clearly a dump, especially by Monaco standards, which were the only ones I had. People drove lowly 2 CV Citroëns, and there were no Rolls-Royces. People spoke French with an accent I did not understand, the hotel was not clean, even I could see that, and the bed had springs like the suspension of an old World War Two GMC truck. And during dinner, the worst thing happened. We had ordered steak. The cook had walked through the dining-room to go get them in the refrigerator, and on the way back, he had dropped one of the floor. And horror of all horrors, he had simply picked it up and continued to the kitchen. I had to alarm my parents of this fact. We simply could not eat a steak that had been dropped on the floor. My grandmother Lainey would never allow it to happen, and she would have left immediately for another restaurant. But neither my father nor my mother seemed concerned, telling me that the microbes would die on the grill. How could they know? I had heard about microbes from my grandmother who worked so hard to keep them away from me, and now, not even a day out of her sight, my parents were taking me to a place where they dropped steaks on the floor and ate them! I inquired whether Saint-Afrique was Limousin. To my relief it was not! But, then I remembered about Auvergne, which was supposed to be close to Limousin. I wanted to know if we were close enough to Auvergne that we should worry about these volcanoes my grandmother had talked about. I was not sure that my father's explanations were consistent with what I had heard before. The volcanoes were dormant, which meant they were sleeping. But when would they wake up? Would they wake up in the morning? Or in the middle of the night? This is when my mother said that they would never wake up because they were dead. Dead? Volcanoes could die? Just like that? This is when the steak arrived, and I did not recognize the steak that I had seen fall on the floor. But I still did not like this Saint-Afrique place. And to think that Africa was even more dangerous!

The second day of the trip was worse. We woke up to pouring rain, while I was sure that the sun shone brightly in Monaco, as I knew it did every day of summer. Instead, we rushed to the car, trying to stay dry as we repacked the suitcases in the trunk. When we finally started on the road, there were no longer any thoughts of meeting my father's travel schedule. We started by getting stuck behind a tractor trailer on a winding Départementale road, with no way to pass, as the Renault Dauphine shared with us another of its features: the ability to fog up entirely all windows of the car once it was raining. It now became an all-hands-on-deck task to find dry rags, handkerchiefs and other assorted pieces of material to keep the windshield from fogging up. In the backseat, due to the angle of the windows, I experience the pleasures of the rain forest, as the condensation started raining on my head. I expressed my discontent by saying that I had never seen this happen in a Peugeot. I should know, since my friend René and I had driven with his parents back from Nice when it was raining one day, and I had not seen his father wiping the windshield from inside. My comments did not amuse my father, who now realized that the defogging system of the car was rather inadequate, and he told me that I should shut up or he would leave me on the side of the road, and I would find out what rain was all about!

When night fell, we still had not reached our destination, and we had to stop for supper. There was no hope of arriving before well into the night, as we were still over one hundred miles away from Limoges, and had to contend with the very winding part of N20 on the way to Uzès. When we finally got to Card, at almost midnight, I had been sleeping for a while, and as we stopped in front of the house it was still raining. There were no street lights, and I wondered what type of town it was that did not have any street lights. I did not know then that Card was a hamlet. On our northern side of the hamlet which was divided into North and South by the Départementale 56 (D56), there were five houses and six barns, ten people and eighteen cows lived there. The lane leading from the road was a dirt road, which that night it had filled with water and was a hybrid between a raging alpine creek and a mud pool. The closest real village, Ambazac, was about two miles away. We had driven through it, but I had not seen it, because I was sleeping. My father's aunt, Marie Lepetit and her husband François lived there.

CHAPTER 4
A Disastrous Arrival

The people living in Card were all more or less related. As we turned from D56 onto the lane, at the very corner of the road on the left was the house of Robert Teulier and his mother, Merlatte. I never understood what the name Merlatte meant, and when I knew her I always thought her name was Mère Latte (Mother Latte). Actually her name was the feminine of the French word for blackbird "Merle". Now that I know her name was Merlatte, I still don't know why a woman would be named after a blackbird. Back then, I had figured out why her name was Latte: the poor people from Limousin did not know how to pronounce Italian, since her name "latte" meant milk in Italian. And she had a farm where the cows produced milk—I knew that because my grandmother Louise and I would go drink milk there when the cows were being milked. So this lady had an Italian name meaning milk because she owned a farm where the cows made milk, and the people of Limousin did not know Italian, so they called her a female blackbird. In any case, both Robert Teulier and Mother Milk were related to our family, since Mother Milk was my grandmother's cousin and Robert Teulier was her son.

The next house up was on the right hand side of the lane. It was peculiar in two respects. First, it was the only house on the right side of the lane, and second, it was the only house the owner of which was not related to our family. The Père Christophe was the sole occupant of the house. He did not have a wife, and he had a couple of cows he kept in the barn right next to our house, which was the next up on the left. Our house was attached to a barn which was attached to another house. Our house was normally empty, as it belonged to my grandmother Louise and she lived in Paris. But the next house was very active. The Père Marzet, who was to become one of my best friends lived there, with his son, Robert Marzet, and his daughter-in-law Alice. They were related to us since Alice's mother had been one of grandmother Louise's other cousins.

Finally, there was the Guérin family. They were not on our lane, and had their own entrance from D56 into the hamlet. But if you entered Card by Robert Teulier's house and made a very sharp left turn past his barn, you would see the Guérin's farmhouse on the right. The Guérins were kind of outcasts in the small community. They were the richest farmers, since they owned almost fifty percent of the cows in Card, and they were the only complete family with two parents and two children. The two children, men in their thirties allowed the farm to prosper while the other inhabitants of Card, who did not have access to such help, simply survived while either receiving a pension from the government or working outside the farm as well. Robert Teulier was the sawmill foreman, down the road in Les Loges, Alice worked as a seamstress at the Mavest garment factory in Ambazac, and Robert Marzet was a mason who worked in Limoges.

Limoges was the closest major city, and for the people living in Card with its ten year-round residents, it was enormous with about 150,000 inhabitants. Located some fifteen miles away, it had been a renowned center for enamel before becoming the capital of French porcelain which it still was in 1959. But despite its proximity, people in Card would rarely if ever go to Limoges, except for Robert Marzet who worked there everyday. Today, the manufacture of porcelain has all but vanished, but when I first visited the city with my parents there were many factories, and everybody in Limousin had a set of the famous Limoges china.

Our arrival in Card was truly dismal. If I had known about such historical events as the rout of the French army on the Berezina River in Russia on 26 November 1812, I would have compared it to it. As it was, I did not have such frames of reference, and I thought we had just arrived in a haunted house, such as were set up on the harbor wharfs in Monaco when the carnival visited for the Prince's birthday in November. I had never actually gone into a haunted house amusement because my mother did not want me to have nightmares. Entering the house in Card, I thought her concerns to have been highly illogical, because this house was absolutely guaranteed to give me nightmares. First and foremost, there were no toilets. The reason there were no toilets, is that there was no running water. Now, in the middle of the night, in pouring rain, I had to go to the bathroom in an outhouse or in the garden, like the bums who occasionally sneaked into Monaco. Second, there was no electric either! So that to find the outhouse, one either had to go with a candle or suddenly develop a cat-like ability to see in the dark. And since it was raining, and I could not use a candle, there was no way I could find the outhouse. Actually it was so dark that I could not even find the wall of the garden which my father had told me to use as a urinal. So, that first night, in beautiful Limousin, I simply peed in the middle of the lane, adding my modest contribution to the water rushing down to the road. And I quickly ran back into the house.

My absence had given enough time to my parents to light the oil lamps. I had never seen such contraptions, although I had heard that people used oil to light their houses in Monaco a century before I was born. There were two of them in the house, one with a yellow globe to hold the oil and the other with a blue globe. They each had a thin glass chimney, through which smoke escaped, and became extremely hot as the oil burned. Frankly, they looked very dangerous to me. The future showed that my assessment was correct. Having turned on, or rather lit with a match, the two oil lamps, my parents and I were now confronted with one of the most miserable sights ever seen by a traveler reaching his destination in the middle of a rainy night. The house had been closed up since the previous summer, and humidity had penetrated every square inch of everything. The walls, which I assumed to be white, were nicely decorated with the green and black marbleized designs of growing mold fields; the furniture was gently covered with the turquoise shade of thriving fungi; and each room was infested with an invasion of every species of spiders leaving in France at the time. The disaster was crowned by the beds. They had been left untouched in a year, and the sheets, which again I assumed should have been white, were damp and had turned a lovely shade of grey as rot had starting to settle in. I swore I could see signs of liquefaction as my mother tried to make sense of this ghastly spectacle.

My father optimistically declared that the only thing we needed to do is heat the house, while my mother emphatically stated that there was no way we could stay there. I thought it was interesting that my father would want to turn on the heat since my terrified eyes could not even detect the slightest trace of a stove or heater. This is when my father went out, and to my horror came back with tree logs which were sure to harbor yet more spiders. The way to heat the house was to light a fire in the fireplace. Of course! How could I have not thought of that? The only problem was that the logs were also damp and humid. So how, do we resolve this little problem in Limousin? Well, we simply go to the barn, find the most convenient container of gasoline, pour it onto the logs which were set in the fireplace, light a match, and voilà! We have a major explosion in the house, my father's hair is suddenly shorter, and we have flames shooting out of the chimney, while the explosion knocks over the yellow globed oil lamp, which crashes on the floor, spills the oil all over the concrete floor, catches on fire and starts warming up the house! We had been in the house less than twenty minutes and already needed the fire department! This did not deter my resolute father, because he had now succeeded in warming up the house. He had three fires going: one in the fireplace, because the logs were actually starting to burn, one in the room, because the oil was burning all over the floor, and one in the chimney because the violence of the explosive heat had ignited the soot that has collected inside it. True to himself my father confidently declared that the two unwanted fires would soon run out of combustibles, while the wanted fire needed more, and he rushed outside to get more logs, leaving my mother and I to wonder whether the house would burn down that night.

Now that the fire was raging and raging is the correct word, in the fireplace, it was time to proceed with the cleaning of the bedrooms. My father went to get a pail of water at the well, and he and my mother starting washing down the walls of the bedroom I was to use in the front of the house. While this was going on, I stayed out of the way terrified by the room I was supposed to sleep in. In the meantime, fresh sheets were found, some that had not been discolored by the onset of the rotting process, and they were put on the back of chairs facing the fire, to "take the dampness out of them". I was told to sit there, and ensure the sheets did not catch fire. At least it was warm and dry! After about an hour of work, the room was ready for me to go to bed. This is when I had to go pee in the middle of the lane for the second time, and the horrible realization that there were no toilets really set in. What if I had to the bathroom in the middle of the night? Proudly, my father pulled out of a closet what is commonly referred to in France as a "hygienic pail". An enameled container with a matching lid, in which you are supposed to take care of business in the middle of the night. In the morning, you simply take it downstairs and empty it in the outhouse. How about gross? Was I supposed to do the emptying before or after breakfast? By the way, I thought it was a sign that this particular pail was light blue, matching the color of the Renault Dauphine parked outside. I went to bed, terrified by the spectacle I had just witnessed, wondering if the house could burn down, trying to see in the dark if spiders were gathering into squadrons of death ready to come attack me, wrap me in spider web materials and suck the life out of me during the night.

CHAPTER 5
The Père Marzet

The next morning, the entire place had completely changed. Instead of the pouring rain, I could see the sun filtering through the shutters and outside I could hear the mooing of cows and the thumping of their hooves on the lane. I had never seen real cows in my life. My curiosity was such that I jumped out of bed barefoot, oblivious to the fact that you could not have paid me to walk on that floor barefoot the night before, and rushed to open the shutters. At first I struggled with the reluctant latch, but when I succeeded, below me (I was on the second floor) I discovered the most beautiful animals I had ever seen. Four cows were waiting in line to drink from the water trough set against the wall of the well, while a farmer was cranking up pales of water to refill it as fast as the cows drank the water. And these were not your simple stupid cows you see on pictures, three of these were absolutely magnificent Limousin cows which my father had talked about, and one, well this one was really special: it was a red and white cow from the province of Normandie, the same one that was on the lid of my favorite camembert cheese, the Lepetit Camembert. I was so excited, I believe I fell in love for the first time of my life, I had never seen such wonderful creatures. The Normandie cow, especially was the cutest, with its short curved symmetrical horns, and the most attractive face, she was instantly my favorite. That's when the farmer saw me, and he said what I assumed was hello, in a language I did not understand. This was my first exposure to the Limousin language.

In my excitement to see the cows from closer, I put my shoes on and went downstairs. I opened the door and stood in the frame, in my pajamas, bathed in the warm glow of the sun, and seeing cows at eye level for the first time. The farmer grew concerned as the cows showed nervousness at my presence, trying to back off sideways, and he warned me not to move. The spectacle was huge. The four cows were now lined up two by two, two drinking in low heavy swallows, from time to time turning their head to the side to see what was going on, water and slobber dripping from their chin, while the other two patiently waited their turn. This is when one of the farmers—in my desire to see the cows, I had not even noticed that there were two farmers—came toward me, took me by the hand and led me to the cow that was drinking on the right, the Normandie cow, and let me pet her. This was my first touching of a cow, and my first meeting with the man I would for ever know as le Père Marzet. He was not a tall man, and wore worn out work blues—in France workers wear heavy blue work clothes—with several patches on the knees and the elbows. He had a more white than grey handlebar moustache, and a welcoming smile. He smelled just like the cows, a mixture of scents I had never experienced before, and he was so kind that he had let me touch his cow. He asked me my name and I timidly answered it was Patrick. To which he added "you are not from around here, are you". I told him I had come all the way from Monaco, and he seemed very impressed. I did not know it then, but this encounter was the beginning of a friendship between the two of us that lasted until the day he died in 1981, and goes on even today as I remember him so vividly. Alice, his daughter-in-law, later told me that the day he died, the Père Marzet inquired about how I was doing, and if I would come and see him. When she told him I could not because I was then an army officer in the United States, he said that he was proud of me, and that he knew I would fight well, like he had done in the trenches of World War One. He asked her to say goodbye to me, which she did in a tearful reunion we had a couple of years later.

You see, le Père Marzet was a veteran of World War One. He had done all of the campaigns starting with the Battle of the Marne in 1914, the Chemin des Dames, the Somme, Verdun in 1916, and the final offensive of the Aisne in 1918. And as I grew up and went working in the fields with him, or watched after the cows, he would tell me the stories of the war, how miserable he had been, and how deadly it had been, and how the Germans had surrendered to him one day after his unit had assaulted their trench. He did not care about the history of the war, he had not been an officer, but through his stories, the trenches came to life, with their daily share of sacrifices, and senseless killings. The companions he had lost, and some who were still alive, were right there in front of my eyes fighting in the mud and the rain, with shells and bullets falling all around them. Above all, le Père Marzet was the most decent human being I ever met, and as I think of those days when we worked together with the team of cows in the chestnut tree forests of Limousin, these are some of the happiest days of my life. Since then, I became an artist, and I painted a portrait of him. Everyday I go so hello to him, and I feel the great fortune I had to meet, know him, and be his friend. Now that I too have served as a soldier, I have even more appreciation for his stories. Wherever you are, Père Marzet, I salute you.

When my mother found out that I been out of the house in my pajamas, without combing my hair, and washing my face, she was terribly cross with me. And when she found out I had petted the cows she was alarmed. I told her never mind, that I had to hurry, because le Père Marzet wanted me to go and help him feed the cows. She did not really agree, but when my father told her that this is why we had driven a thousand kilometers, she reluctantly got me my clothes, I got dressed, and without even eating a piece of bread, I ran out of the house to the cows' stable. Le Père Marzet was already there changing the litter, and he asked if I had eaten breakfast. When I told him I had not, he said that neither had he, and together, we went to his house to have breakfast. I was really surprised when he pulled out cheese, ham, a loaf of pain de campagne, and a bottle of red wine. I objected that this was not breakfast food, that we should have tartines, or croissants, with coffee and milk. He explained that this was city food, and that in the country people work hard, and they have to have breakfast that looks like lunch otherwise they would collapse in the fields while they were working. And so it is that on this glorious morning of July 3, 1959, I had my first breakfast as a farmer! I did not get to have wine though, and le Père Marzet got me a glass of French sweet cider. That was another discovery for me, as I had never had any in Monaco. When everything was done, he took my glass, washed it, and put it above the sink, next to his, just like farm hands do. I asked him how this was, and he told me that they only had enough glasses for the number of people who lived or worked in the house. And that I was lucky, since his nephew could not come and work here any longer, he had the extra glass. "What about when you have guests" I asked him. He responded "we don't have the time to have guests here; we work every day, from sun up till sun down"! Well, maybe I thought I did not like to be a farm hand that much. This was way too much work.

Feeding the cows was a lot of fun. The only thing I regretted was not to be able to pet them while they were eating. Their heads were enormous compared to me, and although I should have been afraid, I simply like these animals who seemed so peaceful. But I soon discovered that le Père Marzet had another wonderful animal in his household, and this was a red dog named Torpille. I had never really been fond of dogs, but this animal was so friendly, so kind, and so forgiving, it must have come from another planet. Torpille became one of my Limousin friends and as soon as she heard me move inside the house, she would come to the front door and wait for me to come out. The entire time I was outside, she would follow me, or at times anticipate where I was going, and lead me around the country side. I don't know what breed she was, she was probably a mix, but this was the ideal dog. And I did not have to make her soup, or pick up after her. She was simply a companion. And every time I left the Limousin to go back to Monaco, Torpille would get depressed, and lay around for days, waiting for me to come back and go walking in the fields with her.

About eleven o'clock that day, I had to go get ready to meet with my other family, starting with my father's aunt, Tata Marie, who owned the biggest grocery store in Ambazac. Ambazac is a small village in the heart of Limousin. It sits at the crossroads of four roads: two roads come from Limoges, one from La Jonchère, and one from Saint-Léonard de Noblat. These four roads converge in the center of town, in front of the church dating back to the twelfth century. At the time, the village itself may have had about three thousand inhabitants and as much as a third of them were minors from the nearby uranium mines in La Crouzille. The village had not changed much since the beginning of the eighteenth century, were it not for the memorial of the two world wars on the left side of the road coming from Saint-Léonard, well before arriving on the church square. The night before, as we had driven through, I had been sleeping, and although I was not happy to already leave le Père Marzet behind, I was curious to see what this famous

Ambazac looked like. As we left Card, we made a hard right, followed the Départementale (D56), and went down a very steep hill at the bottom of which was a sharp left curve leading up another hill, and down again as we joined up with the road from Saint-Léonard. To the right we could see the railroad station on a hill, and we had to go under the railroad bridge which was single lane. Then the road took us down a gentle slope into town, and back up toward the church. Less than two miles, and a few minutes later, I saw the store for the first time, on the left side of the church square, with a sign in large faded black characters on an ivory background, spelling the word "EPICERIE" (grocery store). My father parked the car opposite, in front of the newspaper store, and we walked by the church front door and across the street.

When my father opened the épicerie door, the first thing I heard was the little bell attached to the top of it that would alert my aunt of the arrival of customers. Entering the place was like walking into the Cave of Ali-Baba. I knew about the cave, since my le Père Noël (Santa Claus) had brought me an illustrated version of it for Christmas. And what I saw could not even compare with the pale efforts of the poor artist who had illustrated the book for the Père Noël—in my opinion the Père Noël had been gypped. The épicerie had a wonderful enchanting aroma, a mixture of French butter, bee's wax, coffee, saucisson, cheese, ham, pepper, cantaloupe melon, chicory, and other subtle yet undistinguishable flavors. But most of all, it was a place where there was everything. In Monaco, I was used to go to different stores to buy different things. For example, Madame Chiabaud would only sell diary products, cheese, and ham, and next doors, Madame Bartaldi only sold bread and baked goods, and to buy vegetable cans and coffee you would yet go to two other stores, and I knew nothing of a store selling fruit—this was done at the market. But, here, in this strange and extraordinary place, there was everything: fruit, vegetables, coffee, tea, ham, delicatessen, cheese, milk, cans of everything imaginable at the time, sugar, flour...And there were the famous Alsacienne brand cookies. My favorites, in quantities and varieties I did not know could exist—I had an eye for the Alsacienne cookies and could tell their distinctive wrapping with the beautiful Alsacienne girl anywhere. This was a store I had never imagined could exist. And behind the counter, a diminutive woman, dressed in black with a gray print jacket, her graying hair tied being her head, with two light gray eyes, taking care of her customers, cutting butter, weighing cheese, slicing ham, while talking about the customer's family, wrapping, adding the totals, taking the money, making change, and moving at a speed I had never seen in a human being move, from behind the counter, to the shelf with the cans of French beans, back to the counter, and to the fruit display. This woman was Tata Marie. She was clearly in charge of the store and she was devoted to her customers, whom she considered to be her guests in the store, chatting with them in this unavoidable language I would never master, Limousin.

When we came in, she did not even acknowledge us, so focused she was on her customers. As it was close to noon time, there were many waiting, and more coming in. She immediately said something to my father and within an instant, he had gone to the kitchen, washed his hands, and he too was helping customers, while Tata Marie explained to her customers in French for my mother's benefit, that we were her relatives from Monaco. One of her customers must have said something to her, because she suddenly interrupted her ballet, kissed me, and turning to the customer, she declared that I was cute, to which the customer readily agreed. I must have turned as red as the radishes the customer was buying. Tata Marie invited my mother and me to go the kitchen, so that we would be out of the way, while she took care of the midday customers. I reluctantly complied, but I had soon sneaked back into the shop to be a witness to the show. Tata Marie's husband, Tonton (uncle) François, had a communicating shop where he made wooden clogs, which like in Holland, were at that time the standard footwear of farmers in Limousin. There were two reasons for visiting with Tata Marie. First, we needed food and cleaning supplies. But second and foremost, she had invited us for lunch despite the fact this was a work day. All over Limousin, I found out our relatives would stop everything they were doing, and extend hospitality I had not seen before. Tata Marie was my grandfather Léon's sister. She was an energetic woman who ran not only the only grocery store in Ambazac, but also the town's biggest business. She did not have time to mess around, especially between ten in the morning and one in the afternoon. This is when she closed the shop and had lunch with Tonton François.

Tonton François and Tata Marie had met back in 1911, when she was sixteen, and the single picture I have of her at the time shows a very attractive young lady. By that time, François Lepetit was in the fourth year of his military service. At that time, France had conscription, and there was a lottery that determined how long people would serve. My uncle, being unlucky that day, had pulled a ticket for the maximum time of seven years. When he was finally released on June 30, 1914, he thought he would go back to Ambazac, marry Marie, and be happy ever after. That was without taking into account World War One, which started on August 1, 1914. Tonton François was recalled to active service and was incorporated into the 168th Infantry regiment, where he served until the end of 1919. Bureaucracy was slow in those days, especially for the privates and the corporals, and it had taken the French army over a year after the end of the war to discharge him. I should not sound outraged or bitter for him, because of all the times we talked about it, he never complained once, never blamed anybody. He was simply proud of having served France, and he would simply comment thoughtfully "these were hard times…these were hard times". He was lucky that my aunt waited for him all these years, and they were finally married on February 28, 1920. They never had any children, and when war broke out again in 1939, Tata Marie took my father under her protection in Ambazac while fighting was going on, and bombing raids were taking place around Paris. This had established a special bond between my father and Tata Marie, particularly since she and Tonton François never could have children.

Well, Tonton François was a cool guy. He had tons of incredible tools in his shop, again the sort of which I had never seen, knew nothing about, and could not even have imagined existed. I started asking all types of questions about them. Tonton François stopped what he was doing, and tool by tool explained what they were all about. But, now I had to help him. So when he called for a nose-tip pair of pliers I had to go get them and give them to him. And when he was done using them I had to put them back in their place. That summer I learned much about tools, observed how to use them, and got a taste for what you can accomplish with them. It was another discovery. My mind was absorbing everything, and I was sure that by the end of summer, I could build my own pair of wooden clogs. Tonton François had the unusual habit of giving nicknames to people, and for a reason that will forever remain mysterious to me, he dubbed me "l'ami du placard". I wish I could inform my readers of the meaning of such a nickname, unfortunately, even in French I have a hard time understanding what it means, as it literally translates to "the friend of the pantry". When I walked into his shop, he would say "Ah, here comes l'ami du placard!" But Tonton François also wanted to know about Monaco. He had never been there—he could not go on vacation because the grocery store had to remain open all year long—and even after he and Tata Marie retired they never made it there. So, he had me describe the harbor, the boats, the color of the sea, the casino, the palace, the oceanographic museum. He asked me if I had ever seen Princess Grace. And most of all he wanted to know about my Monaco family, about my grandparents, and where they lived, and what they ate. So, all summer, as I visited his shop, I would sit there by his bench, help him with the tools, and I would tell him about Monaco.

What was striking about Tonton François is that he was bald, his face was round, and he had a beautiful white handlebar mustache. His light-brown eyes expressed joviality and openness to good humor. His cheeks had coupe rose, and it turned out he liked his wine. He did not drink for the sake of drinking, but he did not have a single meal without red wine. And he even added wine to his soup, like the soldiers did in the trenches of WW I. He never seemed to get angry at anything, and he was good friends with le Père Marzet, although they rarely saw each other. They lived only two miles away, but they never visited. On occasion, le Père Marzet would come to town for a funeral or a wedding, and he would stop by to say hello to Tonton François, but my uncle never once went to Card in all the years I knew him. So it happens that I also became a messenger between the two veterans. Upon every visit I had to report how everything was going, just like a courier in the trenches, they would joke. My uncle would receive customers all day long when I was there, and he would introduce me as his apprentice, telling his customers that the business would go on after he retired, especially with such a gifted apprentice. The customers would then take a coin out of their pocket, and give me a little tip. Once I had collected enough, this allowed me to go back next doors to my aunt's épicerie and buy one of these fantastic things known as "surprises". These were long cones made of bright paper, yellow, red or blue, the top of which was sealed. Inside were surprises, and since you could not tell what was they contained ahead of time, you picked at random from the basket in which ten to fifteen such surprises were stored, and you hoped to get a marvelous game, or candy, or even money. These surprises were so much fun, except when a boy would buy one, open it, and discover that the toys inside were meant for a girl. There was a rumor that one of them had a five hundred Francs bank note hidden in it. That would have been a surprise!

As the last midday customers left the épicerie Tata Marie went to the kitchen and lunch was ready. For on top of taking care of her store starting in the early morning, serving the customers, and replenishing the shelves, Tata Marie had also prepared lunch. As she showed me my seat, I fell under her spell, because not only did I have special silverware which was made out of red plastic, the same color as the Maserati, but my plate had the picture of a beautiful Alsacienne girl in the middle of it…While the meal went on and adults started to forget themselves into endless conversations that were of no interest to me, Tonton François, who definitely was more in tune with me, introduced me to the garden that was hidden behind the store. It was a vegetable garden that he maintained for their use. I had seen the garden of my uncle Georges in Monaco, where tomatoes, peppers, fava beans and eggplants grew on well tended terraces, but what struck me with Tonton François' garden was how big it was, with the rows of cabbage all lined up, and the white butterflies flying around, the strawberries—he even had strawberries—the rows of pole beans, all perfectly arranged, in squares, and around every square of vegetables, a single row of huge pansies of all colors. And then, in the back, massifs of flowers: gladiolas, dahlias, aromas, roses, irises, many others I did not know—but no carnations. And Tonton François kept a surprise for the end of the visit: tucked away in a corner of the garden next to the tool shed, he opened the door, and here were about sixteen cages, with rabbits! These were healthy beautiful rabbits eating grass and carrot greens, and there were of all colors as well: black, brown, white with their red eyes, mixed, with straight ears, with floppy ears. I would have given anything to pet them, but Tonton François did not allow that. He explained they did not know me, and I would scare them, which was not good for them. These were no pets; these were rabbits which were being raised with but one purpose: being eaten as sautéed rabbit, mustard rabbit, or civet de lapin!

CHAPTER 6
The Père Christophe

Everyday that I stayed in Card, the same scenario would unroll. At about eight in the morning, as the cows came back from pasture, they would wake me up, and I would rush downstairs to see them drink at the water trough. First there would be le Père Marzet's cows, quickly followed by the Père Christophe's as they were on the same schedule. Then, Robert Teulier would bring his own cows, but they were not allowed to drink in front of our house, they had to drink from Robert Teulier's own water trough, with water brought up from his own well, down the lane. They would rush past the house, shaking the ground under their hoofs. But, more spectacular, because there were eight cows, were Guérin's cows. When they came by, they would literally shake the house, almost running home to the Guérin farm to be first at the water trough. The Père Christophe's cows were both of the breed that we call Hollandaise cows, but which are called Holstein in the United States. They produced his milk, and allowed him to raise a couple of calves a year which he then sold to the butcher. The Père Christophe was a tall elegant man, who always wore a black smock and black pants, an unusual combination in a country where everybody wore work blues. Because of his tall size, he had served in the cavalry in World War One, and seeing how tall I was already for my age, he had declared that I would be a cavalryman just like he had been. This had caused me some concern, because unlike he, I had visited the French Army exhibit during the big fair in Nice, and I knew that the French Army did not use horses any longer. Even more troublesome was that I had seen the new French cavalry tank, the AMX-13, and even as a child, I could hardly fit in it. I could not imagine someone the size of the Père Christophe in this tiny machine. I would have liked to have a discussion with him about the merits of his choice of a career for me, but I then said something which he did not like at all. I volunteered that my great-grandfather, Auguste, also had been a cavalryman and that he was tall like him. I went on to tell him that my great-grandfather had been a gendarme.

I don't know what triggered the answer, but the Père Christophe somehow did not like gendarmes. He said "I hate gendarmes and I don't associate with people who like them. You have to go". Now, I could not understand what was going on. Gendarmes are like the Military Police of the French Army, and they also serve as a police force in rural areas. But my not understanding why the Père Christophe did not like them was the least of my problems. Because seizing his stick he clearly indicated I had to leave. Immediately. That would have been fine if I had been in his house, across the lane from mine, but we were watching the cows graze, far from the house, where we had gotten after following a maze of cow paths I was not sure I could remember. Faced with the raised stick of a very angry man and the alternative of finding my own way home, I decided to chance it and try to find my way home. It went well until the second turn, and all of a sudden, I knew I was in trouble. I tried to find my way back, but a seven year old is not exactly the best person at guessing directions. After walking for what seemed hours, and were actually hours, I ended up on a road. I assumed it was the road that would lead me back to the lane in front of our house. Well it was not. Soon, I noticed the sun going down, and the light decreasing. For sure my parents would now come looking for me. I should have asked for directions, but I had read the tales of Grimm, and I knew that children should not knock on the door of houses in the forest or for that matter of houses on the side of the road. So I kept on walking.

Meanwhile in Card, the Père Christophe had gone back, and had put his cows in the stable. And I was not with him. When my parents went to inquire where I was, he simply raised his stick at my mother and muttered "gendarme's grandson!" To which my mother answered something even more unpleasant, and all communications were lost between the Père Christophe and my family. The family needed a mediator, and there was only one, le Père Marzet. He quickly figured out what had taken place, and he set about finding me, by having Torpille follow my scent. By this time, it was dinner time, and the small hamlet, safe the Père Christophe, set out to find me. I had sat by the side of the road, certain that I had walked for miles and without food and water, I started to cry in the grass, hoping that someone, anyone, even the old witch in Hans and Gretel would find me. Eventually, I fell asleep, right on the side of the road, abandoned by all, and not knowing that the greatest Search and Rescue Operation in the history of Card was going on. My mother kept a vigil at the house, while my father drove up and down the roads looking for me, assisted in this task by Robert Teulier on his bicycle. During this time le Père Marzet with Robert Marzet and Torpille set up a search in the various cow paths leading in and out of the pasture where I had last been seen with the Père Christophe. At about ten at night, Torpille's wet snout woke me up, and the relationship between Torpille and me would never be any stronger than in that moment.

The next day, to commemorate the event, my parents took a picture of me and Torpille in front of our house. I still have the picture and look at it remembering how this dog was the best dog in my life, ever. My parents consoled me and forbade me to ever talk to the Père Christophe whom they labeled a nasty old man. But I did not know until much after his death that the poor man was haunted by the picture of the gendarmes taking away his brother to be executed. In 1916, as the French Army was fighting the battle of Verdun, French soldiers desperate to survive the massacre and the madness of the war started to desert in droves. The supreme commander, the then-loved and now disgraced Maréchal Pétain, gave the order that everyone of these soldiers should be found and court-martialed. The Père Christophe's brother, an infantryman in Verdun, had cracked, and had taken refuge with his mother in Card. His mother hid him as long as she could until the fatidic day when the gendarmes on horseback showed up to carry him away. They searched the farm, the surrounding fields and finally found him, hiding in a chestnut tree grove. They tied him to a rope, and dragged him back behind their horses without even allowing him to say farewell to his mother. The poor chap knew he was going straight for the firing squad, as over two thousand French soldiers had been executed in 1916. By the time the gendarmes managed to get him back to Verdun, the battle had been won, and the urgency to make examples had waned somehow. Escaping the murderous obsession of the Maréchal, the Père Christophe's brother had been sentenced to hard labor for life. Promptly shipped to the French penitentiary colony of French Guyana, no one had ever heard of him again, and his mother died, always hoping to see her son walk through the door one day. In those times when entire families were wiped out, she could not even share her grief with friends or family. The Père Christophe had never forgiven the gendarmes. This incident taught me one lesson, which was never to volunteer information until I had to. Like Mémé Lainey had told me before "If nobody asks you the question, don't give the answer!" Despite this incident, I still liked the Père Christophe, and fortunately, I disobeyed my parents' orders not to see him again. From time to time, I would sneak into his house, and he would give me a glass of water with black current syrup he made from the bushes growing near our well, and he too, would talk about World War One.

This also showed that I needed to get familiar with my surroundings, and that I should know all of the cow paths in and around Card. Le Père Marzet volunteered to educate me in this matter, and one Sunday morning, after we had fed the cows, he took my hand and showed me where all the paths led. But we did not go very far. As we left the house, with our companion, Torpille, we went to the first crossroads, and as we turned left to go to the field with the leaning apple tree, le Père Marzet noticed that one of the field markers had been toppled. I had no idea what he was talking about. I had no idea that these famous field markers, known as "bornes" were the most sacred stones of Limousin. In later days, I would be able to compare them to the famous menhir alignments of Carnac in Brittany. But at that moment I had no such information that explained why le Père Marzet immediately rushed back to the house and grabbing the two essential tools of borne mending practically ran back to the site of the accident with a spade and a heel bar. Then, while asking me to stay out of the way, like a druid priest officiating over a sacred rite, he started straightening out the famous borne. After a long time—at my age I still did not have a clear concept of the duration of time—sweating and covered with dirt, he decided the work was done, and carrying his ceremonial tools, we walked back to the house for a glass of fresh water from the well. I still had no idea what act I had witnessed. The funniest thing is that my grandmother Louise suffered from the same type of obsession about bornes. As soon as she would arrive in Card, she would ask my father if he had inspected all of the bornes. In this rare case my father and I thought alike that my grandmother was crazy, arriving from Paris, and immediately asking about bornes. Well, what was ever crazier is that the next day, she grabbed me by the hand as soon as I was done with breakfast, and she dragged me all over the countryside to check for her bornes. I soon found out that she, like le Père Marzet, had a quantity of bornes scattered all over the place. So we went, through pastures, bramble fields, chestnut tree forests, marshes, across creeks, until we had found every one of these bornes. And it was not easy work. They were overgrown by vegetation, buried under piles of leaves, swallowed by the massive roots of the chestnut trees, sunk into the soft marshy ground. On all fours, my grandmother and I would be searching for these miraculous stones, disregarding our most elementary safety, oblivious to the omnipresence of vipers, and the danger of wild boars. At one point after finding a borne at the angle of the woods with Robert Teulier's, she turned to me and said: "I think he moved my borne!" I assumed that Robert Teulier was "he", but I could not understand first why anyone would want to move a borne and second how it could be done. The smallest of these sacred stones must have weighed five hundred pounds, and they were ninety percent buried, with only the tip sticking out, just like the icebergs I had learned about in school. And now that I had seen le Père Marzet work for hours simply to straighten out one, I doubted very much that Robert Teulier could have moved an entire borne. My grandmother authoritatively decided that I knew nothing of the matter, and that she would have to talk to Robert Teulier about it. She was actually quite upset that I did not share her suspicion of foul play. The good part about looking for bornes was that my grandmother showed me where all of the good bushes were. As we crisscrossed the area, she knew where to find the raspberry bushes that were still growing in some remote corner of a field she owned, she would remember the red current bushes that her father had planted half a century before, and we would stop and gorge ourselves on the succulent berries. She knew where a certain blackberry patch was way behind a wall that sheltered it from the northern winds, and she would find a clear water spring in a field that had not been polluted by cattle for over seventy years. We would sit there, refreshing ourselves with this pure water filtered by the volcanic sands, under the shade of a huge oak tree. These were the days of happiness, when my grandmother enjoyed life at its fullest and taught with me the simple joy of drinking fresh water from the palm of my hand. In these short moments I remember how happy my grandmother was, away from her worries, from the sorrow of having lost her husband and from her constant aversion of having to pay taxes. I never saw my grandmother happier than on that day.

But then, she would remember how we had gotten there, and why, and the hunt for the sacred stones would be on again. Upon returning to Card, she did not even freshen up—after all she was from Paris, and you would have expected that. She went straight to Robert Teulier's house. He was in the barn, milking his cows. He did not lose his composure, simply replying that she must be confused, and that how could he move such a heavy stone, and that it was crazy to think that he would have done that. He defused the situation completely by offering my grandmother a glass of milk still warm from the cow, and the matter was filed away. My grandmother still had the last word, telling him that regardless, no one could convince her that that stone had not been moved.

I found out later that day that these famous bornes were the field markers, the precise location of which was recorded with the town clerk, and that they served to measure the fields when they were sold. Most of them had been in place way before the French Revolution in 1789 and they also had a blood link, since most of them would have been set by the long-ago ancestors of the present owners, ancestors whose names were now forgotten. So, it was absolutely taboo to touch these bornes, because moving them without proper authority reflected an intention to steal land from the owner, and was an arrogant display of disrespect to a long lineage of ancestry. If you were not from a particular family you had no business touching the borne, and it was indeed a desecration of the family. Once I understood this, my grandmother took me to a borne in one of her most isolated fields, and laying my hand on it, she said: "The last man who touched this borne was my grandfather Joseph about one hundred years ago. My father never came here because he did not like this place. And even your father does not know where it is. You are now part of the chain of custody of this borne." I was really impressed. And every year when my grandmother arrived in Card, I had to report to her (since my father refused to do it) that I had inspected all of the bornes, that they were in their appointed place, and that our special borne had not been disturbed in any way from the previous year.

CHAPTER 7
My First Visit to Fondanèche

In 1959, the house in Card actually belonged to my grandmother Louise, my father's mother. It was not a Faure house, but a Desjouannets house which she had inherited from her parents, and had been in the family for several generations. That the house was labeled 1895 above the front door was actually no indication of its age, but of the date when cement had been added to the front wall made of heavy stones and a mortar made of volcanic ash and sand. Based on the age of all the other houses in the hamlet, it would appear that the house had been rebuilt in the late eighteenth century on the foundation of an even older structure. The house had two floors, with the front door on the right and a window on its left, and above these were two windows on the second floor. Upon entering the house, one faced the wooden staircase going to the second floor, while entering the large common area, with its dining table, the fireplace and tiny stone sink, in front of which we kept the pails of fresh water. The floor was made of concrete. In the back of this room was what was grandiosely referred to as the kitchen with a two burner propane stove (the propane was supplied by a propane bottle, right under the cooking area), and a huge bread oven which had not been used for decades. The floor of this room was made of stones laid directly on top of the dirt. Climbing the stairs to the second floor, one arrived at a small landing, with two doors: on the left was the main bedroom, which for some unknown reason I had been given on this first trip—and this bedroom overlooked the hamlet lane; on the right was a smaller bedroom which opened over an inner courtyard used in the past to keep a couple of pigs. The outer limit of the courtyard was a dry stone wall, retaining one of the Guérin family fields, and which was level with the bedroom window. Between the house and the wall, perpendicular to the house, was the small stables which has been used to shelter the pigs. And there, in the angle between the stables and the wall was the outhouse!

The house came with all of the land that had been the farm's to start with. There were grazing fields, chestnut tree forests, vegetable gardens, fields used to grow wheat, and a few unusable parcels that were marshy, down by the La Boissarde creek. But in front of the house, across the lane was the parcel that had been used to grow fruits and vegetables. Fully surrounded by dry stone walls, it included a small tool shed, and gently sloped down to a cow path parallel to the hamlet lane. This was the cow path used by Lemaunier's tractors, and it is at its intersection with the path coming from Card that le Père Marzet had noticed the problem with the "borne". While our vegetable garden was now simply covered with grass, it still had three major plum trees that produced enormous amounts of fruit every year. Unfortunately, we were unable to collect all of them, and beginning in mid-August, the entrance to this parcel became the domain of the yellow jackets that gorged on the fallen fruit and defended their booty with unrestrained dedication and aggressiveness. But next to our uncultivated vegetable, was the garden of le Père Marzet. Like my uncle François's, this garden was a model on how to grow vegetables. Each type of vegetable was identified, set in even rows, and delineated by boards set flat on the ground. There was not a single weed to be seen, and like my uncle, le Père Marzet had an area dedicated to flowers. From the moment I discovered this garden, I wanted to learn how to do it. So it was that over the course of the summers I spent there, I became more and more knowledgeable and involved on preparing the soil, planting, pruning, caring for, and finally collecting vegetables and fruits. These preoccupations distracted me completely from playing with my toy cars and trucks for weeks on end. Instead, as soon as I got up, I "helped" with the cows, feeding them their ration of beets after they were finished drinking, collecting vegetables, going to the fields with le Père Marzet to weed potatoes, coming back for lunch, taking a little nap—just like le Père Marzet who unlike me got up with the sun—collecting our things to take the cows grazing, and coming back in time for milking them before having supper. This was nothing like Monaco. I could not imagine that anyone in Monaco knew any such skills.

All the while, I learned about my Limousin family, and visited them little by little. Mostly, we visited with Tata Marie every day as we went grocery shopping, and every day I spent a couple of hours with Tonton François. It was not long before he allowed me to take scraps of wood and build my first bird house. During this first summer in Limousin, I simply learned the lay of the land, but I knew that I could help. I was too short to reach the top shelves in my aunt's épicerie, but soon I was given the task of replenishing the lower shelves with the cans of tomato sauce, green peas, and sugar, which came in tins rather than bags in those days. And this restocking had to be done right. I had to go into the reserve, get the cans, clean them with a rag (a yellow "torchon à poussière), so they would not be dusty, pull the left-over ones from the back, put the new ones in their place, labels facing to the front, each can precisely on top of the other, and put the old cans in the front of the newly stacked ones. As I grew in size and was able to reach more shelves, my aunt increased my range of responsibilities, but she always asked me to do the bottom rows so that she would not have to bend over.

It was a small price to pay for all the Sunday meals she prepared for us. During our stays in Limousin, we ate every Sunday meal at Tata Marie's. There was only one exception, and that's the day we were invited at Fondanèche. Fondanèche, like Limousin a few months sooner, had never been part of my personal lexicon. I had a difficult time understanding the word, first thinking that my parents were saying Fondeneige, which sounds very much like Fondanèche, and has the great merit of actually meaning something, which is melting snow. In my mind, I had this image of a perpetually snowy mountain, and like Santa Claus in the North Pole, the people of Fondeneige, would be working in cozy warm factories while the snow slowly melted outside. Well, this was not exactly the case, since the day of our visit, rather than wearing a snowsuit or my regular tennis shoes, my mother insisted on my wearing knee high rubber boots, which we had acquired at the Ambazac market. However, I thought that I must have been right, and this was to better walk in the snow, and not get my blue and white canvas tennis shoes wet.

Fondanèche—it turned out this was the proper spelling—was home to my grandfather Léon's brother Emile and his family. By being my grandfather's brother, Tonton Emile, as I was told to call him, was also the brother of Tata Marie. And this was the only reason why Tata Marie had reluctantly conceded that we could have Sunday lunch there. Tonton Emile and his wife Marie—who became a second Tata Marie, whom I had to call Tata Marie de Fondanèche to distinguish her from the real Tata Marie d'Ambazac who owned the épicerie—had a big farm by Limousin standards. They ran it with their two sons Maxime and Gustave, and an array of day laborers who came and went depending on their actual state of sobriety and how much money they needed for wine that week. Amongst all of them, the Père Gouraud was the only one who was a regular help. Why he was called Père Gouraud rather than simply Gouraud, I have no idea. Probably because he was older than fifty which made him an automatic father, even if he had never been married. And what made his name popular was that there was a French song that went:

"As-tu vu la casquette, la casquette
As-tu vu la casquette du Père Gouraud?"

and which we all sang cheerfully every time he came into the house or the dining-room. He enjoyed this little attention which made him the hero of the household for a few seconds each day.

In any case, Tonton Emile had a farm with three different barns, eighty sheep and thirty-two cows plus a massive Limousin bull. His land extended as far as one could see from his house which was at the top of a hill, and he even had a tractor, an orange Allis-Chalmers from America. They had tons of hens and roosters, five dogs, two pigs, and cats, so many cats they never even counted them. And then came the reason for the boots…With so many animals around and precious little time to hose down the place—it would have been a waste anyhow—once we parked the Dauphine between the "bergerie" (sheep stable) and the second "étable" (cow stable), we had to make our way through layers of cow pies of various freshness and consistency. And unfortunately, most were of the fresher type. I was appalled, especially that the first thing that dominated the farm, right outside the front door on the other side of the narrow street, and immediately next to the drinking water spring, was an enormous pile of manure, with thousands of flies buzzing around. And the head rooster of Fondanèche was crowing on top of it as if to defy us to penetrate into his domain. The stench was unbearable, and was similar to what townspeople refer to as the smell of the country. The main cow stable door was open, and an equally throat grabbing infection was rushing out from inside it as we walked by. My parents must have been delirious to come for lunch in such a disgusting place! And they had turned down Tata Marie d'Ambazac's invitation to come here? That topped it all! And what was I supposed to do with the tons of crap attached to my boots as I went in the house?

Before we could go into the house Tata Marie (de Fondanèche) came to welcome us. She was smaller than either my grandmother Lainey or the other Tata Marie, and she wore all black garments: a black dress, a black top with a black sweater, and black stockings. Her hair was short and gray, and she also wore a pair of glasses with a pinkish rim that was repaired with Scotch tape. She had a soft and at once commanding voice, with a pronounced Limousin accent. She immediately took charge of me, wiped my boots on the grass, next to the front stoop, and taking a toilet brush from a bucket of water standing by, she washed them with so much energy I almost fell over. Then she handled the brush to my father and mother and told them to do the same with their own shoes. She grabbed me by the hand and up the three stone steps we went, into the hall, and left into the common room, which served all purposes except sleeping. I was even more shocked in there than I had been outside. Imagine a long rectangular room, lit through a single small window on its narrow side, with a large fireplace on the left side, a recess made by the stairs going up the bedrooms on the right side, and at the far end a series of cabinets containing papers and dishes. And in the center a large dining table with a row of benches on each side. Every wall, the floor and the fireplace were made of granite blocks, and the ceiling showed the beams supporting the wooden floor above. But also imagine the whole room blackened by tens of years of soot and smoke from the fireplace. Everything, every inch of the room, be it walls, cabinets, shelves, furniture, table, benches darkened black. It was like entering a tunnel. And the small window was fighting with all of its heart to give the room any semblance of light. The place was scary and fascinating at once. A place where things could be lost, where gestures could remain unseen, a place where these people operated in a clear obscure the likes of which I would never see again. And in the fireplace, a powerful fire on which my aunt was cooking our lunch. All the while the flies which had not found a place on the manure heap were looking for one in the house. Every non removable object specked by their passage. Several fly traps were hanging from the ceiling, most in dire need of being replaced, while flies explored the dining room table, the dishes, the glasses, the floor and the silverware. This was truly another horrific sight. But the room smelled good of food being prepared and the heat from both the fire and a wood oven in which meat was cooking provided warmth that was both soft and enchanting. I said absolutely not a word, so shocked I was by the aspect of the place. I observed and wondered how it could be. How I could have been forcefully kidnapped from Monaco and its impeccable white marble apartments, to this place that was without doubt a remnant of the Middle Ages. I came to the conclusion that time travel was possible, and that I had just experienced it.

And then the person I surmised to be my uncle came in the door, embracing my father and then my mother before lifting me in the air so that he could take a good look at me. "He looks just like you!" he exclaimed to my father while he kissed me. What struck me about him was how hard his unshaven beard was. Like Tata Marie he was all dressed in black and he smelled of what I know now to be the smell of cattle. He had just come back from the stables taking care of cows. He was not very tall either, maybe a bit taller than my grandfather Léon. He had the biggest handlebar mustache of all my Limousin family, and he spoke with a deep scratchy voice in a manner that was used to command. There was no arguing with him. He also had a severe limp, a leftover from World War One, he told me, beating on his left leg with the walking stick he had carved from a chestnut tree branch. As the time of lunch approached, more of the people came in, first the Père Gouraud—to the tune of his song—then another farm hand, then my father's cousin Gustave, who impressed me by his size, especially compared to his parents. He had just come back from the fields with the tractor. And finally Gustave's brother, Maxime, who was the elder son and took care of the cows, came in. It was way past my Monaco lunch time (in Monaco we ate at noon) and I anxiously looked at the grandfather clock indicating one thirty. At my grandmother's house, by that time the dishes were washed and put back in the closet, ready for the next meal. Tata Marie, who was the only woman of the entire household simply said "lunch time", and every person immediately found his place. We were finally ready to eat. I sat on the bench next to my newly-found aunt as if I had always known her, with my back to the fire, which was now really intense, and we proceeded with the biggest feast I had participated in. We started with pâté made from the pig they had killed in the previous fall, followed by a mushroom omelet made from their own eggs and mushrooms they had collected in the fields and woods they owned, and then there was a roasted hen with carrots, both products from their own stock. I thought for sure we were done with lunch, as I was already stuffed. But there was simply a lull in the action, as Gustave took out the biggest leg of lamb from the oven, which was served with roasted potatoes and green beans, all from their herd and from their garden. After that it was time for salad, and outside of the bread, it was the first time we had to resource to brought in ingredients: they did not produce oil or vinegar. The cheese was a white cheese they made from the milk of their own cows, and desert was cherry clafoutis from the cherries of their own cherry tree and eggs from their hens. The meal must have lasted three and a half hours, and by the time I had ingested the last bite of clafoutis, I was ready to go to sleep. While the grown-ups had coffee, my aunt sat me on her armchair by the fire, and I fell asleep in this house that had scared me so much when I had come in. The welcome, the warmth and the kindness of these people had made me feel right at home.

 My uncle woke me up so that he could take me around the farm to see the cows. In addition, it was time to take them to their second grazing of the day. I found it hard to leave the comfort of the house, and yet, I wanted to see more cows. Contrary to le Père Marzet whose cows each had a name, my uncle did not have a name for every one of his. He had names only for the four cows that were properly trained to pull the farm wagons and carts, the ones they worked with almost everyday to supplement the tractor. A farm this size should have had two tractors, but since they only had one, the second was replaced by a team of two cows that were trained to the tasks of farming. The visit lasted over an hour, as my uncle and my father discussed the difficulties of being a farmer. I was vaguely interested. There were only two things I wanted to do: see the big Limousin bull, and ride the tractor. The bull, with his massive head and impressive genitalia, I did see that day. But he was a sad sight. Farmers had the habit to keep the bull in the stable all day long—he basically never saw the light or the fresh grass prairies—as a means to manage the herd. Thus, despite his strength and beauty, the poor yet impressive animal was used only for reproduction, once or twice a month, and never came out except for these short spells. I loved the animal, but I could not understand how my uncle could lock up an animal in this manner and feel right about it. As for the tractor, I could not ride on it that day because Gustave had already returned to working in the fields and needed it. The "bergerie" was also interesting with the sheep constantly baying. And suddenly there was a great commotion, as my cousin Maxime organized the cow herd to take it to pasture for the afternoon. The thirty plus cows fought to fit into the cow path off to the left past the house, and Tata Marie told me to follow her as she was taking out the sheep. That day I was going to go with her. The sheep were a lot calmer than the cows, and Tata Marie was helped in her task by three dogs that were in charge of keeping the sheep going where they were supposed to. I was amazed that my aunt only had to say a few words in Limousin to the dogs who would turn into the right path, and get the entire herd to the right pasture. My aunt and I sat down on the grass, and she too, like Tonton François asked about life in Monaco. She had never been any place but Fondanèche and Ambazac. She had not ever been to Limoges, not even ten miles away. She had been born in the house where we had had lunch, she had been married there, she had given birth there, and not once over the course of her sixty-six years had she spent even one night away from her house. She decided right there and then that I would be an explorer because at the right age of seven I had already done more travel than she would ever. When Tata Marie fell sick in her later years, and had to go to the hospital in Limoges for overnight treatment, she refused to go, calling her sons assassins for daring to separate her from her house. And she got her wishes dying in the house of her childhood, of her life and of her parents at the age of ninety-five just one day short of the New Year in 1992.

That day as we were watching over the sheep, or rather it seemed to me, taking a break from housework, I asked my aunt about uranium mines. I could hear the humming noise of the machinery over the next range of hills. But she did not seem to know much, or care about it much. This proved to be highly ironic because in the seventies the French government passed a law stating that only the French government could own uranium. Since Limousin was the number one producer, the French Atomic Commission sent geologists to survey the area, and make arrangements should uranium be discovered in private hands, to exchange the uranium fields for equal value fields where there was no uranium. When the geologists showed up on this very field where my aunt and I were watching the sheep graze that day, their Geiger counters went crazy. They immediately cordoned off the pasture and declared it off limits. It turned out that at some places, high-grade uranium was not even a foot below ground, and that this was one of the most amazing uranium finds of the time. The Atomic Commission then sent doctors to survey us, and to find out why not everybody in the family had died of cancer. They were baffled by the health of the Fondanèche people, and they would be even more baffled today if they knew that none of them ever died before the age of ninety—despite walking and breathing uranium, and eating lamb that had grazed on what papers called "uranium pastures".

CHAPTER 8
La Fête Nationale
I Learn How to Ride a Bicycle

    By the time we got back to Card that night, it was again well past midnight. After the sheep had been brought back to their bergerie, it had been the turn of the cows to come back. My aunt and I were on the top step of the stoop watching the cows, when suddenly I realized how dangerous these animals can be. Spooked by my presence, one of the cows decided to investigate the matter closely, and climbing the steps to the house, pushed its huge head against me, causing me to fall backwards, while my aunt beat the cow back with her stick and my mother yelled in back of me. I had done nothing wrong, but my mother told me to immediately come inside and watch from behind the window. Then she declared that she did not want me near cows any longer. That order lasted about ten seconds, as my uncle took me by the hand, and leading me to the stables ensured that each cow could smell me and thus remember me the next time I came. I had not been as much scared as surprised, as had my aunt who had never seen any of her cows go up the stairs before. But cows could be dangerous my uncle related. Down in the town of Saint-Sylvestre, he knew a fellow farmer whose wife had died because of a cow. Two winters before, this farmer's wife had gone to get the cows out of the stable, as she has done thousands of times before. It was a cold day, with ice on the road. One cow slipped on the ice, another freaked and charged the farmer's wife crushing her to death against the stone wall of the barn. Then the cows had stood there like nothing had happened, incapable of comprehending the tragedy of the event, and not knowing what to do next. The farmer had gone for his shotgun, had killed the guilty cow on the spot, had buried his wife, sold the cows, and abandoned the farm. He had left Limousin, and nobody had ever heard from him again. My uncle told me that if I walked passed the house today, I would see it with it broken windows, the door gaping, the roof already leaking, and the weeds growing in between the stones of the entrance. It was a shame, he said. He told me to remember that cows were nice animals but their intellect was not highly developed. He said "they are here for one purpose, give us milk and meat". I guess that explained how he treated the bull.

Coming back to the farmhouse, it was already dark, and Gustave rode home on the tractor. Fondanèche in all of its backwardness actually had electricity (unlike Card). The house and the barns used it, although all of the milking was done by hand—there were no milking machines then in Limousin. When we entered the house I could not believe that the table was set anew. After all we had eaten, my aunt had prepared another meal during the afternoon, and we were to eat again. Rather than the white bread we had eaten for lunch, my uncle served a huge round pain de seigle (actually it was buckwheat bread, not rye bread), and it is with thick wide slices of this delicious bread that we accompanied our meal. There was soup, ham, left over lamb from lunch, salad, cheese and fruit. As the men drank red wine I slowly drifted to sleep again to wake up only when I arrived in Card, ready to go to bed.

Two days later was the much-awaited Fourteenth of July, the national holiday of France which Americans know as Bastille Day but which we simply call Fête Nationale, or Quatorze Juillet. Alice and Robert Marzet were both home since this is a national day off. In the morning instead of going to feed the cows, my father told me to get dressed to go to the bicycle race. There was a bicycle race every Quatorze Juillet and local riders tried to get enough points to advance to the next level of cycling. I was already a fan of cycling, and every day I impatiently waited for news of le Tour de France which only le Père Marzet could give me because in his house there *was* electricity and he had a radio which gave him the news of the race every night at eight o'clock together with national news. It was the year when the French had clearly intended to win le Tour de France, starting the race with stars like Anquetil who had won in 1957, Bobet the French world champion who had won the Tour three times, Rivière, and Geminiani. But in the middle of the race, the rivalries in the French camp had allowed the Spanish climber Bahamontes to take the lead, while the first Frenchman was the unexpected Anglade, over four minutes behind! For the Fête Nationale we were all hoping for a miracle worthy of our republican ancestors who had toppled the king. In this mood we went to the race, but in our hearts we were hoping to hear that Anglade had beaten Bahamontes. At the race I witnessed my first real bicycle crash, when coming out of the narrow railroad tunnel from Ambazac, some riders got tangled up and fell. Several remained on the ground, unprotected by modern helmets, bleeding, and the ambulance had to get into action and take them to the hospital in Limoges, while the rest continued on to Saint-Léonard. I was so impressed that I told my father I wanted to ride in races as well. Always a pragmatic, he stated that I had to learn how to ride first. I replied that I already knew how, since in Monaco I had my own bicycle and rode well enough. But it was a child's bike and I needed to ride on a grown-up bike.

After the race we walked down the hill to the War Memorial where the mayor of the little town, accompanied by the municipal band conducted a ceremony to honor the sacrifice of those who had died in the world wars. This was his way to celebrate the Fête Nationale, while in Paris the President attended the annual Fourteenth of July Military Parade. There were many names on the memorial, and although none were related to us, many soldiers were named Faure. In 1959, on this hot summer day, blasting with hope of a French victory in the Tour, the memories of both wars were still very vivid, and there were many relatives of those who had died. There were also the comrades of the veteran associations with their French flags decorated with the gold letters of the battles they had fought in, there were war invalids in their wheelchair tricycles who had returned home unable to take care of their farm and their families, and there were also a few soldiers serving in the on-going war in Algeria who were home for a short leave. At exactly eleven o'clock, the band played "To the Dead" (in the US, it is known as Taps), and after the minute of silence, the mayor laid the wreath in the name of the town of Ambazac, while many in the assistance cried softly at the memory of their relatives and friends. Le Père Marzet was there, and the Père Christophe, their decorations pinned on the left breast pocket of their suit. And Tonton François was also there, decorated, holding the flag of his regiment, and when our eyes made contact, I saw there were two long tears rolling down his cheeks. The mayor, overcome by emotion—he was also a World War One veteran—made a hurried speech, before he too was overcome by emotion and unable to speak, and the band burst out into La Marseillaise, the French national anthem. In those days everyone in France knew the words, I included, and as the band played we sang along, there was such a strong sense of pride and thankfulness for these veterans, that everybody was teary eyed by the time the band finished playing. Deep inside everybody was also hoping that a Frenchman would win the stage of the day. Then the band organized for a little parade and marched on towards the church square playing various military marches such as La Madelon, and Sambre et Meuse, and the entire crowd followed on to the bar across the square from my aunt's épicerie. The bar was a mob scene, with people calling to each other, shaking hands, socializing and drinking wine or Pastis, celebrating this Quatorze Juillet joyfully despite the memory of so many who should have been there. So many good soldiers. I drank a glass of Vichy grenadine, which is a mixture of Vichy water and red grenadine syrup. If it was not wine, at least it looked like it! At lunch time we crossed the street and went into the épicerie where Tata Marie had prepared a real feast for the Fête Nationale, to include a cake known as Paris-Brest purchased from the pastry shop. In the afternoon, we went to the little soccer field behind the Gendarmerie and watched the game as the Ambazac team faced off against the much stronger La Jonchère, and tied the game before finally losing two to one on a corner kick in the last minutes of play. When we got back home, Tonton François turned on the radio for the six o'clock news and we found out that no miracle had taken place on the roads of le Tour de France: an Italian had won the stage and Bahamontes was still in front. The only consolation was the fact that our only French hope, Anglade was now second. That year Bahamontes would go on to win the Tour, thus becoming the first Spaniard to ever do so. As the day lazily waned into evening, we had soup and we all waited with anticipation for the fireworks which would be fired just outside the village, on the other side of the railroad bridge, not far from where we had seen the bicycle race in the morning.

The next day was to be one of the most challenging days in my life. My father pulled out his old bicycle, dating back to the forties, and proceeded to fix it so I could ride it. After at least two trips to the bicycle shop to purchase tubes, tires, and brake parts, three hours of labor, maintenance and oiling of the chain, my father conducted a test ride and decided himself satisfied with his work. I was finally ready to embark on my grown-up bike adventure. It was easier said than done. Even with the seat as low as could be, I had a hard time reaching the ground. To add to the difficulty the lane in front of the house was not a hard top, and had ruts, stones, and grass. And this bicycle had brakes on the handlebar, while mine had brakes activated by the pedals. I am glad that there are no pictures to document the event: I was hesitant but pretty well managed the first two or three test runs of a few hundred feet in front of the house. This is when I decided to go down the cow path to the crossroad where a few days earlier le Père Marzet and I had discovered the sabotage of the "borne". This was downhill, in a rutted path, and suddenly, I lost contact with the pedals, the bike went flying as I was unable to brake due to the bumps, and just like the riders in the race I found myself kissing the ground with my nose, which immediately turned into a fountain of blood. Le Père Marzet and my mother came to my rescue, and like the rider in the race I imagined I was being carried to the Limoges hospital. Like him, as he was laying on the gurney, I waved at the crowd which showered me with applause. Suddenly I was in le Tour de France, and as I had seen in the news at the movie theater, I got up from my wreckage, got back on the bicycle and raced to victory. Well, pampered by my mother who that day again issued a tern interdiction, this one never to get on the bicycle again, I did not exactly rise from my wreckage. After an hour of trying to stop the bleeding, my father took me to Ambazac to the doctor, who decided I had probably broken my nose, needed to have medical cotton shoved into it as far as possible, which he took great pleasure in doing, had to breathe through my mouth, and that within a day the cotton could be taken out, and I could ride again. The next day, my father and I sneaked out of the house, pushed the bicycle out of the barn, and within a few minutes I had mastered enough skill to ride. I had been riding around the lane and the cow paths for about two hours before my mother came out and realized that I had disobeyed her orders. And the fact that my father had helped me in doing so facilitated neither my case, nor his when he came back from visiting Tata Marie in Ambazac. My mother was like the Maréchal Pétain: she wanted to make an example, and she wanted an execution. Fortunately she chose to make an example of my father, and she refused to serve dinner for three straight days, while telling me that if I wanted to go and kill myself I was free to do so, and that she would not cry at my funeral.

Unfortunately for my father, a few days later, after he had borrowed a bicycle from Alice, he decided that we should go together on a ride as father and son. We went down the lane and turned left on the Départementale in the direction of the small village of Les Loges. At that time, there was still a bar in Les Loges, and when we reached our destination, my father had a beer, and I had a Vichy grenadine. All was well until I expressed my concern about the big hill I had to climb to get back to Card. "Don't worry", minimized my father, "it is not a big hill"! Well, as I had experienced many times before, he was wrong. As I desperately tried to find the strength to climb the hill while staying on the bicycle, I lost my balance to the left—I found out since then that seventy-eight percent of the time cyclists fall on the left—and suddenly found myself zooming across the road toward the unforgiving barbed wire fence that kept the cows in that farmer's field. There was the equally unattractive alternative of hitting a tree, or a patch of stinging nettles, or perhaps not as bad a bunch of hazelnut trees. In a desperate move I lunged off the bicycle toward the hazelnut trees, while the bicycle crashed in a noise of crunched metal, broken glass and scratched chrome behind me. When I came to, my father and a stranger were looking at me, and pouring water on my face. I managed to stumble up, but it was painful. My head hurt, and I had a significant bump on it, my knees were scraped, my hand was bleeding, and the headlight of the bicycle had been broken. My father insisted I get back on the bicycle, and we managed to get home. There was no way to hide my mishap, and the first thing my mother said was "I told you so"! By that time, I did not care much about what she said because I had had a good time with my father, riding together, having a drink at the bar. And so what if I fell. That was the first time I ever rebelled against my mother as she demanded that anti-bicycle sanctions be taken against me.

Limousin was making me discover an entirely new universe both outside and inside me. Sights and feelings I had never experienced were becoming part of me, and in these first two weeks of my first summer in Limousin, I matured so much that for a time I forgot Monaco, and playing with my toys. There was so much to do, to discover, to learn, so many people to meet, animals to feed, and so many conversations about war, about the danger of cows, about uranium mining…So much more than in Monaco. It seemed that these people lived by different values, and despite the lack of comfort, no running water, and working every day of the year, they were so much more welcoming and cared so much more about each other, that I started to look at my Monaco family in a different light.

CHAPTER 9
Visiting Family:
Tata des Quatre-Vents

As the days passed it became more and more urgent to make trips to visit family, as our vacation was drawing to an end so much quicker than anticipated. With every Sunday taken by lunch at Tata Marie's, there were not many days left to visit the other members of the family. There was cousin Jean (John in English), and cousin Hortense, and the aunt of the Quatre Vents (the Four Winds), and the cousin of Saint-Priest, and cousin Michel in Limoges, who was a school principal, and cousin Marcelle, Gustave's and Maxime's sister who lived in another town. There it was already July fifteen, we had to leave on July twenty-eight to go back to Monaco, and that left only nine days to visit all of them, not taking into account the invitation for a farewell dinner at Fondanèche which we had accepted. And I had to ride the bicycle, and my father had started wiring the house so that we would have electricity next time we came. A decision had to be made. But not before we went to Limoges to buy wiring and materials to do the electric. This was to be an expedition indeed. The day before we left, my father had spent the better part of the morning measuring, calculating, making plans, as he usually did when he had a major mission. He had then made a list of everything he needed since Limoges was far away, no store in Ambazac sold everything he needed, and he did not want to have to go back for more materials. That afternoon, the workers of the Electricité de France had showed in their grey Citroën truck, and had actually connected the circuit breaker box to the electric wires. I was fascinated by how simple they made it look, while my father had spent so many hours simply making plans. I was excited about going to Limoges until my father told me we would spend our time there in a hardware store and gave me the choice to stay with Tata Marie for the entire day instead. Given this choice there was no choice, because spending the day in the épicerie was like spending the day in Ali-Baba's cave. So, off my parents went to Limoges while I got ready to help Tata Marie. And there were so many things to discover there yet. Like the wire used to cut butter and cheese. I could not understand how a piece of wire could cut anything. And what about using a knife? What was wrong with that? That morning my aunt showed me why, and how much easier it was to use the wire than the knife.

By the time my parents dropped me off, the épicerie was already in full combat alert, especially since the market was in town, and the entire church square had been taken over by the stands of the merchants who had come from as far away as the Atlantic coast to sell their goods. And it was an important day for Ambazac, as this was the townspeople's only opportunity to buy fresh fish. But it was an equally important day for Tata Marie as customers came from all around to the market and often took advantage of this opportunity to buy their regular groceries as well. That day my aunt found out that having me around actually boosted her sales, as she used me to get the fruits from their crates and her customers thought it was so cute to see this little boy from Monaco helping his aunt. After we were done with the morning rush, we had lunch with Tonton François who ate soup twice a day, and always added wine to it. Then my aunt went back to serving more customers, as I helped her prepare for the evening rush. She would never leave the grocery store alone. And not even for a moment would she think of putting Tonton François in charge. So, she spent her every waking hour in the store. When she was not selling, she was restocking or receiving deliveries which were stored in a big warehouse next to my uncle's wooden clogs shop, or she would clean and wax, and ensure the épicerie remained in top shape. So that afternoon when she told my uncle she was going out with me for a minute I was really surprised. She took me to the store stuck between the two roads coming from Limoges, and this store sold clothes, lamps, sheets, towels, and toys. And there, to thank me for all my work in the previous two weeks, she told me I could have any Dinky Toys car I wanted. I was awed, and had not considered this possibility at all. Which car to choose? I did not want to blow it. Racing cars, were there any racing cars? No racing cars. I panicked. I sure had wished that they had had racing cars in this store. But all was not lost, because I discovered the car that was the hottest car that year, the cream colored Peugeot 403 Cabriolet. Surely, this was the car worthy of all the work I had done for my aunt. This is how I became the new owner of this prized car, which I never intended to leave out of my sight. This car was so much cooler than the stupid Renault my father had bought. If only he had listened to me. But I did not care, and as soon as I got back to the épicerie I started testing it on the waxed wood floor of the shop. It was a dream car. But my aunt did not take lightly to someone playing in her épicerie. I had to go and put the car on the kitchen table and I had to come and continue to help her with the chores. If she had waited nine years for her husband, I guess I could wait a few hours to play with my car...

But with all these distractions, my apprenticeship with Tonton François did not go very well. He told me he could not possibly continue this way and would have to demote me if I did not show up for work. Tonton François always liked to joke and make serious situations easy to solve through humor. He was always ready to tell a joke, play a trick on someone and have a good laugh. That's the way he operated. Sometimes people took him seriously, and he laughed even more. Like the day that one of his customers came with a terrible toothache and the village dentist was no where to be found. Tonton François told him he was a dentist too and he could pull that tooth and save him a bundle. The poor guy was in so much pain that he could not have cared less who told him what. So the two of them with me in tow crossed the street and went to the bar, because this feat had to be done in public, like in the Middle Ages. The patient was holding his mouth with both of his hands, ready to pass out from the agony of the pain. Tonton François had brought over a couple of his best pliers, to include the ones lined with leather, and I followed, wondering how my uncle would pull a tooth. It started with a glass of "fine" (pronounced "feen") which is the plum alcohol produced in Limousin. After two glasses each, both the patient and the would-be dentist were ready for surgery. My uncle, used to pulling nails out of wood, pulled the tooth without effort, and brandished it like a trophy above the heads of all who had gathered to witness this feat: the wooden clog maker filling in as the dentist! A couple more glasses of fine, and the patient was about just as pleased with the surgery as the dentist himself. There was minimal bleeding and the pain was gone. That's when the real dentist showed up. He did not take lightly to this incident. He was absolutely furious, threatening to get the gendarmes in there and get Tonton François arrested for practicing dentistry without a license! But everyone in the bar stated that they had not seen anything, and that they knew nothing of a tooth extraction taking place in the bar. The dentist had two factors against him. First, he was an outsider, an out-of-towner, a "Monsieur" who was tolerated as long as he did not pester anyone. Second, he had just mentioned the word gendarmes and that was a big no-no in the villages of Limousin, where gendarmes were despised and often ridiculed. Now, the dentist beside himself with rage spotted me and pointing his finger at me screamed "truth comes out of the mouth of children, so I am going to ask this child if he saw anything". Of course, the dentist could not have known that Tonton François was who he was (that is my uncle), and he could not have known of the bond already created between my uncle and myself, and he could not have known that I was ready to lie to protect my uncle, and finally, he could not have known of the valuable lesson I had learned in my incident with the Père Christophe. Without a nanosecond of hesitation, I advanced that I had seen nothing as remotely resembling "someone pulling a tooth". The entire assembly of men in the bar exploded with laughter caused by the confidence with which I had made this false statement. The dentist, as close to explode from rage as the frog in the Frog and the Ox fable of La Fontaine could not believe it, and turning to the patient, grabbing his chin, he yelled "and him, who did that to him? Did he lose his tooth by himself?" The patient in question had in fact been in the same infantry regiment as my uncle in the big war. This, the fact that he had had a few glasses of "fine", and that the poor man wanted to celebrate with his friends, led him to declare that "this asshole could go f…himself" and he threw the dentist out of the bar. My uncle, he and I had become instant heroes and the raucous and joyful celebration was in full swing when my parents showed up at the épicerie to pick me up! To say that the stuff was about to hit the fan would be an understatement…

It was decided that I had had enough excitement for the day, and with my uncle slightly under the weather, we headed home with all types of threats of punishment since I had lied to the dentist. What had made me a hero at the bar brought about my condemnation with my mother who declared that from now on I would be locked in the house, and would only go out under her own supervision. My father said nothing, which was a good indication that the sanction would not be carried out.

And indeed it was that the next morning I was out helping le Père Marzet feed the cows. Alice was home, and she asked me if I could climb a ladder. I had never done such a thing, but buoyed by my Limousin adventures, especially after becoming the hero of the Bar de l'Eglise the day before, I assured her that even though I had never done it, I could certainly do it. Well she said, "I have a very special mission for you". "You need to take this basket, climb the ladder to the henhouse" and she pointed to the henhouse, "and collect the eggs for me". I thought about it for a second and asked her what I should do if I met a hen in the henhouse. I had seen them fight amongst each other, and I knew they had sharp claws and a sharp beak. Alice assured me that there were no hens in the henhouse at this time of day, and that I would not have any problem. Well there are two things Alice did not know. First there *was* a hen in the henhouse and second, I did not know the difference between the fake eggs that were placed in the henhouse to entice the hens to lay their eggs, and the real eggs. As soon as I was at the top of the ladder, I saw the black hen sitting on the bench, and I immediately realized that she did not want to be disturbed. This made me very scared, as it got agitated and beat its wings in a threatening manner. I hurried to pick up the eggs, and rushed down the ladder, proud to have accomplished the mission without the loss to my limbs. Alice laughed when she saw that the only eggs I had collected were the fake ones. Of course, until that day I had not even known that farmers used fake eggs to show the hens where to lay theirs. And she did not believe there could be a hen in the henhouse at this time of day, about eleven o'clock in the morning, because all the hens lay their eggs before ten usually. Well, this was an unusual hen, who decided to defend the henhouse even against Alice. When the climbed the ladder to put back the fake eggs, the hen attacked her and scratched her face. Alice—I had never seen her mad before, but now she was—closed the door to the henhouse, and cleaned up the scratches for fear of catching an infection. She then charged up the ladder swung the door of the henhouse open, grabbed the hen by the neck, and broke it. When she pulled it out of the hen house, the hen was already dead. Two days later, Alice and her family were eating that hen for lunch. I found out that there was a simple rule in Limousin: any domestic animal that attacked its owner was killed. This was true for cows, for hens, and for pigs.

That same day my father started the electric installation in earnest, and by noon time he had installed the conduit and the wires in the common room. I was fascinated by their colors: blue and red, and white for the ground, the colors of the French flag. I liked electricity a lot! Unfortunately, that afternoon we had to go visit the aunt of the Quatre-Vents. I had no idea who this aunt who lived at the Four Winds was. But I will never forget her or the place she lived in. After getting in the Dauphine, we drove on the lower road to Limoges, about halfway to the city, and arrived at a perfect four directional intersection. I guessed that the Quatre-Vents name came from there: there were four roads representing the four directions. Nobody explained anything to me. As my father parked the car on the side of the road in front of the wall surrounding the house and the garden, I saw a farm house just like my uncle's in Fondanèche, except this one was no longer a farm house and was pretty, with flowers growing all around and curtains in the windows, and even an electric bell at the gate. I had not been warned, and almost did not recover when the aunt of the Quatre-Vents opened the door of her house to come open the gate. She was a witch! There was no other word to describe her, and I held my mother's hand tighter, because I was sure we had fallen into the trap that poor Snow White had fallen into in the movie I had seen, where the witch had poisoned her with the apple. The so-called aunt was dressed all in black, with a black hat which had a large rim, and in my confusion at the time it seemed pointy, and she was the oldest person I had ever seen. Her hands were skin and bones, with long fingers and sharp fingernails, and her face was emaciated, making her nose look like if was straight out the Grimm's story. I was scared beyond reason, and my mother had to struggle to get me going into the right direction. And I was supposed to kiss her? And the nightmare continued, as Tata des Quatre-Vents bent forward and greeted me with a kiss. I closed my eyes, hoping that she would turn into a princess. And this is the precise moment when I lost faith in any of the fairy tales that I had read. There was no way any of this stuff could happen. I decided there and then that a queen could not possibly turn into something as hideous as this creature—and if she was supposed to be my aunt, where was the uncle that came with her—and such a hideous creature could not possibly be turned into a princess.

But my father seemed comfortable with her, as we went in. Now, having been at Fondanèche already, I was expecting the worst in this house. To the contrary, everything was immaculate, the common room was bright, painted white, the stove—a gas stove—was modern, like the one at Tata Marie d'Ambazac, and the sun shone brightly in the room. We sat down, and I did not dare move still petrified by the aunt. My eyes followed her every move, and it was not too difficult since she moved slowly with the help of a cane. She managed to take out three glasses—and I got even more scared since it meant she would not drink. She offered my parents a glass of cold cider, and for me, she pulled out a special container—I was going to be poisoned—of Orangina. She poured it, and I simply let it sit, not daring to touch it. She came over and said in her diminutive voice that I could take my glass, and could go drink it under the "tonnelle" (an approximate translation of this word is arbor). That was a good idea! She added that she knew exactly what I was thinking, that I should not be afraid, she was not a witch, but that when people get to be almost a hundred years old like she was, this is what they looked like. She said "go ahead go outside, look at the flowers, run in the alleys of my garden". I was embarrassed and did not say anything, as I took my glass and went sit in the tonnelle. Since that day I have not seen a tonnelle as beautiful as this one. It was made of thick ivy that kept the sun from penetrating it, and it was a full tonnelle, a cylinder topped by a half sphere, and an opening slightly smaller that a regular door. Inside was a bistro table with four chairs. I placed my glass on the table and sat on the chair facing the door, trying to assimilate everything the aunt had said in these couple of sentences. Limousin was definitely a land of discovery and of firsts in my life: I had never seen a person who was almost one hundred years old, and even if I had seen one, I certainly had never talked to one; there were people like the aunt of the Quatre-Vents who could guess exactly what you were thinking—this was dangerous, and I immediately thought that maybe my mother also could figure out what I was thinking, which could get me in terrible trouble; then, there was this stupendous piece of learning that when people got old they looked liked her. This had to be a disconnect because I knew old people, my grandparents, my parents, my aunts and uncles, and none looked like her, but then they were not one hundred years old…Maybe I was not so interested in becoming one hundred years old if I had to look like that! I would have to consult with my grandmother Lainey when I got home. The rest of the visit was uneventful. I played in the garden as she suggested, and soon it was time to leave. I had to kiss her again, and we got in the car. As soon as the Dauphine was on the road my father turned to me and said "this was not very nice what you did this afternoon with Tata des Quatre-Vents—next time we come I expect you to be a lot nicer to her. Do you understand me?" There was no replying, and no arguing. I understood, and I was glad that next time would be the following summer and I would have the time to overcome my fright and hesitation to be nice to such old people.

I would have a few more opportunities to be nice to Tata des Quatre-Vents, who turned out to be my great-grandmother's sister, and died a few years later. It also turned out that she had been born in Card, that there had been an uncle des Quatre-Vents, but that he had died in World War One, and the only remembrance of him was on the War Memorial in Ambazac. His name was there, carved on the granite of the monument, and gilded, and it is still there today, two word "Jean Périchon" the only testimony to having been of this world, as his body has never been recovered.

CHAPTER 10
The Secret Mushroom Hunt

A key principle of life in the country was to get everything possible from the earth. Unlike in Monaco, where the entire landscape was urban, and food was brought in miraculously to the market every day, here in Limousin, people were pre-occupied with food on a constant basis. If le Père Marzet wanted potatoes, he simply went to the potato field and dug them up. If it was shallots, we would simply go to the vegetable garden and pull a plant from the ground. And if it was a chicken, he would go to the poultry-yard, catch a chicken, kill it, and eat it the next day. But there were still some food items they did not produce, or could not make. For these items, the cooperative store would dispatch a van on a weekly basis to travel to every remote village and hamlet, and the van would deliver the food stuff not available from the farm. The cooperative truck came to Card on Wednesday afternoons between four and five. It was a Citroën van painted in a cream color, and it bore the logo of the store in red letters placed diagonally that spelled "COOP" (pronounced co-op). When it arrived, it would stop right in front of our door, and the Card neighbors would line up with their lists to purchase oil, vinegar, salt, pepper, sugar, coffee, flour, rice and pasta, and the occasional yoghurt or commercial cheese such as camembert or brie. The arrival of the truck was always awaited with great anticipation. The women of Card, and that included my mother, would gather ahead of time, and gossip, and talk until they were ready for their limited shopping. When the truck left using the narrow cow path, it was gone for a week, and unless you could go to Ambazac, whatever you got, is whatever you had until the following Wednesday. The same system applied to the baker's deliveries. Each boulangerie had a specific day to deliver bread, and not all of them delivered bread. On Monday, the Boulangerie Lechat stopped by Card. He would park the gray Peugeot 203 station wagon at the entrance of the lane, on the left hand side and would beep his horn to announce he was there. At that time, everyone who needed bread would rush to the car (or they may already have been waiting), purchase the bread they needed and the Boulangerie Lechat truck would move on to its next stop in the hamlet of La Boissarde. On Wednesdays the same scenario would repeat itself with the Boulangerie Faure which came from the rue de l'Eglise with its newer Peugeot 403 station wagon, and on Thursday it was the Boulangerie Péricault, the brother of the Péricault who owned the Citroën garage who would stop by in his brand new and impressive ID 19 Citroën station wagon. I remember running down the lane with the money in my hand to buy the bread for our family. With my shorts and my tennis shoes, I was a serious competitor to the housewives to get there first! And we did not buy the scrawny little pieces of bread sold in Monaco or Paris, which we know today under the generic name of baguettes. No, we bought hearty big pieces of bread, just what a farmer needed after a long day in the fields. We dealt with mélées and tourtes. The mélées were twisted pieces of bread, about six times the size of a baguette and about time and a half as long, with a thick crunchy crust. Their taste was so much better than today's baguettes: they had the full wheat flavor and they did not turn stale after one day either. You could keep them three of four days, and they were still good to eat. The tourtes were big circular breads, like today's round pain de campagne, but they were about six or seven times their size and they were made from buckwheat flour. These tourtes were a favorite of Limousin to make sandwiches, and to cut in small pieces that we added to the soup in the evening. Each boulangerie had its specialty: nobody would have bought tourtes from Lechat, he could only make mélées well, which was the opposite of Faure. As for Péricault, people really looked forward to his pastries more than to his bread. Today in Ambazac you can still buy this same bread, and the Boulangerie Lechat has survived, under another name, but you can still buy the famous mélées there, avenue de la Libération.

But there were other things that did not grow in the gardens of Card but were collected by the farmers and by le Père Marzet, and these were the mushrooms. Although July was a bit early for hunting mushrooms, they still could be found. However, the topic of mushrooms was a highly controversial one, that was not approached lightly, and certainly not in public. One day, when I saw le Père Marzet preparing mushrooms for an omelet, I asked "Where did you find these mushrooms?" He answered "Oh, malheureux, keep quiet!" He made it clear that the topic was not to be raised again, and certainly not outside the house where everyone could hear what was being said. He took me inside the house, closed the door, and in a whisper explained about mushrooms. They grow only in certain areas, and different mushrooms grow in different areas. They also grow at different times. Therefore, a keen mushroom hunter like le Père Marzet knew which mushrooms grew where and when, and this knowledge had been acquired through years of experience, of trial and error, and it was not to be shared with anyone. It was important to make sure that any mushroom hunting expedition would be kept absolutely secret—even from my parents, and that if somebody asked me by chance how the mushroom collection had gone, I was to answer that we had not found a single one. He made me promise that I would never talk about mushroom hunting outside the house, that I would never ask him to take me on a mushroom hunt (he would tell me to get ready to go the wine store and wink at me in a certain way when it was time to go), and that I would never ever reveal where I had found mushrooms—even to my parents.

A few days later, when we were watching the cows in the pasture of La Boissarde, he leaned over and told me that the next day he and I would be going to the wine store—wink, wink. It had rained two days before, and the sun had been shining ever since: he said the wine should be particularly good. He then explained that there were five types of mushrooms that could be picked, not more as all of the other ones would kill you. First, there was the king of all mushrooms, the cèpe, which we know as porcini, but it was too early for this one, and we would not find any until late August. Then, there was his brother, the bolet (boletus in English) that was the same shape but a bit smaller and with an orangey stem—and it was a trickster, because the cousin of the bolet was the poisonous bolet, which had enough poison in one bite to kill you, and le Père Marzet called it Satan's mushroom. The third type was the chanterelles or giroles, which were easily recognizable because of their bright orange color, but they hid under the chestnut tree leaves, and you had to have a stick to move the leaves around. Never with the hands had he cautioned, because the forest where these mushrooms grew was also the domain of the dangerous aspic viper. And a bite of the aspic would be deadly, "especially for someone your size", he added. That was not reassuring. So when you come tomorrow, make sure you wear your knee-high rubber boots, the vipers cannot bite through them. That was some relief. And he continued with the mushroom classification. In the pastures, I would find the colomelle (lepiota), a tall white and brownish mushroom with brown flakes on its beautiful umbrella top. But he warned, be careful to see that it is not more brown than white and to notice what the ring looked like on its stem: if it was thin and grooved it was a colomelle, but if it was thick and smooth, then you had just touched its poisonous brother, the brown colomelle, or death angel, a single gram of which would kill the unsuspecting eater. And finely there was the rosé des prés, the relative of the Paris mushroom, which could be picked safely, since it had no poisonous relatives. Le Père Marzet continued that all other mushrooms should be considered poisonous, especially the red amanita which was the deadliest of all French mushrooms. All of these explanations made me a lot less eager to go collecting mushrooms, and for a while, I would only tell le Père Marzet where the mushrooms were, not daring to touch them myself. Then le Père Marzet said we had to leave before sun up so that nobody could follow us in the dark. I had never gotten that early in my life, and now came the very practical question of how I was supposed to wake up, get dressed, have breakfast, and get out of the house without my parents knowing about it. After all, I was seven, and by now I did know that some things are simply impossible to do—and sneaking out of the house at five in the morning without my parents knowing about it was one of these things. Le Père Marzet simply commented that everything would be taken care of.

That night I went to bed knowing full well that I would miss out on the mushroom hunt, and I would not wake up on time. Yet, as if by magic, my father came to my room, got me dressed warmly, it was always cool in the morning, got my boots on, and gave me my tartines and a couple of Alsacienne cookies from Tata Marie's épicerie. I grabbed my viper stick and I was on my way with the recommendation to be careful of snakes. And there, by the front door in the very first light of the starting day, le

Père Marzet was waiting with a canvas bag to put our mushrooms. We took paths I had never known existed, we crossed the Départementale, went up hills, and down ravines, and finally, le Père Marzet stopped. He listened intently to make sure no one had followed us, and for the first time that morning he talked, revealing in a whisper "we are in the Camp de César". I had heard of Caesar's Camp. In fact in Monaco, I lived just below the mountain that had marked the border between the Roman Empire and Gaul until Caesar had decided to conquer Gaul, and there was a Roman camp, and the famous Tower of Augustus on top of the mountain in La Turbie. But I had never been in Caesar's Camp. I imagined Roman legionnaires walking around, and the throne of Caesar in the middle of the woods under a red tent. Later, I would find out that there are many places called "Camp de César" in the Limousin. Nobody is really certain why they are called that, but these places seem to have been used between the first and the eleventh centuries, either as a fortified encampment, or as a mining community. There is always a mysterious way in Limousin about why places are named as they are. People have simply forgotten why places got their names. In World War II, the Camp de César had been used by the French underground to store weapons, and to plan operations in the neighboring countryside. But this role as a Résistance movement base had been much embellished over the recent years, and its modest contribution to the war effort had probably spared Ambazac and Card the fate of the town of Oradour-sur-Glane.

That morning however, there were no traces of Roman soldiers, fortifications, mining or Résistance fighters, as we made our way first through a thick forest of chestnut trees, and then physically fought the tight grip of bramble to reach the right location. After what seemed an eternity fighting blackberry bushes and their sharp thorns, and the undergrowth of countless trees, there, in front of us, in the still dark underwood were hundreds of the chanterelles, shining bright yellow against the dark humus. Le Père Marzet showed me how to collect them, making sure I only took the bigger ones who had already matured and leaving being the smaller ones which would grow to adult size within a couple of days. He was careful to ensure neither of us would walk on the mushrooms, and within a few minutes, his canvas bag was full. He turned to me and asked in a whisper "where is your bag?" I did not have a bag.

So he pulled another bag from his coat pocket and gave it to me to fill with my own mushrooms as he had explained. During that time, he pulled slices of tourte from his satchel, and he prepared tartines with crème fraîche. Once I was done, we sat on a patch of green moss, listening to the birds singing in the light of the new morning. We returned following a different route than the one we had taken on the way there, as the key to success was to avoid encounters with any other human being. We got back to Card from the North, having avoided all of its farms, and especially having avoided walking past Robert Teulier's house, from where he could see everybody walking in and out of Card.

I got home, and triumphantly gave my mother over a kilo of mushrooms, not telling her anything about how I got across so many chanterelles. She was relieved to learn that I had not run into any vipers, and that I had not touched any poisonous mushrooms. That lunchtime we enjoyed the best mushroom omelet ever made, after which I went and took a long afternoon nap.

CHAPTER 11
The Mercier Family

For almost the entire month of July I had been around adults, and I had learned how to work on a farm, in a grocery store and in a wooden clogs artisan shop. In other words I had seen no children even remotely close to my age. That's when my father said that we were going to visit his cousin Marcelle who had two children about my age. I was looking forward to this eventuality. Although by this time, I was not missing children my age, and I had found no need to play with toys, as my mind was occupied with cows, chickens, pigs, the danger of vipers—I was always on the lookout for one—Torpille, bornes, tractors, mushroom secrets, and so many other things that I hardly found the time to sleep. Marcelle was my Uncle Emile's oldest child and single daughter. She had married a farmer from Saint-Pardoux, Jean Mercier, and lived on his family farm. She had two sons, Raymond who was two years older than me, and Louis—known as Petit-Louis, like the famous cyclist—who was two years younger. Saint-Pardoux is a very small village with just over three hundred people on the other side of the N20 from Ambazac, and not far from Fondanèche. About half an hour after we left Card we arrived at a farm that was very similar to the one in Fondanèche. Several buildings of granite stone made up the complex, and although they did not have sheep like in Fondanèche, they had a good quantity of cows, over thirty, which unlike in other places I was used to, they let graze outside all day long. As we came to a stop, cousin Marcelle walked out of the house to welcome us. She was a beautiful, tall, and energetic woman of thirty-seven years of age, tanned, wearing blue and yellow farm clothes, and she was quickly followed by my two young cousins, who were anxious to play with me. We immediately hit it off, and they asked me what I wanted to do. I asked them to go see their cows. They thought it was strange, and we set off to visit the cows, and I to make them laugh so hard they would soon be rolling on the ground. My problem was that I had never seen an electric fence for cows. In Card or at Fondanèche there was no need for them since someone was always watching the animals, but at Saint-Pardoux, where they let the cows graze all day long, they needed a fence to keep the cows in, and they had installed an electric fence. The principle of electric fences is that they shock the cows when they touch them. After one or two such instances, the cows understand they need to stay away from the fence, and the farmer can leave his cows unattended. Well, the electricity that shocks the cows also shocks humans. And these two new cousins of mine, of course did not say anything. As I approached the fence, they said we should go in the field to see the cows at close range. Because the wire was too low for me to get under, they invited me to go first, and I grabbed it to lift it, to allow me to pass. At the same moment I got shocked, let go, backed up, tripped and fell in puddle of muddy water which just happened to be there. My two cousins started laughing, they were laughing, crying, bent over in pain from laughing at their own trick, and at my falling into the puddle of mud. Finally, my younger cousin Petit-Louis who was laughing even harder than his brother lost his balance and fell in the puddle as well. That brought my other cousin to his knees, and caused me to laugh as well, and we laughed like idiots for at least ten minutes before we could catch our breaths. That was the most fun part of my entire trip to Limousin.

As we walked back to the farmhouse, I made them laugh even more as I was concerned how I was going to explain this—I meant the dirty clothes—to my mother. To my cousins this was an everyday occurrence that was not even worth mentioning. But what was worth mentioning to their parents was how I had grabbed the electric fence, fallen over, and ended up in a puddle of mud! Marcelle was cross with Raymond for having set me up, and then, of course my mother became cross with me for being so stupid as to fall for a trick like that. My father, as always, calmed down the ardor of my mother to punish me for my foolishness, and he and Marcelle sent the three of us out to play. That was easier said than done because my retarded cousins did not even have toys. By this time in the afternoon I was rather angry with these two jerks, and I kept telling them that in Monaco kids had toys, not like them. To my consternation, they did not even know what a Ferrari was, and they had never seen a Rolls-Royce—and they had no idea what I was talking about. Now it was time for me to have fun with them. I invented brands of cars, asking them if they knew them, just to tell them they were stupid because these cars did not exist. Raymond got tired of it, and asking me to follow him told me he was going to show me the best toy. I was now on my guards, and let him and Petit-Louis lead the way, well ahead of me. They took me to one of the barns, and there in its glory was an orange Renault tractor. Turning to me, Raymond said "I bet in Monaco you don't have one of these to play with!" He climbed on it and boasted that he could drive it. I told him he could not, and soon we were exchanging enthusiastic can-cannot while Petit-Louis looked anxiously as if he already knew this could only end badly. After so much taunting Raymond could not hold himself any longer, just like the crow in the fable of the Fox and the Crow, when the fox taunts the crow to sing, thus releasing and dropping the cheese he was holding in his beak to the delight of the fox waiting below. In my mind, my cousin Raymond on top of the tractor was the crow, and I on the ground was the fox. It was unavoidable. Raymond cranked up the tractor and started idling the engine. He put it in gear and drove it out of the barn—the doors were open—and made a turn down the road toward the house where my parents were visiting. This is probably when Raymond realized he was not supposed to play with a tractor that was towing a fully loaded hay trailer. In a panic he stopped in the middle of the road. He now had to accomplish a complex maneuver that even I had not mastered with my trucks: I could not turn around a tractor trailer in the streets of my living room in Monaco. And this is exactly what Raymond had to do, because unfortunately for him, there was a trailer attached to the tractor, and the trailer was full of hey!

I also realized that this was a situation where a witness could easily be construed to be an accomplice. I knew already that this incident could only develop into a major disaster, and I told Raymond that the only way out was to get his father. But simply having driven the tractor out of the barn was enough to deserve some type of punishment. Petit-Louis wanting nothing to do with the whole thing had already scampered and I was about to do the same when Raymond put the tractor in reverse. This was going to be too good to miss! Taking shelter behind the corner of the building, I watched as Raymond first succeeded in backing up slightly, but lacking the experience, and unable to see around the trailer, he overcompensated to the right when he started going left, and this is when it happened. The right wheel of the trailer slipped down the ditch, and the weight of the hey took the tractor with it down into the ditch as the trailer haplessly flipped to the side finally resting at a forty-five degree angle, the tractor bottoming out on the high side of the ditch. I desperately looked for Petit-Louis as I knew this could not have a good ending. Raymond ran after us, and decided he was going to hide for the rest of his life, which I thought was a good idea. Actually, joining the French Foreign Legion sounded ever more splendidly adequate. Since I could not play anymore, and Raymond was going into hiding, and Petit-Louis did not have any tractors to flip over, I decided to go back to the farmhouse. As I entered, my mother, like Tata des Quatre-Vents, read my mind and did not even ask if anything was wrong. Instead she inquired "What have you done this time?" Well, it was not me really, but I blurted that there had been a tractor accident. Jean Mercier rushed outside—it could only be his tractor since there was only one tractor in Saint-Pardoux, swearing as he saw the disaster "Putain de merde, mais putain de merde! Where is this fucking son of mine?" While he was running to the tractor, my mother turned to me and said "And you, what were you doing? You were watching him or helping him, tell me!" I knew that both Raymond and I were going to get a spanking; there was no doubt about that.

Jean assessed the situation, and with the help of my father, found out that nothing was broken. The tractor still ran, and by pulling gently forward there was hope of reaching a spot where the ditch turned into a culvert under a path. Slowly, I watched as Jean applied his driving skills, pulling the whole load with only the right wheels of the tractor touching the ground, then righting the Renault, taking it back onto the road, while the trailer squeaking and squealing slowly inched back on the road as well. Then, Jean backed up and parked it back into the barn it should never have left with the help of his wife. Now came the task of finding Raymond. He had run into the woods, and Petit-Louis would not betray his brother. So I was sent after him, and within an hour I delivered to him the message that he would not be punished because nothing was broken. He would not believe it—and frankly neither did I—but I told him our parents were waiting for us to have a snack and he reluctantly agreed to come along. When we got back to the house, Jean declared that the three of us should never be left alone again. We were too much trouble. This was easy to do during that visit, but there would be more, and our parents would forget the wise words of Jean Mercier.

We set down for our snack, and Jean Mercier, instead of going to the kitchen to get the ham, went to the fireplace, untied a rope, and lowered a ham that he had been smoking inside the chimney. We, the visitors from Monaco, were amazed. Jean explained that this is how he smoked all of the meats he produced at the farm. The pain de seigle, the smoked ham, the farm made butter, the pâté made by Marcelle, the fresh pears, all tasted so sweet that afternoon…especially after escaping the punishment. Today at the age of eighty-six, cousin Marcelle still lives on the farm. Her husband Jean Mercier, who proved so magnanimous that day, died in 2002, as for my cousins Raymond and Petit-Louis, life did not prove very kind to them. Petit-Louis became a roofer, and when he was about thirty, the father of a son and two daughters, he fell of a roof, ending up in a coma that lasted over three months, and becoming paralyzed on the right side. He refuses to see visitors and lives as a recluse in the farmhouse with his mother. His wife worn down by the stress of having to take care of him and three children finally gave up and left him. As for Raymond, his wife Marie-Joe fell victim to cancer after he had just retired from the French Postal Service. After all of these years the souvenir of the few hours we spent together on these vacation days when we had our entire life in front of us is even more bittersweet. If we had only known that these were the happiest moments of our lives…

CHAPTER 12
Laundry Day

    One of the biggest chores for a woman living in Card was to do the laundry, or as we say in French "faire la lessive". There was no running water in any of the houses, there certainly was no washing machine, and there was no hot water, except the one that could be boiled in the huge "marmites" hanging from the trammel hooks in the fireplace. Alice had to do laundry for two men and a woman. She would start by boiling water in the marmite. Once the water was boiling, she would take an iron tripod and put it in the fireplace over the red hot ambers. She would then set her "lessiveuse", or wash boiler, on top of the tripod, and transfer the boiling water to the lessiveuse with a ladle, while at the same time mixing in chips of soap she had purchased at Tata Marie's. She then would put the central percolator inside the lessiveuse, and she would place the light colored and white clothes, which included the heavy linen sheets used in Limousin at that time, into the lessiveuse, which was soon percolating and washing the clothes. Once the light colored and white clothes were done, she would transfer them to another lessiveuse using big wooden clips, and she would start over the same operation with the work blues and the dark colors. The entire process lasted a full afternoon, and the fire had to be kept hot enough to keep water boiling. While this process soaped up the clothes, it certainly did not rinse them. This was the second phase of the washing which took place the following day.
    Rinsing the clothes meant going down to the pond which was located in South Card passed the house of the Roussel family, at the edge of the hamlet, where the pastures began. To transport the clothes, Alice had a

two-wheel hand-pulled cart. The first step was to get the two lessiveuses on the cart, and since they were full of clothes and water, this was a task that required two people. After this was done and Alice had added her brushes, her washboard, a cube of Marseille soap, and her knee pads, she would walk down the lane to the small pond, and her main job was to make sure the heavy cart did not run away from her.

The pond was in fact a wash pond, with stone emplacements where the washers could kneel into, and a big slab of granite slanted at a forty-five degree angle that extended into the water in front of each washing position. Once Alice was there she went to her preferred wash emplacement and one by one she took the garments out of the lessiveuses and onto the slanted piece of granite. She would then simply pour the soapy water out, wash out the empty lessiveuse and set it next to her. Then, one by one she rinsed and pounded the soap out of the blues, some times rewashing tough stains with the piece of Marseille soap and the brush. Once she was done with the dark colors, she would switch to the whites, and proceed exactly the same way. When she was done, usually after an hour or an hour and a half, phase two of the washing cycle was complete. Now, she had to reload the lessiveuses onto the cart—since they contained no water she was able to do it—put the clean clothes back into the lessiveuses, pull the cart uphill back to her house, and hang the clothes to dry on the cloth lines that were installed all along the main alley of the vegetable garden. I was fascinated by how much effort this took, while in Monaco, we only had to sort the clothes, put them in a washing machine, forget about them for an hour, and bingo, they were done!

This was back-breaking work, which also explained why the farmers were reluctant to change clothes and sheets as often as we did in Monaco. It was during my last week in Limousin that Alice asked my mother if I could accompany her to the pond. I was always looking for something new to discover, and both Alice and Torpille were going to be there. I had never been passed the Roussel farmhouse—or so I thought—and I wanted to see what was beyond it. We walked down and in the Lemaunier farm I saw my first live domestic turkey. When we arrived at the pond Madame Roussel was already there washing and she invited me to come and visit with her sometime. While Alice and Madame Roussel were speaking, I realized that I had been there before, because on the other side of the small valley below our feet were none other than the hills of the Camp de César. At that very moment I almost got in trouble, almost spurting out that this is where le Père Marzet and I had collected the mushrooms. In extremis I remembered his orders to keep this a secret, and I pretended to discover the hills for the first time. When Madame Roussel told me I should come down and she would take me mushroom hunting in the Camp de César I almost choked, and had again to pretend I was really excited about it. I was going to be in trouble with le Père Marzet for sure!

Fortunately, the entire conversation was derailed by the appearance, at the bottom of the water of the inhabitants of the pond. Several salamanders were the permanent renters of the pond, and two of them had come into sight, a black and red one and a black and yellow one. Again, I had never seen such creatures, and they were elusive. Both Alice and Madame Roussel warned me never to try to catch them: they would trick me into following them down, and once I was down at the bottom of the pond, they would make me lose my way, and I would drown. This, they said, had happened to a little boy about my age at La Boissarde, when he had tried to catch one. Holy cow! Did this story keep me away from the pond! Thankfully there were other animals to look at and to try to catch. The far side of the pond was overgrown with rush plants and insects were flying around, the most magnificent of which was the huge dragonflies which obviously benefited from the mosquito breeding ground provided by the water. There were also smaller blue dragonflies, and a whole bunch of different butterflies. On the other side of the pond where we were standing was the wall of the chateau, and this wall was covered by flowers of all types which fell back towards the pond. The main ones I remember were the nasturtiums, and the morning glories.

The chateau was kind of a mystery house, and nobody talked about it. When I asked about it, people changed the topic of conversation, and as far as I knew no one had ever been there. It was hard to see the chateau from the road, and because of the huge fir trees growing between the road and the chateau, I had never caught a clear sight of it. Most intriguing to me was the fact that the pillars at the entrance, the ones supporting the big forged-iron gate bore the family name of my great-grandfather "Couty" on a cement plate, as if the chateau was the property of Monsieur Couty. When I had asked my father, he had simply responded by a question "Are we the only Faure family?" I had to answer that we were not, to which he had added "And what makes you think there is only one Couty family?" End of discussion. But through all of the years I went to Card on vacation, I could not keep from thinking that there was some dark secret linking our family to the chateau, that everyone in Card except my mother and I knew about it, and that I would never know the truth.

While I decided that one day I would figure out why our name was in front of the chateau, I became a quick study in butterflies, as I pestered Alice to tell me all of their names. There were the white ones, simply named large whites that were the most prevalent, as their caterpillars loved cabbage, a common vegetable crop of Limousin. The yellow ones were the clouded yellows, and the small blue ones that loved to drink from water puddles were the algon blues. There were also Cleopatras, large tortoise shells, painted ladies, ringlets, and meadow browns. But my favorite butterflies above all others were the swallowtails. They were rare, and it was a real treat to see one, but down by the flowers of the pond, there were several flying around at all times.

While I was concentrating on the best way to build a butterfly collection like the one I had seen in Monaco at the Oceanographic Museum, which also had insect collections, Alice tried to pull one over on me, as she innocently asked "Have you ever been to the Camp de César?" I had learned so much in that month in Limousin, that I did not hesitate one second, and denied any knowledge of the place. I must have been convincing, as she dropped the subject and I continued to pet Torpille, who followed my every move, as if to ensure I would not fall victim to the vicious salamanders. On the way back I asked Alice how she washed the clothes in winter, for surely in winter you could not use the pond. She said that in winter she did the same thing, except that she had to break the ice on the surface of the pond first. When we got back to Card, I helped Alice hang the laundry to dry, by giving her the clothes pins needed to keep the clothes from falling on the ground in case of wind. As a reward, she let me feed the chicken in the chicken coop behind the garden.

But I really wanted to see the pig the Marzet family kept. In the previous three weeks I had not been allowed to approach it, because it was a dangerous and vicious animal that would bite people it did not know. I could not believe that a lowly pig could be a dangerous animal. I would learn otherwise during my successive summers in Limousin. The pig was kept in a small building by itself and it was not allowed to come out, much like the bull at my uncle Emile's. This was a sad life I thought, but le Père Marzet had explained that they wanted a fat pig, so that he would have more tender meat and nice fat-layered bacon, and running around wasted his energy and made him leaner. I had almost convinced Alice it would be fine for me to sneak into the pigsty, when Madame Roussel ran up the path, out of breath "You need to get inside! Get inside!" she yelled in a panic. "You know the big Percheron horses that Lemaunier keeps? Well one of them has gone mad! It is running around knocking over everything! You need to get inside! I am running back down to the house!" Alice immediately rushed me to the house and convinced Madame Roussel to seek shelter in her house as well. Alice locked the heavy wood door and we watched from her window to see if the Percheron ran by. I did not know it then, but Percheron horses are some of the biggest horses around, can be almost seven feet tall and weigh over 2,500 pounds, and while I was waiting for a light horse like those I had seen running at the horse track in Nice, my thoughts were soon interrupted by a thunderous noise coming from the cow path. The ground was shaking, and I soon saw this monstrous horse running full speed past our window, almost falling as he made the turn from the cow path to our lane. He was wet with sweat and foam was hanging from his mouth, and he was gone. A few moments later, the poor demented horse ran by again, stumbling as he took the right turn onto the cow path, almost falling anew. I was sad to see the poor animal gone crazy, and I sought refuge by the fireplace and by Torpille who was lazily lying on the warm stones in front of the hearth. About an hour later le Père Marzet who had been in the fields tending his potatoes came back to the house and said we could go out again. The beautiful Percheron had run himself to death, and Lemaunier had taken him away with the tractor to bury him.

CHAPTER 13
Encounter with a Sanglier

Le Père Marzet used his cows for several purposes. First the Normandie cow, whose name was "Brette", provided all of the milk needed by the household, and many times for our household as well, because unless she had a calf she had much more milk than needed by three people. Second, the Limousin cow, which was raised for its calves, was a source of revenue for the family, and over the years, I saw several of her calves being loaded in the butcher's truck while she simply watched with total incomprehension. Once a cow could not bear any more calves, she too would be taken away in the same butcher's truck. But le Père Marzet hated to do this as much as I would have hated seeing it, and fortunately, it never happened during any of the summers I spent in Card. Third, the cows' manure was used as fertilizer in the fields and in the garden, and finally, the two cows were trained as a team to pull heavy loads in the "charette", the cart used for hay, wood, or wheat, or in the "tombereau", the heavier dumper used for loads such as manure, or sugar beets. The days when the cows were harnessed for these tasks were special for me. It was an opportunity to see more of the animals, but much more gratifying, I was allowed to ride in the charette, while le Père Marzet walked in front of the cows guiding them where they needed to go for that day's task. I was always intrigued by the black product he brushed on their foreheads and on their hindquarters. This was a product that kept the flies and the nasty horse flies from their eyes and from their legs as the cows labored and sweated. It was some type of tar that made me cough if I breathed it. The cows were placid, well behaved, and patient animals who would sit still for hours in the fields or in the chestnut tree woods, while we loaded the cart. They would simply stand there and ruminate, waiting for le Père Marzet to give them their next instructions. He did that with a long stick about ten feet long, which he would simply rest on the yoke while walking in front of them. He would also control them from the side and simply tap one cow or the other to make the team turn right or left. All the while, Torpille would accompany us and walk tranquilly by the team of cows, never asserting her presence more than necessary except to warn us of danger, such as that of "sangliers", or wild boars.

Sangliers are common all over France, and they are probably the most formidable wild animals of France. They are fearsome with their indestructible front shoulders, their heavy skulls, their determination, and their protruding fangs. In Limousin there are stories of hunters wounding a sanglier and not being able to kill him, and the sanglier turning around, reversing roles by hunting the hunter, and killing him. Every story ends up with the hunter's wife, worried not to see her husband come home, alerting the gendarmes—when it comes to search and rescue, people will call the gendarmes even if they hate them for all other matters—the gendarmes organizing a search party, and finding the husband laying in his blood, disemboweled and the sanglier no place to be seen. Le Père Marzet had warned me of the danger early on, and he had told me that if a sanglier should show up I should find the biggest chestnut tree, climb it, and make myself comfortable while the wild boar walked around, dug for food, or even took a nap. Torpille knew to jump in the charette, and the sanglier would not bother the cows which presented no threat to him, and were much bigger anyhow.

That day, it started when Torpille suddenly stood up from her slumber on the forest floor. This alerted le Père Marzet, who stopped working on collecting dried-up eagle ferns for the cows' stable litter, and motioning to me not to make any noises. As he listened intently, I could make out the rustle of leaves and branches—a noise which was unlike any I had heard in the woods before. Le Père Marzet dropped was he was doing while Torpille started barking. He ran to me, grabbed me, and pushed me up the trunk of a big chestnut tree telling me to climb up to one of its big branches. He then grabbed Torpille and put her in the charette, which was partly loaded already, and was higher than any sanglier could reach, and then he himself climbed up another chestnut tree. We waited a few moments, as the noise became more distinct, and we soon could hear the grunting of the sanglier, and then, she was there digging the forest floor with her snout for roots, chestnuts, mushrooms, and insects. And she was with four small young wild boars which we call "marcassins" in French. The little ones were light brown, their backs spotted with light cream, but she was huge, with high shoulders, dark brown and black, a true menace. I clutched the tree harder to make sure I did not fall. She went right away to the place where le Père Marzet had been working. Because he had disturbed the forest ground, there was plenty to eat and it was easier to dig. Torpille had stopped barking by then, but the sanglier did not even pay attention to her anyhow, knowing full well that a single dog was no threat to her. The cows showed a certain level of nervousness even trying to get away, but le Père Marzet had set the heavy wood brakes on the wheels, and they could not go anywhere. We sat there in the trees while Madame Sanglier went around her business, and it seemed her business in this clearing would last a long time. After a while I needed to go to the bathroom, and I told le Père Marzet who told be to pee from my branch. As I did it attracted the attention of the sanglier, who came over and started bumping and pushing against the tree, as if she wanted to bring me down. Fortunately, the tree had a trunk about six feet wide, and I realized then why le Père Marzet had told me to pick the biggest tree I could find. The pushing and shoving against the tree producing no results, she started to simply charge it. It did not produce any more results. Finally the frustration got the best of her and she went back to grazing and forgot all about me. We must have been there for two hours sitting on the tree, and le Père Marzet looked anxiously at the sun, knowing that the cows should be soon taken to their evening pasture. But there was no way to get away.

The stalemate got broken by the noise of the Lemaunier's tractor. He had fields up from the woods we were stuck in, and was probably driving there that day. The engine hum clearly disturbed the sanglier, and as the engine got closer, she nudged her marcassins, and trotted away, finally allowing us to get down from our trees. The first thing le Père Marzet did was relieve himself. Then, he packed up our entire troop and we made back for home. We had been alerted by Torpille, but he told me that I should always be vigilant to unusual noises in the forest, as they could be those of sangliers or even vipers. Certainly, in all the times I went to Limousin, it would not be my last encounter with sangliers, nor the one that scared me the most, but this one was the first, and it remains very clear in my mind today.

Another one happened several years later, when le Père Marzet entrusted me to take the cows to pasture on my own. I was at La Boissarde, when I suddenly heard the telltale noise indicating a sanglier. This one was almost running toward my location. In a panic, I forgot to pick the *biggest* chestnut tree around, and went instead for the closest one, which was barely two feet in diameter. I climbed it easily enough. But the sanglier, a massive male knocked it around just as easily. I had to hang on for dear life as he beat the crap out of that tree. I was sure he could have uprooted if he had wanted to. Each charge brought me further to surely falling. I grabbed for some of the yet unripe chestnut husks, which hurt quite a bit, since chestnut husks look like green sea urchins, with all of their pins, and threw them on the ground in an attempt to distract the sanglier, as I had seen the cowboys do in movies. This actually distracted the monster enough that he forgot about me, and went on his way disappearing into the thickets of the nearby woods. The cows had not finished grazing, but following le Père Marzet's example that day of the first encounter, I opened the gate, got the cows back on their way home, and gave them twice their ration of sugar beets.

These experiences were in no way meant to increase my mother's level of comfort about me running around the fields alone, and she gave me instructions that I should not do so. This was yet another set of rules set forth by mother that I totally disregarded, and she was not happy at all about that. Unfortunately for her, I now knew how to ride my bicycle quite well, even on the rough cow paths, and I could pedal on these for miles unencumbered by cars, traffic or people. Everyday I went further, and soon, I knew every inch of every path. I knew where the big stones were, where the puddles formed when it rained, where the sandy parts were, and I knew I would never get lost again like the day the Père Christophe had sent me home. I knew who owned which fields and which woods, I knew where there were electric fences—I had found out that Lemaunier used those—I knew where to find mushrooms, where the vipers liked to sun, and where I could see the blue jays in the forest. In a short month I had explored the land and become as familiar with it as a native, like le Père Marzet said. But my stay in Limousin was coming to a close too quickly. There were so many things to do. And I did not want to go home. It was such a change from the little boy who wanted to stay in Monaco. I did not dare say it for fear of my father telling me "I told you so", but I had fallen in love with Limousin.

In the meantime, we still had to visit the remaining members of the family. It was a visitathon of relatives in Limoges, La Jonchère, Saint-Priest, and Ambazac, where my father had more cousins. And then, there were the visits to say goodbye to the closest relatives such as the ones in Fondanèche. And my father was also struggling to find the time to install electricity in the house. After the trip to Limoges, my father had successfully installed electricity in the common area, and he had suspended a forged iron chandelier that gave us a welcome light during evening meals. We now had light to eat by, and we could actually read at night as well. My mother had insisted that I bring books from Monaco, and that I read a few pages every night, so as not to forget how to read during the school vacation. But faced with the double challenge of competing with Limousin and le Père Marzet on one hand, and the lack of acceptable light on the other hand, she had given up. Now that electricity was installed, every night before I went to bed I had to read a chapter of a book, any book. I had to write down every word I did not know the meaning of, and look it up in the Larousse dictionary. I had been smart enough to choose interesting reading from my father's collection of acceptable books, and I was reading the adventures of a young man drafted into Napoleon's Army in 1815. Every night I would read my chapter of "The 1815 Conscript" and in the morning I would summarize the chapter for le Père Marzet who had never read it. This gave him the opportunity to talk about the "Guerre de Quatorze"—the 1914 War, as everybody called the First World War in France. This is how I discovered le Père Marzet's own adventures, if one can call war an adventure.

CHAPTER 14
La Guerre de Quatorze

As I write this book, I realize how significant number fourteen is in the history of France. We have Louis XIV, the Sun King, le Quatorze Juillet, and finally la Guerre de Quatorze. Therefore, it is not by chance that this chapter, number fourteen, relates le Père Marzet's life as a "Poilu". Poilu is the term used to designate the French infantry soldiers who served in World War One and means hairy, because the soldiers let their beards grow for lack of razor blades and shaving cream. Le Père Marzet was proud to have been a Poilu, and he had story upon story of what had happened during his four years on the front lines. He would always start his stories with "Ah, mon petit!"—Oh, my poor boy—which was the signal that he was going to talk about the war. The first time he talked about it was to tell me the story of the Chemin des Dames. When these words are translated into English, they mean the Pathway of the Ladies, and upon hearing these words I first thought he was going to tell me about some romantic story. I did not know that this had been one of the worst failures of the French Army. The Chemin des Dames offensive was launched on 16 April 1916, and 285,000 Poilus had died in five days, at the rate of three soldiers killed per foot of battlefront. Le Père Marzet had been there. Engaged with his unit from the beginning; "Ah, mon petit, there were no heroes that day! We tried to dodge the bullets, and our soldiers were falling all over…There was no ground to walk on, you just ran on the bodies of the wounded and the killed. There was not an inch of ground not covered with blood. And then the shells started falling. You had to run fast to find a shell hole to hide into. And there was no running away. The officers were behind us with their revolvers and they would kill us if we ran away. Ah, mon petit! To see all of this and to live!" He was going back to that day, telling me how his best friend Mazuret had been blown away by a shell, a few feet from him, and how he had been covered by the fragments of his body. He would stay silent, trying to regain enough composure to continue the story, but still after all of these years, he would cry when evoking the memory of his long departed friend. "I was covered by his flesh, by the flesh of my best friend!" I did not know what to do. I had only seen one man, Tonton François, cry before, but that day, everybody was ready to cry because of the emotion of the ceremony. But le Père Marzet? I would not really comprehend everything he was telling me that day until years later, after I had grown up a little more, and he would tell me the stories again. And he would continue, lamenting about all these Poilus who were still buried there at the Chemin des Dames without even a cross.

When I had gone back to Card that evening, and told Alice that le Père Marzet had talked about the Guerre de Quatorze and had cried, she had scolded him telling him that he should not talk about these things, that it was bad for him, that it was too painful. Yet, day after day, after I told le Père Marzet about the battle of Champeaubert that my book conscript had been in, he would tell me about the second battle of the Marne. "Ah, mon petit, we had mud up to here" and with a gesture of his thumb, he traced a line across his chest, right below where his shirt pocket flaps were. "We could not go to the latrines, the rats were swimming all around us, and the dead…The dead…They were coming back up from where they had fallen or from where we had buried them, with their eyes eaten by the rats; they would look at you with big black holes in their face, if they had a face at all…At night, you had to sleep standing up, and hope you would not slip, for fear of drowning in the mud. And you never knew whether the Poilu next to you was alive or whether he was one of the dead ones who had risen back up! This is how we got the saying "Debout les Morts!" as we were calling for our dead comrades to join back into the fight. Many times, we would grab them and prop them up against the side of the trench. The Germans would believe we had received reinforcements, and they would waste their ammunition on them. "Les pauvres vieux" (the poor old bastards) were already dead, what did it matter that they got shot again? They would never see their family again, so they might as well help us survive. Many did not even have their ID tags any longer, and nobody ever knew their name". Le Père Marzet would shake his head from side to side, while drying his eyes with his right sleeve. These were terrible moments. But at the same time, the Poilus had saved France. When Clémenceau, the Prime Minister, had stated "they [the Germans] will not go through [the French lines]", the Poilus had made sure of that. And he said with pride that France owed everything to the Poilus de Quatorze. And le Père Marzet would tell me again and again how the German soldiers would surrender, throwing up their arms, and yelling "Kamerad! Kamerad!"

And my grandfather Léon, and all of my uncles had stories about World War One. All of them remembered vividly these horrible days. My granduncle Emile would tell me "…and there were crosses for all the dead, and crosses, as far as you could see, there were white crosses. Some had a name, some were blank. But these were the lucky ones who were actually buried. We knew we were all going to die, and the only thing we would wish was that we could be buried like this instead of being blown to smithereens in the shelling, and the trenches, and being eaten by rats."

As for Tonton François, he was one of the luckiest men alive. During the Battle of the Somme, his infantry company was rotated from the frontlines, and came to find respite from the rain inside a disaffected railroad tunnel. The tunnel was blocked off and sealed on the other side, and the company was comfortable there, sheltered from the elements. After a few days of inactivity—it may have been three, it may have been four—my uncle started to feel restless, and when his company commander asked for two volunteers to deliver messages to the battalion, my uncle and another Poilu had volunteered. In those days, there was no radio to speak of, and once the shells had cut the telephone lines, the only way to communicate was through runners who used the communications trenches to move about the battlefield in relative safety. Well, my uncle and the other guy went on, and it took them a day and a half to find the battalion headquarters, deliver the message, wait for the response, and return to the company. When they returned they could find neither the tunnel, nor the company. Finally, a Poilu from another unit told them there was no use looking for their company. It did not exist any longer.

Every one of their fellow soldiers had been buried alive. What the commander had not known when he provided shelter to his soldiers, was that behind the wall sealing the tunnel was a huge ammunition dump—this is why no other unit had occupied the tunnel before them. The Germans had been trying to blow it up for weeks, and unfortunately they had just done that. A direct hit from one of the big German guns had penetrated the tunnel and blown up the ammunition, exploding and collapsing the tunnel, killing all within. Tonton François had missed being killed by but a few hours. When the two Poilus returned to the battalion headquarters with the tragic news, they were given an extra ration of wine, were reassigned to another company, and the next day they were back on the frontlines. By that time, the carnage had rendered men and officers so callous, that such an event was barely a couple of lines in the battalion log.

One day, when Alice was gone—she would have disapproved—le Père Marzet invited me in the house, and he went upstairs to get his decorations and his certificates. He came back down with a cigar box. It was full of personal mementos from the war. His lighter—because every Poilu smoked the daily ration of tobacco known as corporal (it is the same tobacco used today in the famous Gauloises cigarettes)—a brass cylinder about as big as a finger with a top that was removable and kept the flint dry, a couple of photographs of him in his Poilu uniform in the trenches, photographs of the unit, and of friends, most of them gone, and a couple of shell casings from the Lebel rifle. Then he pulled out his decorations: the Médaille de la Victoire (Victory Medal), with its winged figure and its rainbow ribbon, the Croix de Feu (Cross of Fire), a medal in the form of a thick cross, with the picture of the French army helmet, and red and light blue ribbon, the Médaille des Volontaires (Medal of the Volunteers)—le Père Marzet had not been drafted, he had volunteered to go fight for France—with its dark blue ribbon and the profile of two soldiers, the 1914-1918 Croix de Guerre (War Cross), in the shape of cross of Malta with two swords intertwined, and the distinguishable red with five light green stripes ribbon, and of course the Médaille Militaire, with its yellow and light-green ribbon. With all of these, he showed me the certificates accompanying them. One remains with me to this day, as it showed the gruesome sight of skeleton soldiers, climbing over the trenches in the face of enemy fire, and bore in bold letters the title "DEBOUT LES MORTS!" Le Père Marzet's name was hand-written below in round letters, and I wondered how this certificate could have survived the mud, the carnage and the rain, and who had had the leisure to so perfectly write his name "Jean Marzet". And why would they give soldiers an award with such black humor. And le Père Marzet added, as they had done in 1914, "Debout les Morts, and don't puff up your chest!" He was really disappointed for not having received the very desirable Légion d'Honneur (Legion of Honor) which includes a small annual stipend. Eventually, after a fifty-two year wait, as the paper stated, le Père Marzet was made a Knight in the order of the Légion d'Honneur, and it is only when he was eighty-six that on a sunny Sunday of December 1980, le Père Marzet was able to enjoy this last satisfaction, with the local senator bestowing this supreme honor upon him.

These stories made a great impression on me, and several times, I had nightmares about being a Poilu in the hell of the Great War. But, inexplicably, it also instilled in me the desire to be a soldier, to go after the enemy, and hear him cry "Kamerad! Kamerad!" as he surrendered with his hands in the air. I wanted to defend France as le Père Marzet had done.

CHAPTER 15
Back to Monaco

The month of July came to an end, and with it my first summer of discovery in Limousin. The little boy who had thought his father was crazy for wanting to leave Monaco would never see things the same way. I had to recognize that my father was not mad after all. A great sadness fell over me on that morning of 30 July, as I had to say goodbye to le Père Marzet, Alice and Torpille. As we drove away, they were waving to us, and Alice was crying. On my knees on the back seat, I waved until they disappeared behind Robert Teulier's well, and they were gone. I slumped back into my seat, inconsolable at leaving them behind. My mother tried to uplift my spirits by talking about our trip the following year, but to me this was so far away in time that it did not help. We had said goodbye to Tata Marie and Tonton François the night before, as Tata Marie treated us to one of her fabulous meals, and it had been agreed that we would not stop in the morning. But my father could not keep this promise. We arrived as she was serving a customer, and we hugged and kissed one more time before heading on to Limoges. This time, it was my father's turn to cry. There was dead silence in the car, as I watched the chestnut trees fly by on the side of the road. I was wondering whether there were any sangliers in the woods. Then, we drove by the road to Fondanèche, down by the uranium mines of La Crouzille. We turned south on N20, passing by the road to Saint-Pardoux, we saw our last Limousin cows, and we were in the center of Limoges. My summer in Limousin was over. Tears were rolling down my cheeks, and again my mother tried to console me by telling me how happy my grandmother Lainey would be to see me.

My mother could simply not understand how heart-breaking it was for me to leave all these people behind, and the poor dog Torpille, and the cows. Deep inside I was hoping that the stupid Dauphine would break down, so that we could go back, or that my father all of sudden would come to his senses, turn around and decide that we would live there. Finally, realizing there was only one thing that would help me get over this, my father said "if we lived in Limousin, you could never see the Grand Prix of Monaco again". Whoa! Whoa! Slow down! What did you say? That grabbed my attention! Not see the Grand Prix again? No way. Suddenly, I became interested in going back to Monaco. But it took me until we arrived on the coast and I saw the Mediterranean Sea again before I could smile again.

Over the course of that year, the memories of Limousin faded somewhat, although we received letters from our family. The cousins in Fondanèche had their own sadness to deal with as Gustave, their younger son, had been drafted in the French Army and had been sent to fight the war in far away Algeria. Every day, the list of casualties was published in the French newspapers, and my uncle Emile would refuse to open the paper for fear of seeing his son's name in it, leaving this task to his other son Maxime, instead. Alice wrote for the entire Marzet family at Christmas time, and said that le Père Marzet missed my company, as he had nobody to talk to about the war. We received more news from Tata Marie who wrote to us every other month, saying how the store was going, and trying to make arrangements for our next visit. From the others, in these times when there were hardly any telephones in France, no Internet, no cell phones and no instant messaging, we heard nothing. The letters needed three or four days to reach us, so there was no way of getting information in real time. The entire country was much more concerned about the war in Algeria, and in January, it was my cousin Robert Spinetta—who lived in Monaco—who was drafted and sent to Algeria. Robert was my grandmother Lainey's nephew. We had a big dinner at my grandparents to say goodbye to him, simply hoping that we would see him again, as the list of the war dead got longer every day. By that time I was eight years old, going on nine, and I was calculating how long it would be before it would be my turn to go to Algeria and fight for France.

On 29 May, the Grand Prix did take place, and I watched it from my father's office at Olympic Maritime, the company owned by magnate

Onassis, where my father worked. There were no longer any Maserati cars in Formula One, and I rooted for the second best thing, the Ferraris, but they could not place better than third, behind the brand new Lotus of Stirling Moss, and the Cooper of Bruce McLaren, and I would have to wait another fifteen years to see a Ferrari win in Monaco. Then, in June, school ended, there was the official end of school day where I received many prizes for my scholarly activities—mainly books—and the preparations for the Limousin trip were on the way. Things were a bit different, because my brother Philippe was now a factor on the trip since he was eighteen months old and he obviously could walk.

In the meantime, because my mother had decided to stay home to raise my brother I saw a lot less of my grandparents, although I visited them every day. But finally, one day they decided they would move because my grandfather had saved enough money to purchase an apartment, which he thought was a better investment than renting from the owner of the two-family house we lived in. A family moved in their place that had a daughter named Brigitte—like Brigitte Bardot I told my mother. Despite the mystique of her name, and the fact that Brigitte was a beautiful blonde girl with great intelligence, she and I never got along, and we incessantly quarreled to the chagrin of both our parents who had mutually thought that we would get along and play together, especially on Thursdays because French schools were closed on Thursdays in those times.

In late June, my father received a letter from his mother saying that since my parents were spending July in Card, she had decided to spend the month of August there, and she was wondering if I would like to stay another month alone with her. I was not too crazy about spending an entire month with my grandmother Louise, because she had idiosyncrasies which I simply did not like. For example, she thought I should know the La Fontaine fables by heart, or at least the main ones. I considered the fables to be school work since this was the place where I learned the ones I knew, but she kept insisting it was not, that it was fun to know the fables. So, everyday, she would demand that I recite one with her, be it the Fox and the Crow, or the Wolf and the Lamb, or the City Rat and the Country Rat, but we had to do this every day. After a while it was kind of fun, but it took me a couple of weeks to get used to it. In any case, the choice was to either spend an extra month with le Père Marzet *and* my grandmother

Louise, or miss out on spending time with le Père Marzet. This was not really a choice. This is how, over the course of the following eight years, I got to spend two months in Limousin. It was agreed that at the end of August my grandmother and I would take the train from Limoges to Lyon, where my father would be waiting to take me back to Monaco.

There was only one problem with this arrangement. My grandmother Louise, I called her Mémé Louise and Tata Marie d'Ambazac no longer spoke to each other. So, it had to be negotiated that on certain days of August, I would be allowed to go to Tata Marie's and spend the entire day with her. But there was yet another problem. Mémé Louise did not have a car, so any time we had to go to Ambazac we had to go on foot. Seemingly two kilometers are not a real challenge, especially since there were shortcuts through the woods which I knew well by then, but this would take at least an hour each way, and the return trip was sure to be with bags of groceries, unless my grandmother was planning to buy everything from the vendors who stopped by Card. I knew that none of these sold meat, so we would have to go to Ambazac to get meat a couple of times a week. I was sorting all of this in my head as my father and Mémé Louise planned this entire expedition. They were able to do this over the phone because my father had a phone in his office in Monaco, and my grandmother was an accountant for the telephone company in Paris.

My mother packed twice as many clothes for me because I had to stay twice as long, and off we left for Limousin in the reliable Dauphine. By that time my hate relationship with the car had settled down, and I almost liked it (especially if it did not rain). With less planning and more experience this trip went a lot smoother. The Dauphine did not break down, and we managed to arrive in Card as the cows were coming home from the fields in the evening. We stopped in Ambazac at Tata Marie's and there was much rejoicing at seeing each other again. My aunt could not believe how much I had grown, although she found me too skinny and determined that she would fix that. Poor Tata Marie could not know that I wolfed down food, but it made no difference. My body was to busy getting taller to care about putting on weight. Not much, if anything, had changed in the épicerie since my previous visit. This made the customers comfortable as they knew day after day, that whatever happened outside, their store would remain the same, and Tata Marie would always be behind the counter, ready to serve them. But one thing had changed in town. Up to then the COOP had been a small store with little more than a few bottles of milk and pieces of cheese. But in the fall, it had been purchased by investors who had decided to turn it into a chain. They had expanded the Ambazac store, and it was now competing directly against Tata Marie whose business had started to decline. She had lost loyal customers who preferred to shop on their own in this supermarket style store. And they did not have to go to multiple stores to get everything they wanted. The COOP offered everything: groceries, bread, vegetables, meat, fresh fish (a novelty for Ambazac), cleaning products, toys, writing paper, wine, and even magazines. All of the Ambazac stores were impacted, and although many did not know it, or refused to recognize it, with the opening of the COOP store, life had changed for ever in the small village. Customers did not have to wait in line until Tata Marie was done with an order. They simply picked up what they wanted, went to the cash register, paid, and were on their way. Personal service no longer mattered. People had started to take conscience that their most important asset was time.

The need to save time or to have more time to do other things had changed Card as well. Robert Teulier had purchased a moped, and no longer rode his bicycle back and forth to the sawmill. But the greatest change had taken place at the Marzet house. Alice, intrigued by my stories of washing machines had inquired about them, and found out that they could be used even if there was no running water. It was a simple matter of filling them up with the right quantity of water, and she had convinced her husband Robert to buy one. Now, instead of taking a full day to wash clothes, it would take her a couple of moments to load and unload and to go hang the clothes outside, just like in Monaco. She did not even have to boil the water, because this particular model came with a built-in propane heater that heated the water to the right temperature and started the washing cycle only when the proper temperature had been reached! And there was change in our house as well, because in the spring Mémé Louise had had a septic system installed, and we now had a toilet in the house! This was such a good surprise! The toilet still did not have running water and required that a quarter of a pail of water be poured in every time it was used, but this sure beat the outhouse, which had already been taken down.

When we arrived in Card that night, everybody was already locked in for the night, and we did not see the Marzet family. As we parked the car and opened the door, it was a far cry from the previous year, as my grandmother had hired Alice to come and air out and clean the house prior to our arrival. There was no mold, and fresh clean linen was on the beds. There was still no electricity except in the common room downstairs, but a new oil lamp had replaced the one we had broken the previous year, and the house had taken a new look with a new cement rendering that had been applied to the outside over the crude masonry of the prior year. And it had been painted a nice light yellow that made the house look decidedly modern compared to the primitive look it had presented a few months hence. There were also changes in the cow paths. The paths that had been barely wide enough for a team of cows and a cart had been widened throughout to allow a tractor to drive through. This had been caused by Lemaunier but also by the Guérin family which now had a green Deutz brand tractor. There was no stopping progress. At that time I saw but did not comprehend how much change had taken place in one year. After all, in Monaco, we had the most modern infrastructure in the world, even when compared to America, especially now that we had an American princess. But for Card to move to septic tanks, washing machines, tractors, and widened cow paths in one year was a revolution.

CHAPTER 16
A US Air Force Appearance

That year, because my brother was older, he needed his own bed. Since the front bedroom of the house was bigger it had space for an extra bed my parents took this bigger bedroom, and assigned me the back bedroom. This room was facing west and did not benefit from the rising sun to wake me up, nor did it transfer the noise of the cows as they came drinking in the water trough in front the house. This produced the immediate consequence that instead of waking up earlier than eight, I slept well into the ninth hour. I missed the feeding of the cows, and that first morning of my second summer, as I rushed out of the house to see le Père Marzet, he was nowhere to be seen, as he had already gone to the fields to work. No problem, I thought. I would get on the bicycle, ride in the countryside and find him. I went to the barn, opened the door, found the bicycle exactly where I had left it the previous summer, and pulled it out only to find out to my dismay that the tires were flat. This was a problem that was clearly not beyond my capability to fix. I got the pump, connected it to the valve and starting pumping. The front wheel inflating operation went OK—it was hard to get there, but I managed. The rear wheel was a different matter, as regardless how hard I pumped, the air refused to stay in. I had to solve this situation immediately, but this technical challenge was above my level of competence. I needed help from my father and went back into the house. When I saw him standing on a stepladder and toying with electric wires while whistling as he did when he was pre-occupied, I figured the bicycle would not be fixed anytime soon. I asked nevertheless, and he responded with a lackadaisical "in a minute", which translated into real French actually means "in a couple of hours". My father simply did not understand the urgency of the situation, and I appealed to my mother, who promptly said she knew nothing of bicycle tires, and "go ask your father", which translated into French means "I am doing other things, and could not care any less about your problem, especially since I am busy feeding your brother."

So there I was caught in a catch 22 situation, with no way out. I went back outside, sat on the curb of the newly constructed sidewalk, and pondered what to do, and how I could find le Père Marzet, when my father—was I dreaming?—came out and said "do you think you can ride your bicycle to Ambazac, and buy bread?" Of course, I could! I had ridden my bicycle in the streets of Monaco, and I could certainly do it in Limousin where there were fewer cars and where hills were not as steep. So my father went about the mysterious operation of fixing the hole in the tire tube. I was amazed that a little piece of rubber and "cold vulcanization" would actually fix the flat. But, twenty minutes later, with the leather satchel attached to the bicycle rack over the back wheel, I was on my way to get a mélée from the Boulangerie Lechat, butter, wine, ham and salami from Tata Marie, and steak from the Bonneau butcher shop. It was easy going to Ambazac because there was only one uphill and two downhills. I flew down these hills with the top speed my legs and the single fixed gear bicycle could muster. I first stopped at the butcher's and then went to the épicerie where my aunt was amazed—and somewhat concerned because she thought there was a lot of traffic on the roads—that I had ridden all the way to Ambazac. I made my purchases, and went to the boulangerie, careful to park my bicycle along the curb, and to use one of the pedals as a kickstand. Attaching the mélée to the bicycle rack was not that easy, as I had to use rubber fasteners, and then I had to get back on the bicycle without getting my leg caught in the bread that was overhanging on both sides. Soon I was back on the road, successfully walking up the last hill because the bicycle was a heavy machine loaded with groceries, and I could not negotiate the last steep part of the second hill. This was the first of my daily trips to Ambazac to either shop for groceries, for cakes, or simply to go say hello to Tata Marie, a daily duty that my father had stated I should fulfill. And it had solved the problem of my grandmother Louise not having a car. I found out later that she had agreed to stay with me in Card only if I could go and do the daily shopping for her in Ambazac. But it also opened the door to my riding on the open road for hours, and allowed me to discover even more amazing people and places in Limousin. Life had really changed in a year's time.

I then had a half hour to go find le Père Marzet before I had to have lunch. I found him in the fields "in the back", as the fields to the northwest of Card were called for the lack of a better name. The first sign that I had found le Père Marzet was Torpille running toward me and barking of joy. The beautiful dog was now sixteen and did not run too often, but she ran to welcome me back, jumping up and down as if she had been a puppy. Le Père Marzet was happy to see me—he told me he knew it was me coming when he had seen Torpille run. He hugged me as if I had been his grandson. I know now that he really considered me as his grandson because Robert and Alice could not have children. I had heard that there were people who could not have children, but since the children making part was still very nebulous in my mind, I did not know that it was due to a medical condition. I wanted to know everything about Card: had he gone hunting, had he killed a sanglier, had there been a lot of snow, how was Torpille, how were the cows, how many chickens he had now, where the potatoes growing well, how were the rabbits, how about the water—was there enough in the well—and the bornes, did anybody mess with the bornes? It was more questions than the poor man could handle, especially since he was cutting grass for the rabbits, and did that by hand with a scythe, which he needed to sharpen every few minutes. I told le Père Marzet about my adventures, about the flat tire, about going to Ambazac and not being able to climb the last hill. This is when he quit what he was doing, took me by the hand and led me down a footpath I did not know, that went further along the fields and then through the middle of a chestnut tree forest, and here was the road to Ambazac, halfway up the nasty hill I could not climb. My problem was solved. And the next morning when I left for the groceries, instead of turning right as I should have, I turned left, and my father who was watching yelled at me that I was going the wrong way, to which I answered "No, I am going le Père Marzet's way!"

I was riding back from Ambazac, when all of a sudden a huge roar like the one of thunder shook the air, causing me to stop the bicycle, get off it, and climb the talus on the left side of the path. I was petrified because I had never heard such loud thunder, and it was coming towards me. This is when I saw them. Two war planes flying nap of the earth at incredible speed. They glimmered in the bright midday sunshine, and flew over so fast I barely recognized the American markings on the wings, and they were gone. I could smell the burnt kerosene from their exhaust, and I was so excited by the sight, I decided there and then that I would be an air force pilot. These planes were huge, they were fast, they were macho, they were scary, and it looked dangerous. I wanted to do it. Forget about being a professional cyclist and winning le Tour de France! Forget about the translator career my mother had been planning for me since our trip to Italy! Forget about everything! This was the job for me. I rushed home and asked my father if he had seen them. He said no, but that they had scared him so much, flying right over our house that he had almost fallen off the stepladder, and that he wondered if the tiles on the roof had not been disturbed by the planes, and that if they had, it would surely cause the roof to leak next time it rained. That immediately tampered my desire to tell him about my new career. I asked him where the planes had come from, and he stated that they probably came from Chateauroux where there was a big American air force base. This was interesting, but since I did not know where Chateauroux was, or even what it was, the information was rather useless. I asked my father what type of planes they were. That, he did not know—the planes had in fact been F-102 Delta Dagger with the delta wings that were so distinctive. When I told my father I did not know of Chateauroux, he sent me to the barn to look for the Dubonnet map of France. Dubonnet was then and is still today a brand of French aperitifs. It had printed a large map of France as part of an ad campaign that was linked to le Tour de France, and the map included all of the départements, the main cities and the secondary cities of France. Since I did not know where Chateauroux was, my father had me look for it, and I found out it was about seventy miles north of Limoges. My father then stated that I should learn about the cities of France, and so it is that every day, he picked five cities in France. I had to go find them on the map, and tell him at lunch time where they were located. It sounded like school work to me, but once I managed to tell my father that I wanted to be a pilot, he pointed out that a pilot needed to know where every town was so that he could fly there. This made a lot of sense to me, and it got me enthused to find out where such unremarkable towns as Embrun, Auxerre, or Saint-Dizier were located.

Since we now had electricity, we were able to use a radio in Card. This was a major change over the previous year (another one). My father had wired the entire common area, and the radio was set up on the far end of the dining table. Thus it came about that lunch had to be served at precisely twelve noon when my parents would listen to the "journal de midi" or the noon hour news. This became the inflexible time at which we ate, and if I was in the fields with le Père Marzet, I had to keep track of time precisely to ensure I would not be late for lunch, which of course was unacceptable. It was easier said than done since neither le Père Marzet nor I had a watch, and we had to rely on the direction of the wind, the noise of the railroad and the ringing of the Ambazac church bells to figure out the time. The direction of the wind decided whether we could hear the Ambazac church bells from Card. If it flew from the east, we could forget it, but if it flew from the west, the church bells were clearly audible from any of the fields, unless we worked in the woods, which we mainly did in the afternoon. The railroad tracks were only a mile away, and we could hear the faint noise of trains from everywhere. We also knew the schedule of all the trains, and the eleven fifty-two train that stopped in Ambazac on its way from Limoges to La Jonchère was the signal that I had to pack up and return to Card for lunch. Sometimes, there would be unscheduled trains, such as the military trains carrying soldiers and equipment to the maneuver camp of La Courtine. The military camp of La Courtine was about fifty miles east of Limoges, and I had often seen the trains going over the railroad bridge in Ambazac. German military equipment and tanks with their black cross of Malta, and the soldiers hanging out from the windows, waving as they went by, trying to see if any pretty French girls were around. British convoys, unmarked and undistinguishable. American convoys with the white star painted on tank turrets and truck doors, and friendly soldiers waving and throwing chewing gum and chocolate out of the windows as the train rode by. It was exciting to see the activity of the trains coming and going, and I watched in awe as train after train of military hardware went through. My only disappointment is that I never saw the French army. My father explained that it was due to the French army being in Algeria, fighting to keep Algeria French. There were no more French soldiers and units in France, they were all in Algeria. I was disappointed that I could never see a French convoy.

This is when I started to understand the graffiti that was painted on road signs, walls, and also on the railroad bridge in Ambazac: the Celtic cross of the people who wanted to keep Algeria French at all costs, and the three ominous letters O.A.S. of the Secret Arms Organization, which was resorting to violence to bring the same point home. And I understood how the war in Algeria had crossed the Mediterranean Sea and had moved into France. In Monaco, we had a street sweeper who came by our house every day. I saw him every day, with his blue work clothes on, and his broom and shovel on his shoulder, sweeping trash into neat piles that he would later collect with his garbage cart—a small cart with several round garbage cans in it. The street sweeper was an Arab (we did not know his name and simply called him the Arab), with a small mustache, and you could tell he loved his job. He loved to keep our street clean. He would say hello to everybody, he was jovial, and he was lucky to work in a nice neighborhood with gardens, and fruit trees. Monsieur Léoni who had a lot of fruit trees had told him he could help himself to the fruit, and the Arab loved to pick the figs above all. I really never talked to him, but as I walked back from school at lunch time he would always say "Bonjour Monsieur". He was the first person who ever called me "Monsieur". The housewives of the neighborhood would often feed him, giving him leftovers from the night before, careful never to him any food that contained pork meat. He lived under the municipal wash house, in a place with no running water, no toilets, and a single light bulb hanging from the ceiling. It was more a cave than a proper dwelling. In the evening, when I walked by, I would hear his radio tuned to the Algiers station as he listened to Algerian music and songs. People said that he had been given this good and stable job of a street sweeper because he had fought for France in the Second World War. Whatever the case, he had become part of the neighborhood, and I never heard anyone do anything but praise the way he cleaned our street. One Thursday evening after a boring day of being home by myself, I was looking out of the window, as people were coming home from work. The Arab was walking to his home as well. A black Citroën Traction Avant was driving up the road. A few yards from my house, it caught up with our street sweeper, and stopped next to him. I heard two shots, just like when

I played cowboys and Indians with my toy revolvers, and the Arab lay there on the side of the road, as the car drove away. I had been witness to his murder. I hid behind the window sill, too petrified to move, as I glanced up from time to time to see what was going on. People had rushed to him, but I overheard that he was dead. I did not know what to do. When my parents came home, I told them what had happened, and what I had seen. My father asked me if I knew the license plate number of the car. Of course I did, and this license plate remains engraved in my mind to this day "36 BL 06". My father immediately accompanied me to the police station to report what I had seen. I never knew whether the people who had murdered the Arab were caught, but I know they did it as retaliation to the French who were killed randomly in the same manner in Algeria. It also showed that hatred and stupidity had no limits, and it prejudiced me against the Celtic cross, which from that day on I saw as a symbol of sectarianism and violence.

CHAPTER 17
Aline

Something else had changed in Card. Le Père Marzet had gotten a second dog. His name was Fidèle, which means loyal. I did not understand why he needed another dog, since he had Torpille. He told me that Torpille had retired, and that he needed to train another dog to watch after the cows and to learn about the sangliers. I did not like Fidèle as much as I did Torpille. He was a much more exuberant dog, and much sillier, as I would find out on several occasions. But this also made me sad, because I knew people retired before they died, and it was an indication that Torpille's life would soon come to an end. And indeed, my friend Torpille died that following winter, in her favorite sport by the fire. Le Père Marzet told me he had gone to feed the cows. Torpille by then could no longer follow him, so he had not been surprised when she had stayed behind. When he came back he poured her soup in her bowl also next to the fire, and he had not really suspected anything was wrong when she had not moved. He had gone about preparing dinner, and only then had he become concerned when her soup was untouched. He had petted her and had noticed that her breathing had stopped. She had died peacefully without bothering anyone, a happy dog by the fireplace. He had sat down on his chair at the table and had cried like a child—don't tell Alice he had told me. And he had buried her on the little hill by the farm. He had fashioned a cross, like the one used for the soldiers of the great War, and he had put it on her grave, with a simple inscription "Torpille, 1943-1960", like for a Poilu de Quatorze. When I had returned, that year, we both had climbed the little promontory and we had said hello to Torpille, the nicest dog I ever met. I had collected a few wild flowers and I put them on her grave, and every day that summer, as I came back to Card after watching the cows, I collected a couple of flowers which I laid by her cross. As the pain of her loss subsided, I became less attentive to this self-imposed task, and a several years later, when I went back and le Père Marzet too had gone, the cross had disappeared, and only the souvenir of Torpille and of the few good days we spent together remains with me today. But how I wish I could hold her in my arms again, the dog of my childhood.

Fidèle was a pretty dog, but there was no way I could love him as much as Torpille. However, I did not have too much time to worry about it, as that summer two new people made their appearance into my life. First, there was Aline, the daughter of Monsieur Lemaunier. It turned out that Monsieur Lemaunier was divorced and that his daughter would come to Limousin for the summer. The previous year I had missed her because she had come in August, and by the time she had arrived I had already left. Aline was a pretty girl, two years older than me—and therefore, we could never get married she told me the first time we met—and she lived in Paris the rest of the year. She had long brown hair that was combed into French braids, and she knew a lot more than I did about things. And when the second new person showed up, Frédéric, Robert Teulier's nephew, who was spending a month in Card with his parents (Carole, his mother was Robert's sister), Aline immediately told me that I should not play with him because he was from a bad district of Paris. Aline could explain things, and why people behaved a certain way. For example, she immediately told me that Robert Teulier drank too much wine. Her father had found him passed out on the side of the road to Ambazac the previous winter, and when he had stopped his car to help him, Robert Teulier could not even stand. When her father had tried to put him in the car to take him home so he wouldn't freeze, Robert Teulier had fought him so hard that her father had given up and had left him on the side of the road. She knew how babies were made and why Alice could not have any children. She said that her father had a cow that had the same thing as Alice, she was infertile, and her father had had to get rid of the cow, because it could not produce calves or make milk. I was blown away. Aline knew so much! When I told my parents, they told me this was gossip, that it should not be repeated, and that Aline was a big mouth who should mind her own business. I continued to learn the meaning of what my grandmother Lainey always said: "If nobody asks you the question, don't answer it". I figured that from that point on, if my parents did not ask about Aline, I would not volunteer any information.

The family of my grandmother Lainey, born Spinetta, was from Italy, from a little village named Arma di Taggia. But her family was originally from Corsica, and my grandmother had all types of rules related to how one should mind one's own business. One of her favorites was "if dogs are fighting, cross the street" which meant that if you happened to see a fight or a dispute, you should simply forget about it and go on with your business unconcerned. Of course, this was exactly the opposite of what my grandfather was doing for a living, and told me to do. My grandfather was paid to go and keep the dogs from fighting! Soon, I was to test the validity of the two theories as an encounter between Aline and Frédéric turned sour. Frédéric was a lonely child whose parents apparently had a good income. As a matter of fact, they drove around in a Simca Aronde, which at that time was the new coolest car in France. It was conspicuously parked in front of Robert Teulier's house, and had a pale yellow body with a black roof. Frédéric, of course, had a pedal car, something I had always wanted but my parents refused to buy me. Frédéric did not let anyone ride it, and I did not care because I had a bicycle, it went much faster, and I could go anywhere I wanted with it. One afternoon, Aline decided that she was going to ride this car, whether Frédéric liked it or not. So, when Frédéric had been distracted by something or another, Aline jumped in and started pedaling away in it. Frédéric ran after her down the lane, at which time Aline made a left turn and she was rolling down the hill on the smooth surface of the Départementale. The car was not meant for this type of speed, and she soon lost control of it and ended up in the ditch. Like a Formula One driver getting out of his car after hitting the barriers at the Grand Prix of Monaco, she was extricating herself from the now wounded machine when Frédéric furious with rage grabbed a rock and rushing to her hit her on the head with her. She fell backwards under the violence of the blow, and spilled over into a growth of stinging nettles. Stinging nettles grow everywhere in Limousin, and they produce the same stinging pain as jelly fish. She was screaming, and Frédéric was kicking her and beating her. I did not have much time to reflect on which theory to adopt, my grandmother's or my grandfather's. I ran over, grabbed Frédéric and distracted him from inflicting more harm to the poor Aline who was dying in pain from the stinging nettles. Frédéric was so furious that he also hit me with the rock, while Aline was yelling at me to kick him in his privates. While this was going on I thought that it would be useful to have gendarmes right then. This kept me from understanding what Aline was yelling, and from seeing that her tormentor was now kicking her, while she was still down. She yelled at the top of her lungs "kick him in the balls", which triggered the right response and immediately brought down the angry and unchivalrous Frédéric to his knees. Regaining her composure, Aline got up and pushed him in the stinging nettles as well, adding "that will teach you".

Aline took me by the hand as we ran down past her father's farm, past the Roussel's farm and to the small wash pond, where she sat down and put her legs in the cool water to relieve the burning sensation of the nettles. There is not much you can do against the sting of the nettles, just bear it and cry in pain, until the body recovers and the stingers fall out, which usually takes a good fifteen to twenty minutes. In the meantime, the pain is intense. More than Aline's pain, I was concerned about the story that Alice had told me about the salamanders. I told Aline, and that made her laugh. "Silly, she told me, the salamanders cannot make you drown. She told you this tale to keep you away from the water, so that you would not jump in and drown on your own. Salamanders cannot do that!" Boy was I relieved. Because Alice had scared me from going near the pond or near any body of water, as everybody knew that salamanders could live in any of those. Aline did know a lot, and she knew all of the tales the people of the country tell or believe in. But the pedal car incident had made the two of us close friends, even if Aline thought I was a bit slow-witted because I believed anything the adults said. As for Frédéric, he was mad for a couple days, but then the need to have someone to play with became more urgent than staying mad, and we started to play together again. That evening before I went home, Aline kissed me for helping her out. Maybe, just maybe, my grandfather's approach was better…

Frederic's mother, Carole, was what people today would describe as "hot". She would wear a bikini, sunbathe in Robert Teulier's garden, and she wanted me to play with her son so he would not bother her. As I was two classes ahead of him in school, although we were the same age, she also thought I would be a good influence on him. My parents, to the contrary did not like that I play with him so much, because he was the same age as me but he was two classes behind, which could not be a good influence on me. My choice was simple because first of all, I would rather work with le Père Marzet than play with a stupid boy from Paris who beat girls. Second, I immediately noticed that Frédéric had the primitive nature of a cave man, and that he liked to break things. When he broke his own things it did not bother me, but when he broke mine, I really did not like it. I had a paratrooper toy that would be flown into the air by unraveling a rope that was wrapped around a propeller. When the propeller stopped spinning, it would release the paratrooper, and his chute would open. Well, this oaf broke it the first day I showed it to him, and when I complained to my parents they said I should be more careful with my things! That encouraged me to avoid Frédéric and not to share anything with him. There was no way I would lend him my bicycle. And then, there was Aline. The day after the incident, her father stopped by the house to thank my parents for my behavior, as Aline had told her father everything. From that point on Aline and I became inseparable, and when I was not with le Père Marzet, I was with her.

It was great because even though I was two years younger I was in the same class as she, but she knew more about life. She asked me if I knew about Brigitte Bardot. She told me that Brigitte Bardot sunbathed in the nude, and that she even let photographers take pictures of her. I could not understand why anybody would go around nude, and even less let other people take her pictures. Then Aline asked me if I had seen the pictures in Paris-Match. When I told her no, she was not surprised, and reacted if it were normal for a retard like me not to have seen them. I did know that the week they had come out, my father had kept the magazine away from me, and that I had not been allowed to read the issue. Aline told me that if I was nice to her she would show them to me. Since my parents had forbidden me to see the pictures, I immediately decided that this was something I wanted to see. But I told Aline that this had to remain a secret between the two of us. She said that would be fine, but I had to give her a secret in return. Since I did not have any, the pictures of Brigitte Bardot were tabled until a later date. Aline was so sophisticated that even I, who was from

Monaco, could not keep up with her. She knew all about Rolls-Royces, Ferraris, the Grand Prix, she even knew that there was a Grand Prix in Italy, and I pretended I did too, even adding "there is even one in France!" to which she responded "as if I did not know!" She might have known it but I had not, and it had been a simple guess that had luckily proven correct. I had a hard time keeping up with her. Not like with my cousin Raymond. I could manipulate him all day long because he thought he was so slick. Not Aline. I had to be careful not ending up holding an electric fence! Again.

While all of this was going on, my father was alternating his days between visiting family and fixing the electricity. One day, when I got home after watching the cows, there was electricity in the staircase and in my parents' bedroom. My father told me that within two days I would have electricity in my bedroom, and I could read in bed before going to sleep. Before that could happen, we had to go visit cousin Michel and his wife, cousin Louise. Who was Cousin Michel? I have no idea. But it was very scary to visit with him because he was the principal of the biggest Limoges high school, he had a college degree—my father did not even have a high school degree—and he was extremely smart. When we arrived in Limoges, I was disappointed because the cousin did not live in the center of the city, like my grandmother did in Paris (I could see the Eiffel Tower from her house), and he had a house with a nice garden well before one arrived in the city itself. The house was furnished with museum quality furniture, the type of furniture my parents would look at in the Galleries Lafayette and quickly walk away from before the saleswoman caught up with them, because they could not afford it. I was offered a glass of grenadine syrup and water, and Cousin Michel proceeded to interrogate me, testing my knowledge, and giving me to read what I know now was a page of a novel of Marcel Proust, one of the most difficult French authors to read. After that I was told to go play in the garden while the adults visited. It was a hot summer day, and the windows were open. I could hear the conversation saying that my reading level was phenomenal, that Cousin Michel had twelfth grade students who could not read Marcel Proust, that I was superlatively intelligent, and then the fatidic words "if he does not get results in school, it is because he does not try. This child should be at the head of the class in every subject matter."

My fate was sealed. From that point on, there was a rule in the house that I should rank below fifth—and French schools at the time ranked all of their students in every subject matter on a monthly basis—that I should read a book a week, starting with Jules Verne, and that I should do class work during the summer vacation to better prepare for the upcoming school year. This summer class work was called Vacation Homework, and was purchased in organized binders that provided two hours of work for every work day of the week. The tranquility of my Card vacation was gone forever, and my parents now expected me to succeed in every endeavor in life simply based on my scholastic achievements that became the national priority program of the Faure family. After that visit, my parents went straight to the first bookstore and purchased the stupid vacation homework book for my grade. From that point on, every afternoon, instead of playing outside, working with le Père Marzet, chasing butterflies or kicking Frédéric in the balls, I had to do vacation homework.

CHAPTER 18
The Deschamps Family Visit

My cousin Maxime at Fondanèche was a lot less willing than le Père Marzet to share his secrets for mushroom hunting. When we got there at about eleven, he was only finishing his tasks with the cattle—his brother was in Algeria in the army—and he had yet to go collect mushrooms as his mother had asked him to do. Upon hearing the word mushroom, I asked him if I could go with him. He laughed and said "I don't think so". Say what? I don't think so? Yes, he refused to take me along. When he came back an hour later, his two wooden baskets were full to the rim, but I immediately noticed that is was a pell-mell mixture of edible and poisonous mushrooms. I told him what I thought, to which he replied "Hush! The Parisians don't know it!", and he walked straight into the house with his load of deadly fungi. When he or the other people in Fondanèche talked about the Parisians they meant the couple who had purchased the farmhouse about three hundred feet down the road. I had seen their Citroën DS 19 car with the "75" license plate parked on the side of the road in front of the house. Like everyone in France the Faure family at Fondanèche despised the Parisians. They despised then so much that my cousin wanted them to eat poisonous mushrooms? No, Tata Marie de Fondanèche said "It is a ploy. First they see us come back with a whole bunch of mushrooms and they think they can retrace our steps to go and collect them themselves. Then, they see the poisonous mushrooms we collected, and they think we are idiots and don't know the difference. That way they don't try to retrace our steps, and they don't find the good ones". As she was explaining the ruse, she had taken pieces of newspapers, and using them to protect her hands, she removed the top layer of poisonous mushrooms, revealing a bunch of chanterelles, cèpes and boletus. Each mushroom she removed went straight into the fire burning in the fireplace. I stopped her when she was throwing a boletus. She said: "Oh, I see that le Père Marzet did not teach about how to tell apart the boletus and Satan's mushroom." She took the top of the poisonous mushroom and cracked it in half. The flesh was in all aspects similar to the regular boletus, but as it came in contact with the air, it started turning blue and within a minute it was completely fluorescent blue. "Sometimes, the stems are so close in color you cannot tell them apart, but once you crack one open, you will always know that if it turns blue, you don't want to eat it."

Protection from the Parisians or from any stranger who might happen to drive by was a major concern in Fondanèche. Fondanèche is tucked out of the way in the Ambazac Mountains and there were only three reasons one would be there: one, to visit a local family, like we did, and there was only one other family living there year round; two, because one was lost, and most of the time people figured out they were lost way before they reached the small hamlet; and three because whoever was there was up to not good. My uncle had hundreds of acres of land, sheep, cows, chickens and turkeys, crops, vegetables growing in fields which they could not see from the house, and hundreds of thousands of dollars of farm equipment scattered all over their fields. There was no way that not enough precautions should not be taken to protect all of these assets. To this end, my aunt kept a calendar from the post office on the wall next to the window—the "calendrier des postes" is the official calendar of France and is sold by the mailman to every household in France. As soon as someone heard a car coming up the hill, it was that person's duty to go to the window, wait until the car was in plain view, and if it was a car that the person did not know, he had to write down the license plate number next to the date on the calendar. This was not a big job because most days there would be only one or two cars making their way to Fondanèche. One day, as we were having lunch there, I heard the sound of a car through the open window. I told my aunt, and everybody went quiet. Conversations stopped, forks were made silent. My aunt rushed to the window and closed it, while from the corner of it, she asked me to tell her the license plate number. It was not a known car, and the license plate ended with "29"—clearly foreigners to Limousin as the license plate indicated they were from Brittany. As the car approached the house, it slowed down, and came to stop in front of the window. But the window was so high off the ground that nobody could see in from outside. When he heard the door of the car open, my uncle Emile told my cousin Maxime "Go get the shotgun". Maxime opened a door in the back of the room and came back with the loaded shotgun. During that time, the stranger knocked at the door. The door was made of heavy wood and was always locked with iron bars. And he knocked again, and then pounded. The room was dead silent. Not a sound was made; the fire itself had gone quiet. After asking us to open several times, the man outside finally gave up, shouting that we were all "paysans de merde" who could go rot in hell for not wanting to help somebody who was lost. Once the car had departed, my uncle told Maxime, "Go put the gun back." And then turning to us, he added "if he were lost, he should have said so at first!" Everybody laughed after these tense moments, and started eating again as if nothing had happened. I found out later the real reason for the concern that day. My uncle, like all farmers in the region at the time did not use a bank. What profit they made, they exchanged the money for gold coins called Louis d'or—Gold Louis. They collected the coins in a coffee can, and the coffee can was buried under a stone, in the ground below the floor of the small room where Maxime had fetched the gun from. There were tens of thousands of dollars in that coffee can, and this is really what the entire family was protecting that day.

Things were not that bad in Card because it was not as isolated and because there was a lot more traffic on the Départementale—at that time there was a least a car an hour. But that did not mean that protecting assets and livestock was not first and foremost on anyone's mind. And strangers had actually no business turning into our lane and venturing into what was almost a gated community. So, when our friends from Monaco, the Deschamps family showed up to visit with us, and my parents had omitted to tell Robert Teulier, when the black Peugeot 203 made its way carefully down our lane in first gear, Robert Teulier—the keeper of the gate—ran behind them with a pitchfork, in the most classic rendition of French farmers revolting against the king during the French

Revolution. I was the only witness to this potential massacre, and quickly entered the house to alert my father. Instead of welcoming his friend, my father had to temper Robert Teulier's desire to defend Card. Robert had these famous words "they scared me". Maybe it was the other way around as Deschamps came out of the car ready to fight for his life and wondering in what savage country he had landed. And he was not even from Paris. This little incident was soon forgotten as my father opened a bottle of wine, and the men ended up toasting glasses in the common room while the women talked about dinner, and I took my friend Gérard on a tour of Card.

The dinner was a lot of fun, the house was full of the activity three more people can add, and since we did not have enough beds, I gave up mine to Gérard parents, and he and I slept in sleeping bags on air mattresses in the common room. Gérard assured me that this was how soldiers slept, except they slept in a tent. In the morning, we went to get a bicycle from Alice who had agreed to lend hers to Gérard so we could both go cycling on the roads around Card. When I was not busy with le Père Marzet, the vacation homework, Aline, Frédéric or shopping in Ambazac, I would take the bicycle and ride around the area. My father had given me a limit to how far I could go on the Départementale but fortunately, he had "forgotten" to give me a limit on the side roads. These side roads were called Chemins Vicinaux (CV)—vicinal roads—and branched out from the Départementales at random but frequent intervals. Most went to hamlets like Card, some went to tiny villages with no more than twenty houses, and some went to single farms. While I was limited on my main roads to a course that extended from Ambazac to the "Propriété" a large walled farm about four miles south of Card, I had not received instructions on other cycling restrictions. Since I had only one bicycle, my grey bicycle, which I used to go get groceries, Gérard used Alice's, a beautiful light metallic green Peugeot which she did not ride any longer. Because there were two cars, and my father wanted to show his friends Ambazac, I was dispensed of the groceries run that day. Gérard and I started down our lane, and at first simply rode a couple of kilometers to Les Loges to get used to riding together. But we soon started riding down the Chemins Vicinaux, first to La Boissarde, to the big farm which was run by the "Italians". I was always welcome there because I could speak Italian, and every time I showed up Signora Marroni would ask me to go in and have a glass of water with syrup. She liked the orgeat flavor, made from almonds, and I really liked as well. So it was a nice match. We would talk in Italian for a few moments, and I would be on my way. That morning was no exception.

After Gérard and I had finished our drinks, we rode away, and suddenly Gérard was racing me. He had taken me by surprise, and before I realized it, he was easily three hundred feet in front of me. I thought he would wait for me at the intersection with the Départementale, but he turned left through the stop sign without event slowing down. My parents had taught me the rules of the road, and I would never run through a stop sign. I stopped, and by the time I turned left, Gérard was now a good six hundred feet ahead, and he turned right on to CV 27 that went down to the little village of Mieux. I thought I would be able to catch him on the flat, but he would not slow down. That's when he made a mistake, and instead of going straight to Mieux, he decided to turn right onto the fast downhill that went no place but to the farm of the one people called the "Fou"—the madman. The Fou had never recovered from the war—nobody knew whether it was the Great War or the Second World War—and he believed that anyone who trespassed on his road or on his farm was a "sale Boche"—a dirty Kraut. And the road Gérard had taken was a dead end straight into the Fou's farm! I yelled at my friend to stop, to turn around, but he thought it was a trick to get him to slow down so that I would beat him. I knew immediately that Gérard had run into the Fou because of the way he locked the rear wheel of the bicycle and skidded to a stop. There is this thing about running into a demented man who wore his World War One helmet and held a loaded shotgun that made you suddenly want to stop and turn around. I came to a stop myself, and peeking around the bushes in the middle of the curve, I saw him aiming at my friend who had dropped the bicycle in the middle of the road and was running back uphill as fast as he could. And that's when the Fou fired. Now, three thoughts came to my mind: first, what about Alice's bicycle? She is not going to be happy when we don't bring it back; second, we are going to be late for lunch—for sure; third, how are we going to explain that to our parents? There were no thoughts of calling the gendarmes, because before they could be alerted and they arrived, the Fou would have killed both of us.

There was no thought of figuring out if Gérard was hit or killed, because there was no way the Fou could miss at that range. This is when Gérard decided to give my position away and call my name. He ran up to me, white as a ghost, and asked "why didn't you tell me about him?" I told him I had tried, but he was too busy trying to win the race. In the middle of his barnyard the Fou was reloading. I asked Gérard "how close did the round hit?" He said that it was not even close, that either he had fired in the air, or he was the worst shot in France. During that time the Fou was yelling at us "I see you! Dirty Krauts! Murderers! You will not get through!" Well, I knew now that the Fou had not recovered from the Great War—"you will not get through" was a dead give away. How were we going to get the bicycle back? Especially since the Fou was now running toward our position. I climbed on my bicycle, and went up the hill, while Gérard was running as fast as he could. The Fou let go of two more rounds, and finally turned around to go back to his farm. As he walked by Alice's bicycle, he kicked it, yelling more anti-German profanities. We stopped running. We needed a plan of action to recover the bicycle.

This is when what le Père Marzet had told me about trench warfare proved to be useful. I hid my bicycle as best I could in the bushes in the side of the road. Then Gérard and I got into the ditch, and using the ditch as if it were a trench, we crawled down the hill, so that no one could see us. We could still hear the Fou yelling and carrying on, talking to himself, and swearing that next time, he would not miss. When we got to where the bicycle lay on the road, that's when things got difficult. There was no way we could escape without attracting the attention of the Fou. Gérard proposed that I should go back and that he should pick up the bike and run uphill with it. That was tough because the Fou surely could run faster that a boy pushing a bicycle. I thought of le Père Marzet rushing over the trench in World War One, and all of a sudden, Gérard and I were Poilus de Quatorze! He laughed at that, but we were both scared beyond our wits. Only the dressing down we would get from our parents if they learned about this was scarier. Between the fear of the dressing down and facing a shotgun, we chose the shotgun. We decided that I would grab the handlebar, turn the bicycle around, and start running uphill while Gérard pushed. We rushed over the ditch, moved according to plan, and the noise of the metal mud guard scrapping on the road as we righted the bicycle alerted the Fou of our presence. By then he had reloaded, and he let go of one round, then the next round. We felt the blow of the second round as the shot pelted the leaves to our right. We ran even faster. My lungs were hurting, my arms were giving way, but Gérard kept pushing and pushing, until we were passed even my bicycle. He would not stop. We could hear the steps of the Fou running behind us. They were less rapid, but he had reloaded and let go of another round. We were out of range, but we kept running, and running. Finally, I lost my balance and we both fell on the road, panting, out of breath and sweating like crazy. The Fou had returned to his farm. This is when Gérard and I noticed that his right calf was bleeding. He had been hit in two places, but in the rush to get out of there, he had not noticed it. He now felt the burning of the wound as the blood was slowly trickling down onto his socks. He could walk, and probably ride, but now we would have to invent a story about how he had gotten hurt. I went back for my bicycle, and Gérard promised he would never race against me again. We rode slowly back to Les Loges, as the burning became more intense in my friend's leg. That's when I decided to go back to Signora Marroni's.

She was surprised that we would be back, and I explained to her what had happened. She laughed about hearing our adventures, and said that the Fou did not use real bullets in his gun. He used salt pellets, which would burn for hours but were harmless. She said she would help my friend. Gérard took off his sock and shoe, and the Signora poured water over his calf. Then, she pinched the area of the wound, and she poured water into in to dissolve more of the salt. By the time she was done, the burning was almost gone, according to Gérard, the bleeding had stopped, and he had two Band-Aids on his leg. Gérard washed his sock in the fountain, and we were back on the road. We swore we would never tell our parents about any of this, or we could forget about ever riding a bicycle. But now we had to rush home because it was past noon, and we were late for lunch. As it turned out, we were early, which gave us time to ride around a little more and take the edge out of our adventure.

Lunch was a special one that day because we had guests, and my father had decided to invite Robert Teulier. Since Robert Teulier worked at the sawmill, and was not done until noon, it had been decided that we would eat at one. Robert Teulier was a true French worker and farmer. Of medium height but strong built with square shoulders, he was slightly overweight, and had a jovial attitude about him. Always dressed in his blue work clothes which he must have washed once a month at best, he kept a yellow corn paper cigarette at the right corner of his mouth at all times. He also wore a beret which he absolutely never took off. His standard footwear was the black wooden clogs which he purchased at Tonton François. His voice was manly and raspy because of his smoking, and his round face was permanently covered with a two day old stub growth. He had a strong jaw and quick brown eyes that were particularly trained to see bottles of red wine. This red wine gave his entire complexion a ruddy look, a feature which was especially noticeable in the appearance of his nose. He liked to joke, and always enjoyed telling a good tale while sitting at the table and drinking a glass of "rouge"—rouge being the cheap red wine sold in France without even a label. Robert Teulier made no qualms that he was a communist, was anti-management, anti-war in Algeria, and would gladly have beheaded the king if it were necessary to do so again, but would be happy to behead a few curés instead. I was from Monaco, where we lived happily with a prince and I was hesitant to hear such speak—I would be plain horrified when I would learn the bloody details of the French Revolution in school. In any case, since Robert Teulier had been invited I knew the meal would be fun, and my parents as well as Gérard's were too busy preparing the food and setting the table to pay any attention to us to my friend's Band-Aids.

CHAPTER 19
A Feast at the Card House

The big rectangular table sat lengthwise in the middle of the common room. On the left of the table was the fireplace, which was lit for the occasion. It was used to keep hot water and to grill the lamb chops that were to be served for lunch. The table was a new oak table that had replaced the old worm-eaten table that had been in the farm for over a century. Wood worms were a persistent problem in Limousin for any wood that was not treated or regularly maintained with wax. The table was covered with the beautiful brand new table cloth which my mother had purchased at the Ambazac market. It had a white background with little blue flowers intertwined throughout, so that is was more blue than white. The table was already set with the "good" ceramic plates, the ones my grandmother Louise kept in the dresser upstairs. They were white with a dark green rim, and were "good" because there actually were enough of them for a setting of seven. They were accompanied by the everyday silverware, except for steak knives with an imitation ivory handle which my father has also bought at the Ambazac market. The glasses were not the standard stem glasses which one would have expected. This was the country and we had thick glasses of the same type our Fondanèche cousins used. White linen napkins were set in the plates, and in the center of the table was a vase with a bunch of wild flowers which my mother had tasked me and Gérard to go collect earlier that morning before we were allowed to go cycling. Madame Deschamps and my mother were busy in the kitchen, and my father and René were placing the chairs and ensuring the salt, pepper and the mélée were on the table.

Monsieur Deschamps, or René, was a wiry very thin man with a triangular face and an energy level that spilled over into hyperactivity. He was quick to look for and find an argument, and even quicker to find a fight. One would have thought that a man as slim as he was could not possibly fight so many times and live to tell about it. But he did, and when he started fighting it usually took the cops or the gendarmes to calm him down. He was an optician by trade, and a good one, but he had spoiled every job he had ever held by getting into a fight with his boss. In the last job in Beausoleil, he had gotten into an argument with the owner of the shop about how to set lenses into a very expensive frame a customer had purchased. The argument had quickly evolved into a shouting match during which René had been fired. That had triggered the fight, and René had ended up throwing the owner into the shop's window, which had crashed, as the owner had gone backward through it and had ended up in the middle of the street. Deschamps—as my father called him—had been arrested, found guilty of assault, and had been sentenced to seventy days in jail in the Nice prison. That little exploit had had three consequences: first, Deschamps was unemployed and had been so for over six months; second, he had been blacklisted by the opticians association, l'Ordre des Opticiens, and he would never be able to practice as an optician again; and third he had had to move his family from Monaco to the small apartment his wife had inherited in the village of La Turbie above Monaco. This had meant that I had lost the opportunity to play with my friend Gérard on Thursdays as I had done in the past. Deschamps was no friends of the capitalists or of the "patrons"—business owners—and this alone made him a friend of Robert Teulier. His wife, Laure, tried to manage as best she could. Between the temper outbursts which were triggered by random events and had nothing to do with her, and the fact that she faced a lifelong of coming in and out of unemployment and reduced income, she had resigned herself to the fact that there was nothing she could do about it and she had accepted her fate with great stoicism.

Robert Teulier arrived in a newly washed set of work clothes, his corn-paper cigarette hanging from his lip, and smiling broadly deposited two bottles of red wine on the table: "I did not know if the lady of the house had wine, so I thought I'd bring a couple of bottles!" which meant that regardless how much wine was served, he expected to drink at least two bottles. Robert Teulier apologized for scaring the Deschamps family, but that as you well know, you cannot be sure of who it is you are dealing with, and it's better to be careful rather than find yourself robbed blind the next day. Of course, Deschamps understood, and it was normal, especially when the "patronat"—the bosses—throws good workers out on the street, and they have to revert to crime to survive. In the end, both of them agreed that the patronat and the capitalists were responsible for the situation. This was a good start! Robert Teulier sat at the head of the table. To his right was Deschamps, and to his left my father—since he was responsible for grilling the lab chops. Next to the fathers sat their respective sons, and next to them the mothers were reversed. Madame Deschamps sat next to me and my mother next to Gérard. The meal officially started with a glass of Pernod. This is the official aperitif of France and is served in a special-purpose glass with one part of Pernod, five times as much water, and ice cubes. Gérard and I were given Berger brand anise syrup which mimicked the pale yellow color of Pernod without the alcohol. The clinking of glasses, the loud voices of the men wishing each other, the sons, and the wives good fortune and health gave the tone of the meal. Black olives were served with Pernod while the adults continued drinking and taking about current news. The war in Algeria, the general de Gaulle who could not make up his mind between fighting and giving Algerians their independence, the threat of all the French colonists coming back to France at once—and they were already arriving Deschamps affirmed—that could not be good for the economy and for us who had never left France to start with. These colonists were nothing but adventurers who should have no rights when they returned! The first real food was saucisson, the French hard salami, which Tonton Emile had given my father. It was from the pig they had killed the previous fall. "It should be well cured" commented Robert Teulier. It was served with butter from the farm which my mother had gotten at Tata Marie's, and this butter was also slightly perfumed with hazelnuts. The first bottle of wine was opened with the saucisson, and before the saucisson was gone, Robert Teulier had already finished his second glass of wine. "Working at the sawmill makes you thirsty" he explained. "There is so much dust, and it is so dry and hot. And you cannot drink there with all the machines, it would not be safe. And even without drinking, you have no idea how dangerous it is. I'll tell you that last year in May we had gotten this new guy. He had come from the North, with recommendations and everything. Well, within two weeks, he fucked up something, I turned around, and before I knew it his right arm had been caught in the big saw, and it was gone. And the guy did not even drink wine! He almost bled to death right there. By the time the ambulance arrived...You know that the ambulance had to come from Ambazac, and then, they had to take him to Limoges. Well, two days later I read in L'Echo du Centre that he was dead. It is not the patrons who are going to pay his widow her pension! Anyway, to tell you we cannot drink—well most of the time—from time to time we sneak in a bottle, when the patron is not watching, hop, a little rouge!" Deschamps agreed. It was a scandal that good workers, grown up men should not be allowed to drink. Why did we have the revolution in 1789, if the Republic is even more a pain than the king? Gérard looked at me and rolled his eyes in his head. He was used to his father's rhetoric and now, with Robert Teulier, it was going to be even better!

After the saucisson was praised for its taste and after it was gone, my mother brought in the diced beets in oil and the radishes. Robert Teulier commented that this was a meal that was starting on the right foot because one should always have some vegetable at the beginning, to make everything else slide down better. The first bottle of wine was gone, and my father opened the wine Robert Teulier had brought. The beets were supremely well done declared Deschamps, and turning to his wife "I hope you wrote down the recipe!" The radishes were just right, not too soft, just biting enough. Where did you get them? These were the radishes from Tonton François. Robert Teulier said that these are the radishes your aunt Marie should sell! And the butter! This was good butter! You could eat butter like this all day long, and not feel a thing. This was followed by Quiche Lorraine which was made from the eggs and the fresh cream from our Card neighbors, and ham from Fondanèche. Then came my father's turn to show his cooking skills as he set the lamb chops on the grill in the fireplace over the red hot ambers. Before that he had buried baking potatoes inside the ambers, and he served the lamb chops together with the potatoes which had the crispiest skin, and the good taste of smoked food, as the wood charcoal had not only cooked them but had also given them the chestnut charcoal flavor. There were more vegetables, creamed spinach and palm hearts, but everybody swore they were full; they could not possibly eat another bite. The salad was a lettuce from Tonton François's garden with Limousin walnut oil, and the cheese selection was of cheese from the region: gouzon (a close cousin of camembert), fresh caillade (similar to cottage cheese, but much finer and creamier), tome du Limousin (a semi hard cheese) and cabicous (a goat cheese wrapped in chestnut leaves). Finally, it was time for desert, which was served with Monbazillac wine. It was a Paris-Brest purchased at the Patisserie Lheureux, recommended by Tata Marie. The Paris-Brest is a circular cake, in the shape of a tire that was created in the late 1890s to celebrate the Paris to Brest bicycle race. Its crust is made of cream puff paste and filled with butter cream. It is so good, it is almost too good. By the time we had finished it an ample supply of bottles of wine had been consumed. My father had arranged them in a corner of the room, and I could count eight bottles, not counting the Monbazillac which was being finished. This is when singing started. From the end of the table, Robert Teulier asked for silence, as he launched the famous song "Les Monédiaires":

Bol d'Or des Monédiaires
Qui regroupe tous les meilleurs coureurs
Qui roulent devant la foule
Sous des acclamations de joie…

Everybody thought that was well performed, and he insisted everybody sing something. Deschamps who was a bit less steady because of the alcohol, found nothing better than "Le Curé de Camaret" and the two mothers tried to drown out his words by yelling" Not in front of the children". Laure yelled at him "You are disgusting!" And turning to my mother: "I don't' know a more disgusting man! If you knew the things he asked me to do in bed!" My mother was even more embarrassed and suggested Deschamps sing something else. But it was too late, and he managed to sing the first verse. Then my father simply sang the nonsensical song "Marguerite aimait les oiseaux" (Marguerite liked birds), which constantly repeats itself without ever ending. I was then asked to sing something. Fortunately le Père Marzet had taught me the words for "La Madelon" the favorite song of the Poilus, and standing on my chair I sang it. Le Père Marzet peeked his head trough the open window, and he was invited in for a drink, as the entire house accompanied me in singing the chorus. Gérard did not have a song to sing, so Robert Teulier gave us his rendition of "La Cabrette au Musette". And then it was time for the Limousin alcohol, fine. Robert Teulier had impatiently waited for it, as the fruit basket was brought in. The table which had been so well arranged was a real battlefield, with wine glasses, silverware, the empty Paris-Brest plate confusedly strewn about as the men started song after song. After the second glass of fine, Robert Teulier switching to the Limousin patois started to sing "Lo Brianço":

Io vau souven di un site acounpli
Per en admira lo richessoLi sai urou moun coeur n'en ei rempli
Co mo rapelo mo jonesso

It did not produce the effect expected since with the exception of le Père Marzet, he was the only one to know the words. Then, it was a cacophony of people wanting to sing, and the entire feast broke up with le Père Marzet going back to work, Deschamps trying to sing "Cochon d'Enfant", my mother and Laure trying to stop him, fearing another filthy song, my father making his own rendition of "Le Tralala", and Robert Teulier finally exhausted by the food and the wine, collapsing on his chair in the loudest snoring ever heard in Card. Gérard and I took advantage of the confusion to escape through the window before we were drafted to do the dishes, and it was back to bicycling into the pathways around Card.

CHAPTER 20
Oradour-sur-Glane

The Deschamps family was only one of the many visitors we had in Card. My parents' friends and family were mainly working class and did not have much of a budget dedicated to their vacation and even less to spend on a hotel room. The few days they could spend in Card were for many the only vacation they could afford. And Limousin was just as foreign to them as it is to the majority of my readers today. Limousin, contrary to what the official website would have you believe is not a "region" of France, but an old province of France, which emerged under the rule of the French kings. The first inhabitants were the Celtic tribes of the Lemovice—meaning those who live near the elm trees (it is ironic that chestnut trees and not elm trees are associated with Limousin these days). The Romans "pacified" the tribes in 51 BC by defeating them at the battle of Uxellodunum, nowadays the village of Capdenac (which is not in the Province of Limousin). Christianity arrived in the third century with Saint Martial, and over the next nine centuries, the province gradually took the shape that it had when the One Hundred Year War started against England. During that war, the Spaniards took advantage of the difficulties of France, and promptly conquered as much of it as the English would tolerate, to include Limousin. France eventually got rid of both invaders, and Limousin became a true French province under the reign of François 1st. It remained a feudal land into the eighteenth century. During the French revolution, the republic banned anything that had to do with the monarchy, and one of these things was the organization of France into provinces. In lieu of provinces, France was reorganized into administrative départements, and Limousin was arbitrarily divided into three départements: Corrèze, Creuse, and Haute-Vienne. The name "Province du Limousin" ceased to exist. That was until the 1970s when the French republic decided to regroup départements into regions, and the Region of Limousin was established with the three départements that were originally the province itself. Like Dane Crook would say, a full "vicious circle" was completed. During World War Two, Limousin was one of the most active Résistance regions, and it paid dearly for its opposition to Germany.

Since so few of our visitors had ever come to Limousin, my father felt an obligation to serve as their tour guide. And one of the places he felt compelled to take our Card visitors was the village of Oradour-sur-Glane. The first time we went there, my father told me we would go visit the village that was burnt down by the Germans during the war. I had no idea he meant it literally. Now, since my father was born after the Great War, when he said "the war", it meant only one thing: World War Two. The first time my father took me there, it had been several years since he himself had been there. As Oradour is only about twenty miles from Ambazac, my father always had a feeling that what had happened there that day could as easily have happened in Ambazac and that troubled him greatly, since he had spent most of the war in Ambazac with Tata Marie. We parked the Dauphine in the big parking lot by the village entrance and walked in. Few people were there (this is not exactly an uplifting visit), and silence reigned supreme, only disturbed here and there by the chirping of a few birds. What happened there is well known, but why it happened has been a subject of speculation ever since.

On the morning of June 10, 1944, six days after the Normandy landings, a convoy of German troops entered Oradour-sur-Glane. As part of their normal procedures, the Germans, who were in fact led by Alsatian officers (hence French citizens), surrounded the village, and by early afternoon they had rounded up all of the inhabitants on the market square, while they searched the houses for weapons or any type of unauthorized hunting rifles, and most likely any type of valuables that could easily be carried away. During that time, the tramway arrived from Limoges, and they let it go on, allowing the Oradour inhabitants to get off and rejoin the other villagers. There was actually nothing unusual about the whole thing, because the German army would often behave in this manner. What was unusual was that the soldiers were not regular German army, but the SS of the Das Reich Division who should have been on their way to the front. They proceeded with military precision, and there was no apparent panic among the villagers. The event started to take an unusual turn when the Germans separated the men from the women and the children, and divided them into small groups. Once this was done, they marched the women and children to the church where they locked them into the building. Meanwhile the SS took the men, and subdivided them into small groups which they led to different buildings in the village. The men were then summarily executed inside these buildings which were subsequently set on fire, while incendiary devices were lobbed into the church through the stained glass windows and ignited. Calmly pillaging the village, the SS watched guard to ensure no one escaped the inferno of the church. It became so hot that the church bell which has fallen from the steeple melted on the stone floor of the church. Of the 642 people living in Oradour that day only a handful survived among which a boy of eight, who ran away as soon as he saw the Germans arrive, and a woman who managed to climb out of the church through a broken window and hid in the hedge surrounding it while the entire village was massacred around her.

My father had not prepared me for the horror I was to witness when I visited there that day, over fifteen years after the events had taken place. In the museum, the everyday objects recovered on the victims or in their houses, told the tale of brutality: crushed eyeglasses, burnt peasant knives, with only the blade remaining, pocket watches trampled by SS boots and keeping for ever the time of their owners' executions, dolls, toys, all of the pathetic reminders of simple lives that were extinguished in torment and sadistic vileness. I could feel what it must have been like to die in terror that day. By the time we got to our next stop, the church, I was already greatly upset by the whole thing. As I entered the church and stepped on the grey granite stones, I walked onto a portion of them that was stained a dark brown in the southern quadrant of the church, and I asked my father why the stones were a different color. When he told me that the blood of the women and children had been baked into the stones and that I was walking on it, I lost all composure, and ran out of the church sick to my stomach. As I ran down the steps with the hope of reaching a grassy area where I could get sick undisturbed, the ever vigilant guard, in the formal blue uniform of republican servants caught me by the ear and yelled at me that it was forbidden to run in this hollowed place. As I desperately tried to control my stomach movements to tell him I needed some privacy, my lunch ran out of patience and exploded forward in a stream of vomit the violence of which was completely new to me. The entire uniform of the guard was promptly redecorated with food residue, stomach acid and other fluids, while he screamed profanities at me "Mais quel est cet enfant de salaud de bordel de merde!". My mother who had attempted to follow my escape out of the church caught up with the scene, as the guard was threatening me with deportation to Devil's Island. Immediately, the altercation turned to my advantage as my mother told the guard that "cet enfant de salaud, c'est mon fils, et je vous emmerde!" and that he must be an imbecile if he thought that a boy as well behaved as me would think of running in this place if not for a compelling reason. The guard retreated and I am sure he ran home to take a shower or a bath and throw away his uniform. After which my mother severely admonished me for yet again getting sick (I guess she was tired of me getting sick in the Dauphine, and this was as good an opportunity as any other to yell at me) and made a spectacle of herself, reproached my father for taking me there. My father was surprisingly happy with himself, saying that it was a good thing, that my getting sick was a clear sign that I could never behave like the German soldiers. He stated that if this was the only thing he ever accomplished in his life, then he was proud of it. He asked me if I wanted to continue the visit, and told him that I could handle it as long as my mother stopped yelling, figuring nothing could top this horror. But I was wrong. We saw the electric company office, where the SS took the time to electrocute the engineer, and the bakery where the SS baked the baker in his own oven, while he was still alive, and the farm well, where the SS threw the farmer into the well, and then taking the structure apart lynched him with the stones, and the garage where they had the mechanic sit in the car he was fixing, the doors locked, and was then ignited with gasoline, burning him alive. All over the village are the words of the survivors: "My group included Brissaud, the village wheelwright, Compain, the pastry chef, and Morliéras, the barber. As soon as we arrived at the barn, the Germans made us remove the two trailers that were in it, and then forced us into the building. Four soldiers with machineguns were standing in the doorway, preventing us from escaping. They were talking and joking while toying with their weapons. Suddenly, about five minutes after we had gotten there, there was a huge explosion that appeared to come from the market square. As if this had been a signal, the soldiers turned toward us, armed their weapons and started shooting at us. The first ones from our group who fell to their bullets protected the others, and I threw myself onto the floor, trying to protect my head with my arms. Meanwhile, bullets were flying all over, bouncing off the walls. I could hardly breathe from the weight of the bodies on top of me. I could hear the wounded crying for help, calling for their wives or their children. As suddenly as the shooting started, it stopped. Our executioners walked onto the pile of bodies and finished off the wounded with a pistol bullet in the head. My left arm was hit, and I was waiting with terror for the bullet that would end my life. Around me, the shouting and the cries stopped, the shooting subsided. Finally, there was nothing but a heavy and worrisome silence, and from far in far the muffled lament of the dying." Survivors who escaped from the first carnage were forced to witness as the Germans burnt the houses and the bodies of their companions, many of whom were still alive.

I pressed my father to know what had happened to the SS who had done that. Surely, they had to have been punished. How could anyone do this and not be? Even today, this issue is highly controversial. The long awaited Oradour trial started in January 1953, with seven Germans and fourteen French Alsatians. The presence of Frenchmen created much embarrassment, and thirteen of them declared they had been drafted into the SS against their will. In response to this situation the French National Assembly voted a law exempting any French citizen from the collective responsibility of the massacre (or any other such massacre). Hence it was established that only the Germans were personally responsible, therefore subject to trial, while the French were collectively responsible, and not subject to trial. At the end of this sorry episode, not a single Frenchman went to jail, and the Germans were sentenced to meaningless prison sentences, the harshest one of which was seven years in jail. By the time I visited Oradour the first time, all of them had already been released from prison. I was outraged by what my father had told me, and scared that justice had not prevailed, and that people who had assassinated children my age were walking free, basically unpunished.

Fortunately, not all sites in Limousin were as gruesome as this one. There are many unlisted sites in Limousin, which are known only through word to mouth, and several of these involve prehistoric sites, such as dolmens, and natural sites such as the so-called "roches branlantes" rocks that are balanced on top of each other, and will sway back and forth through a small push despite the fact that they may weigh over four hundred tons. Again, for the person who has never seen such a rock, it sounds impossible and dangerous as it was for me. "Can't the rock", I asked my father, "fall on top of us and simply crush us?" I was somewhat nervous as I got under the massive structure and pushed up to start it in motion. My father did not really have an answer. Forty years later, the rock is still there, but every time I visit, I am still not sure I want to go mess with it. The one we visited that day was an enormous turtle shaped rock in Saint-Léger-la-Montagne, not far from Fondanèche. The boulder is caught between two rock outcrops that allow it to sway back and forth without even making any noise. We also visited the one in La Jonchère from where you see the entire village. There are no markers, only the locals know the rock is there, and very few people actually visit these sites.

One day I was visiting with friends of my grandmother's from La Jonchère—by that time I had fully graduated to road cycling, and I was allowed to ride all the way there, a good three miles away—because their grandson Pierre was on vacation with them. Monsieur and Madame Martin, who were originally from La Jonchère but now lived in Paris, took the both of us to a special site. Riding in the back of their big Peugeot, we drove about twenty minutes, arriving at a chestnut tree forest. There, Monsieur Martin carefully turned right onto a dirt path, until the car could go no farther. He parked it, and we walked up the hill, under the trees. Suddenly we came up on granite stairs—not the square ones we use today, but steps made of large granite slabs that were overgrown by eagle ferns, trees, lichens and moss. Soon in front of us, there was the entrance to what looked like a cave in the hillside. Pulling out a flashlight, Monsieur Martin got on his knees and went in. What Pierre and I thought was a cave, was in fact a dolmen, a Celtic funeral chamber supported by huge blocks of rock, on top of which had been placed an ever more massive one that served as a roof. Inside, with the flashlight barely able to light the walls, we could see the stone carvings left behind thousands of years before. I could not make out what they really represented, or even less what they meant. There were spirals, what looked like flowers, indefinable marks, and straight lines. It would be tens of years before I would again see similar markings, on the rocks of the Sonoran desert in Arizona. This visit to such a mysterious site was another one of my eye opening experiences in Limousin.

While every one of these visits took me away from Card, le Père Marzet and the animals, it soon came to be that they were what I was looking for during my vacation. Despite the encouraging words of le Père Marzet who was convinced I would make a great farmer, I knew that I would never be a farmer. And even though I loved the animals, I simply could not see myself taking care of them every day for the rest of my life. And when the veterinarian came to give the cows their shots, I knew this was not my calling either. I recognized the fact that my ancestors had been farmers, but I was well aware of the even more obvious fact that our family had moved away from farming two full generations before me. It looked to me like it was a definitive career change, and there was no way that I would ever go back to that. So I let my curiosity and thirst for knowledge take over my life, slowly abandoning the care of the farm to le Père Marzet and went looking for other mysterious sites. In the same time I tried to forget about Oradour-sur-Glane, especially at bedtime, since this first visit had given me nightmares that had lasted several weeks, and stopped only after I had returned to Monaco.

CHAPTER 21
Mémé Louise Arrives

Soon the month of July was over, and my grandmother Louise arrived to take over the house and watch over me during the month of August. This would be the first of many months of August we would spend together in Card. My grandmother Louise, or as I called her, Mémé Louise, was a tall blond woman with a handsome face, light blue eyes, and a determination equal to none. She had been born Desjouannets, in the twelfth district of Paris—and was thus a true Parisian—a worker's district where her father had been a master plasterer. In those days, it meant that he made the plaster decorations on ceilings, decorations that are now manufactured in China with resin, and simply glued on the ceiling. He was an artist, and one of his greatest achievements had been to decorate the main exhibit hall of the Monaco Oceanographic Museum—that had taken place long before my family had been linked to Monaco. Mémé Louise had had several brothers and sisters, only two of them were still alive (Pierre and Adrien, whom we met in the first chapter of thisbook). But in her heart she never forgot the other three who had died before reaching the age of twenty. Georges had died an accidental death at the age of fifteen, and I cannot recall the circumstances of his death. The first Pierre had died while retrieving the laundry hanging off the window on the sixth floor of the family apartment. His mother had gone grocery shopping, and it started raining. Realizing that the laundry would get wet, Pierre who was thirteen had wanted to help his mother, and prevent the clothes from getting wet. His mother had found him dead on the sidewalk as she was coming back with the groceries (the second brother Pierre was named after the first one who had died). But the one my grandmother would miss for the rest of her life was her beloved sister Hélène. She was five years older than my grandmother, and had taken care of her little sister Louise in a way that still touched my grandmother. One day of 1912, Hélène who was then thirteen, had to have her appendix removed. Apparently the surgery had gone well. Well enough that she was released. A couple of days after her release, her uncle Léonard, who did not have any children and who was Hélène's godfather had taken her to the restaurant, where she had ordered oysters, her favorite food. That night, Hélène did not feel right, and she felt even worse the next day. She was taken back to the hospital, only to discover that her incision had become infected. In those days of limited medical knowledge, when antibiotics had yet to be invented, the doctors had basically no recourse but to make her more comfortable as she slowly passed away. My grandmother cried every day for weeks, and one can only imagine the despair of my great-grandmother who had lost her son Pierre the year before. My grandmother eventually recovered from her sister's loss, but always expressed regrets about her sister's short life, often commenting "if Hélène had lived..." and always telling me how lucky she had been to have had such a good sister. It is in honor of this Hélène that my sister received her first name.

My grandmother's life was also witness to both world wars, and during the Great War, she remembered vividly the shelling of Paris by the German gun known as Big Bertha. She remembered the events of June 26, 1918 when the shells fell on her neighborhood. Nobody could understand what it was at first, but people soon figured it out, and they were incredulous that the Germans had a gun that could fire from sixty miles away. All of these events had made Mémé Louise a tough customer. In 1940, while people were running away from the German occupation and were throwing away valuables that they had brought with them and now simply slowed down their escape, Mémé Louise went behind them and picked up these discarded goods, carrying them back to Paris where they adorned her apartment for the following forty years. And when the German troops marching below her apartment in the rue d'Estrées were singing their chants of conquest, she had yelled at them to stop singing from her balcony on the seventh floor, and had not hesitated to spit at them, while my grandfather called her a crazy woman who would end up having them both arrested. But the German officer had told the soldiers to stop singing, and they had passed without further incidents. When the war had broken out, she and my grandfather had sent their only son far from the bombardments or the potential thereof to the closest relatives in Ambazac. This is how my father spent the first couple of years of years in Ambazac with Tata Marie (his father's sister), which explained the special bond between the two.

Mémé Louise arrived in Ambazac on the express train from Paris, where she still lived, since at that time the train from Paris still stopped in Ambazac. Nowadays this train simply travels on to Limoges, and the passengers have to catch another local train to come back to Ambazac. "This is what they call progress" had commented Mémé Louise the first time she had to do it. We went and picked her up in the Dauphine, and before she was sitting in the car, she had already decided that she was treating us for dinner. So we went home, dropped off her bags, and made for the Hotel de France, on the main square of Ambazac, opposite the épicerie of Tata Marie. It was out of the question to visit Tata Marie because the two women no longer spoke to each other. This stemmed from the death of my grandfather Léon who had died in 1958. The circumstances of his death remain a mystery: he was hit by a train while walking on the railroad tracks away from home. The two theories of accident versus suicide were proposed to explain his death, my grandmother clinging to the accident theory, while my aunt accused her of having driven her brother to commit suicide. I was too young when my grandfather Léon died to offer any explanation one way or the other. Regardless of the reason, the two women would not talk again until almost twenty years later. The Hotel de France still operates today, and then as now, it has a simple restaurant catering to customers who are mainly farmers, vendors on market days, and occasional tourists who come to visit the church and see the relics of Saint-Etienne de Muret, the founder of the order of Grandmont, who died before the First Crusade of 1095. The Hotel de France was also the single restaurant in Ambazac and whether it was first class or not, I was destined to eat there many times while staying with Mémé Louise. The point is that Mémé Louise did not like to, nor was very good at cooking. In Paris she ate at the restaurant often because she had a good income as a managing accountant with the French telephone company and lived alone in an apartment that was on rent control since 1936. The house in Card was paid for—she had inherited it—and she had no expense except for paying utilities and taxes.

And Mémé Louise hated to have to pay taxes. She would often start a diatribe, even in public, revolting against the heavy tax burden imposed on French citizens. Inevitably, she would find one, two, or more people immediately agreeing with her, and soon, people would gather around her, as she preached against taxes. The patrons of the restaurant would move closer to hear her ideas, the waiters, would stop serving, enthralled by her revolutionary accents, and passersby (if we were eating outside) would stop and participate in the debate. In Ambazac, the owner of the Hotel de France would even chime in, and soon there was a crowd ready to go and attack the office of taxation and collection, as the revolutionaries did to La Bastille. Realizing that serving had stopped, the cook would call everybody back to order, the owner would tell his waiters to continue the service, the patrons would suddenly remember they had ordered a Meunière sole, or a pepper steak and everything would be back to normal. But for a few moments, Mémé Louise was a hero, the leader of a group who was ready to act, and she had not even had to get up. She should have run for elections, I thought in my mind. I already imagined my grandmother wearing the tricolor scarf of mayor of Ambazac. I was certain of one thing: the month I was about to spend with my grandmother was going to be anything but boring.

Two days later, at about eight in the morning, my parents packed up my brother in the Dauphine, said goodbye to the Marzet family, to Mémé Louise, kissed me on both cheeks, made their last recommendations, making sure my grandmother did not forget about the vacation homework, and they were gone behind the corner of Robert Teulier's well. I was very sad to see them go, but Mémé Louise reminded me I would be able to go work in the fields with le Père Marzet and listen to his war stories. The problem was that I now realized I would never be a farmer, and my passion for working in the fields was somewhat tempered compared to the previous year. Be as it may, my grandmother went into the house and came up with a present she had carried from Paris and had kept for this anticipated awkward moment, when she and I would be left alone in Card. I was thrilled by the present, and guessed from the weight that it must be a Dinky Toys car or truck. It was. In the hard white and blue striped box of the Dinky Supertoys models, there was a Berliet fire truck, with the short climbing ladder, and the rolls of fire hose hanging from the back, which could be removed. I remember it was model number 583, and it was the same truck used by the firemen in Monaco. My grandmother knew how to get to me. And in addition, she brought out a tablet of Tobler brand chocolate, the one with the images of exotic places that you could collect in an album. The first day was not even started that we were already eating chocolate in the common room, and breaking my mother's rules. According to my mother, I was not allowed to eat chocolate before the mid-afternoon snack at four o'clock. And chocolate was certainly not to be consumed in the morning. Chocolate could only be consumed for the mid-afternoon snack, or after dinner. Never in the morning. I liked breaking the rules, especially my mother's. I already knew that my grandmother did not care much about rules either.

My grandmother loved to have company, and in Card it meant that we had the company of Robert Teulier a lot. The Père Christophe kept to himself. The Marzet family had to go to work early in the morning, and they were their own company. But Robert Teulier did not have much entertainment, and he and Mémé Louise loved each other's company. They had many things in common: they liked to laugh, they hated to pay taxes, they were cousins, and they did not have anyone to talk to. Robert Teulier also ran his own farm, and my grandmother loved to go to his stables and drink the fresh milk just milked from the cows, when it was still warm and rich with cream. She often took me with her to visit with Robert Teulier at milking time, and whether I liked it or not, I had to drink a big glass of fresh milk—and frankly, I mostly did not like it. I guess I had good reasons not to like it, as I later found out that all types of organisms can be ingested, and I could have been exposed to listeria (another word Microsoft Office does not know), salmonella, or E.coli. But at that time, we really only concerned ourselves with TB and typhoid, and these were under control because the cows were vaccinated—they had the ear tag to show it. My grandmother only saw the advantages of such a practice, repeating that this would make me strong. Robert Teulier partook in the ceremony, and after he was done milking, he would often come and have dinner at the house, and drink wine rather than milk. He even convinced my grandmother that I should be allowed to color my water pink with a little wine (another one of my mother's rule was broken), and he laughed heartily when my grandmother poured a couple of drops of wine in my water. "Let me do it", he interrupted. And soon my water had the color of rosé wine from Provence. Robert Teulier then decided everybody was ready to clink glasses, and so we did. Evenings would go on until about nine or nine thirty when Robert Teulier had to turn in to be ready for the next day's work at the sawmill and at the farm. It was usually at that time that he ran out of topics of discussion or of stories to tell. He was a keen cycling fan, claiming to be a personal friend of the French champion Géminiani, and it is thanks to him that I discovered there were other races besides the Tour de France. He introduced me to the Tour of Italy, and to the Tour of Spain. He is the one who told me that every year the cyclists competed for the title of world champion. And he described for me the likes of his friend Géminiani, Bobet, Anquetil, Darrigade, Anglade and Rivière, the great French champions of the day. And in that summer of 1960, all of France felt sorry and sad for Roger Rivière—the triple world champion—who had fallen thirty feet down a ravine during the Tour de France, and had remained paralyzed following his fall because of a double fracture of his spinal column. After Robert Teulier was gone, my grandmother would wash the dishes while I dried them and put them away. She would then send me to bed so that I could read and be ready for the next day's adventures.

 I would read a few pages of the books from my father's childhood collection, she would come up say goodnight and close the door. Then in the darkness of the room, I would listen to the trains speeding on the tracks in the night, passing through the Ambazac railroad station. From the duration of the noise and from the speed I could tell whether they were freight trains or passenger trains. I would wonder what it was like to speed down the track in the middle of night and I would try to figure out where the people were going. I already knew that the trains went either north to Paris or south to Limoges, but I played a game in my mind where I tried to guess where the passengers were going. Were they soldiers going to Marseille to board the ship that would bring them to war, like my cousin Gustave? Were they tourists going to visit far away lands like Norway or England? Or were they relatives simply going home like I would do in a month? These games allowed me to slowly drift into sleep and dream of travels to places I did not yet know existed.

CHAPTER 22
Mémé Louise Decides My Future

The month of August was far more exciting in Card than the month of July. It was the time when all of the major crops had matured and needed to be taken in and processed. It started with the alfalfa that would be used to feed the cows in winter, and all of the cereals soon followed: wheat, barley, oat, and buckwheat, a favorite of Limousin. Le Père Marzet now harnessed his cows every day, and Alice and Robert would also work on Saturday and Sunday, their day off from their regular jobs to ensure everything was done in time, and especially before the late summer thunderstorms could spoil the crops. There was a very short window to operate between the time the cereals had ripened and the time when the patterns of fall weather set in. And every day I would accompany le Père Marzet as he walked past his fields of ripening wheat and barley, and tested the cereals to determine whether they were ready to be cut. All of the work was done by manual or animal labor: the cutting, the bundling, the loading and the threshing. He had very few pieces of machinery, and I only remember being scared of having my legs chopped up by the reaper which he used to cut the alfalfa and the wheat. I would participate in the activities by driving the team of cows back and forth from the fields, or as the products were loaded into the cart, by slowly driving them on the field. I was so proud to have such an important responsibility, and to have gained the respect of le Père Marzet who would entrust me with his most praised possession: his two cows. It was even more amazing because a year before, I had not even seen a live cow, even less worked with one. The cows were easy to lead. The Limousin cow, which le Père Marzet had named "Julie", was the leader of the team. Her placid character, her greater maturity, and her good nature controlled Brette who was a lot younger and more eager to go. Julie would slow her down, and really do all the work of controlling the team. When there was a tougher part, when the path would climb up, she is the one who would hunker down and show Brette how to use her weight to pull better. And if the path had ruts, she would know to slow down so that the cart so that its load would not bounce all over the place. Once I got to the farm, Robert or Alice would then take over the maneuvering of the team to unload the cart, and to turn it around so that it would be ready to go again. The two cows knew exactly where to stop in front of the barn, and they would not even need a command to place the cart in the right position for the maneuver. Julie had done this routine for over ten years, and Brette had quickly learned from her. From these days, I have a small black and white picture of a little boy driving these two huge animals, Julie, the Limousin cow on the left, and Brette the Normandie cow on the right.

Mémé Louise was impressed by my abilities to lead the team, but she would also emphatically state that this was not a career for me or for any young man. "There is no future in farming" she would say. She knew well that life in the country was changing, that farming small parcels of land while raising two cows and a pig was a life mode that was quickly vanishing, and that the future belonged to farmers who could control huge expanses of land and run their machinery unimpeded as she had seen the Soviet and American farmers do in documentaries. She was proud of me, but at the same time she wanted to make sure I chose a good future for myself. In this sense, she was a lot more helpful and provided much better guidance than my parents. She would sit down with me at lunch or dinner (when Robert Teulier was not there) and open my mind to the higher institutions of learning in Paris. She would describe which careers one could anticipate having after graduating from these schools. France was and still is an extremely elitist country, and you simply have no chance of getting a top job in France if you don't graduate from the right French school. This is why attending a regular university in France will not get you into the elite that runs the country. Attending the University of Limoges—which is open to any high school graduate who can afford the registration fee of eighty Euros (about ninety six Dollars)—is not at all the same thing as attending the Institute of Political Science of Paris where you need to have graduated from high school with honors (less than five percent of students do), or need to take a competitive exam for the left over slots. The entire purpose of the French system is to weed out competition and eventually select the cream of the crop to attend the elite schools such as the National Administration School, the French Polytechnic Institute, or the famous Ecole Normale. In order to do that, Mémé Louise affirmed, you had to go to high school in Paris, at the Lycée Louis-le-Grand in the famous Latin District (Quartier Latin), right next to La Sorbonne. Anything else was useless! According to her, I had to leave Monaco behind with the utmost urgency before the laissez-faire, the warm climate, the constant vacation atmosphere and the corruption of gambling turned my brain into a useless cauliflower, and I could not aspire to any better a career than that of Robert Teulier. She would add "if you want to turn into a Robert Teulier, then you can stay in Monaco, but if you want to make something out of yourself, if you want to be a Grand Monsieur [by this term she referred to the men who ran the republic], you must come up to Paris and live with me so that you can go to Louis-le-Grand!" Her predictions of my impeding doom and inability to do any better than Robert Teulier haunted me as I went back to leading the cows after lunch, or tried to go to sleep at night. After all Robert Teulier was OK, but he certainly was not he example I wanted to follow. Even Frédéric knew better than that, as he said of him one day "He stinks, he never washes!" So, by the end of summer I was fully indoctrinated, ready to leave the idle pleasures and the laziness of Monaco to move to Paris and like Eugénie Grandet, conquer the world!

My grandmother's biggest shortcoming was her prejudice against people from the South. The Southerners as she would call anyone who came from anywhere south of Limoges were a plague. Whether they were Italians, Spaniards, Portuguese or Frenchmen from the south "gens du Midi", they were simply useless. Nothing good ever came out of them or their countries. And there was no sense in arguing the point. She would dismiss Leonardo da Vinci with "The only thing he ever did was paint one portrait and build useless palaces for the king of France", and Michelangelo would fare no better as "he had only painted a church for the Pope, another Italian we could all do without". Christopher Columbus was not spared either, because "we lived perfectly well before he discovered America!" My defense of the South stopped after these futile and less than convincing attempts, for there was no sense in bringing up Roman emperors who, according to Mémé Louise were nothing but degenerate tyrants who had oppressed their own people and the people of the countries they had conquered. So it is that I had to put up with her constant belittling of Southerners, and I had a real hard time to do so. After all, I was born in Monaco, my grandmother Lainey was as Italian as one gets, and I lived there. I could find absolutely nothing wrong with the South, and even less with the people who lived there. I attended a school where over ninety percent of my classmates were either Italian, of Italian descent or were more Italian than French. This is why I knew that I would never attend Louis-le-Grand. I would never have been able to stand the rhetoric of my grandmother against the Southerners. Even the people of Limousin were somewhat questionable. In her eyes they really were from the South, but she had to make an exception, because her parents had come from there. Nevertheless, in her more anti-Southern enthusiastic moments, she would let it slip, that "in Paris people work a lot harder than that! Oh, no, if anybody worked as little and with as little intensity as these people [the Limousin people], they would get fired! They would not survive five minutes in the Office of the French Telephone Company! When the service is interrupted, we do not have the time to sit down, smoke a cigarette and drink a glass of wine! It is not like working in the South, where people think that you can do tomorrow what needs to be done today!" And she would use the example of La Fontaine's fable entitled The Ant and the Cicada where the ant represented the northerners, the people from Paris, and the cicada the southerners. On and on she would go until I could get her distracted to attack another subject, by simply saying "Yes, but in the North they pay a lot of taxes, don't they?" And this would move her onto a different track all together, the internal revenue track. She would rant and rave for thirty minutes on taxes. How the government was nothing but a bunch of communists who intended to ruin people like her who worked so hard for their money. I had to be careful when I heard the word "work" not to let her slip back into the logical conclusion of this statement, that these people who collected taxes were all from the South because they worked so little they could not actually generate enough revenue to justify collecting taxes: "Oh, it's easy when the only thing you have to do is sit at your desk and wait for the checks to arrive!" And I formed this idea of the tax collector, sitting at his desk, reading his newspaper, simply waiting for the mailman to deliver the mail so that he could open the envelopes and collect checks that he would pile up and simply put in his drawer. Yes, indeed, these tax collectors were lazy people!

Mémé Louise had always lived in Paris, and although I still don't understand what people from the South had done to her to get her so incensed, she behaved as a true Parisian, who thought that people could only live decently in Paris. This is the reason why she liked my friend Aline. My grandmother questioned Aline and found out that she lived in the sixteenth district of Paris, the district where the rich people live (even today), and that her mother was a famous antique dealer, who had recently made the front page of French papers (to include the celebrated Le Monde paper) by selling an Eugène Boudin painting to Le Louvre museum for an outlandish price. My grandmother was duly impressed because four of her most important words were put together in the same sentence: Paris, Louvre, money, and Le Monde. In the middle of this conversation, I felt like the village idiot because I had little concept of what was so important: I did not know who Eugène Boudin was, I had never been to Le Louvre, I did not know what the significance of the sixteenth district was, I had never heard of, and even less read Le Monde, and I barely knew what an antique dealer did for a living. My grandmother had figured out everything, and she was already celebrating my wedding with Aline. This is why I now had to attend the Ecole Nationale des Beaux-Arts, another school I had never heard anything about before, and had no concept what it did or why. I would have to ask my grandmother for a translation into Southern French after Aline left so that I could have an idea of who I was supposed to marry, why, and what career I had to embark on that day. It turned out that Aline's mother family was exceedingly wealthy, and from an old aristocratic family that had managed to survive the revolution, recover their assets when the kings had returned, and had started a business finding and reselling furniture and art pieces that had been stolen during the revolution. The story went about that they had provided over half of the furniture that was now in the palace of Versailles. They had property all over France, and still owned the original medieval castle of the family in the Ile de France, the province that was the birth place of France. Mémé Louise was really impressed and she told me how lucky I was to know such a wonderful person as Aline.

And Aline was wonderful. She was pretty, she was smart, but there was only one problem. She knew way too much more than I did. Maybe Mémé Louise was right and I should move with her to Paris to repair all of the inadequacies from my Monaco upbringing. Aline was not happy to be stuck in Limousin. Unlike me she had nothing to discover there, and her father was too busy farming to actually spend much time with her. She should have been in Saint-Tropez with her mother, spending her summer with Brigitte Bardot—it turned out that her mother knew Brigitte Bardot—instead of being stuck with a bunch of country bumpkins. Fortunately, Aline also has her favorite places in Card and the surrounding area. Her favorite place was the Camp de César. One day that it was particularly hot—the flies were not even buzzing around—she took me by the hand, and down the path, across the Départementale, down to the Camp de César, up the hill, down the hill, and finally to a creek which ran down there. The water was crystal clear and some fish were swimming in it. The water flowed slowly, effortlessly. The bed was pure golden sand, and Aline decided that we were going to swim in her creek—it was on her father's land. I stupidly stumbled that I did not have any swim trunks, to which she replied "You don't need any, you silly!" What? No swim trunks? She wanted me to go into the creek fully clothed? That would never work—my grandmother would not be happy, but my mother! If she ever found out, I would be in real trouble! This is when I saw that Aline was undressing. I was dumbfounded as I had never seen a girl undress, and I had certainly never undressed in front of one. She explained that she was only doing what people do in Saint-Tropez: they don't wear anything, they just go swimming naked. And she encouraged me to imitate her. "And it's OK with your mother?" "Of course, she answered, we do it all the time when we are there!" So, convinced by her confident answers, I undressed and we both went in the cool refreshing water. That day, Aline who definitely knew everything explained to me the secrets and the mystery of how babies were made, since I had noticed a certain lack of body parts on her. She commented with impatience "I have to explain everything to you!" By the time we were to spend our last summer vacation together, she would explain a lot more than that…In the meantime, if she were going to become my wife as my grandmother had already decided, it was only normal that we go skinny-dipping together.

CHAPTER 23
Le Jour de la Batteuse

The exciting time of the wheat harvest was an opportunity for every one to get together for the biggest event of the year at the Roussel farm, the threshing of the newly harvested wheat. Small farms like Marzet, Teulier and Guérin did the threshing by hand, using flails. The wheat was placed on the dirt floor of the barn, threshed, collected, sifted and bagged. This produced an enormous amount of dust and required a lot of effort. This would have been impossible to accomplish for a big farm like Roussel or that of my cousins in Fondanèche. And since it was uneconomical for one farm to buy a combine, farmers would simply hire a company that showed up with a mechanical thresher and provided the service to farms around the region. This was "le jour de la batteuse" or the day of the thresher. Because Roussel had the biggest wheat production, he would hire the itinerant thresher and ask everyone in Card to come help out, carrying the harvested wheat from the barn to the thresher, and then collecting the bags of wheat on one side, and the straw on the other. The bags of wheat were stored in a stone storage facility, while the straw had to be further processed to be packed into bails, which were then carried to the barn anew and stored there for use as litter in the winter. In exchange for their help, the farmers of Card would be treated to a feast that lasted from sun up, well into the night until the work was done. It was like a pagan celebration of summer. Everybody put aside their differences, and worked hard to ensure the threshing was done in one day, since the machine had to be delivered to the next farm the following morning so that the same process could start all over again. In Card, it meant that all of the men worked for Roussel for a full day. This even included Lemaunier who was otherwise not welcome to any social event. Madame Roussel served breakfast before sunrise, and the women of Card would soon come down to help prepare the many dishes that would be served that day on a rotating basis. To this end, a huge temporary table made of wood planks set on sawhorses was installed in the courtyard of the farm, and there, starting at ten in the morning, the finest morsels of meat, cold cuts, egg dishes, vegetables, fruits, cakes and tarts, would be devoured by the hungry crew. Gallons of wine were consumed, and even if you did not work there, you were invited. For example, Mémé Louise and le Père Christophe were welcome to partake in the feast although neither of them would be performing any service. People's good nature prevailed over all else that day. Le Père Marzet, Robert, Robert Teulier and Alice had been working at Roussel for three hours before I even woke up. I was disappointed with my grandmother who had decided to let me sleep rather than allowing me to go down to the Roussel farm with the men. I hurriedly swallowed my breakfast, dressed, and rushed out of the door, while my grandmother was yelling to me to be careful "crossing the road". That should be easy since there was maybe a car per hour…

When I got to the Roussel farm, work was in full swing, and had been for four hours. The thresher was connected with a huge leather belt to the drive pulley of the Roussels' Renault tractor that was working hard to keep the process going. The belt, which was about a foot and a half wide, was only one of the dangerous devices le Père Marzet had warned me about. I had to be sure not to even come close to the intake of the machine, because every year some poor chap would get his arm caught in it and would end up losing it. I was given a task that was more in line with what I could do, and that was to number the bags of wheat that were filled during the day. This would allow Roussel to ensure that the same number of bags was stored in the stone storage as had been processed. To this end I was given a can of black paint and a paint brush and I numbered every bag that was waiting to be filled. At the end of the day, it would be a simple matter of counting the bags and ensuring that they were all marked with my handwriting, and that none was missing. Because even though everyone was helping, one could not assume that a bag would not somehow disappear—especially at the end of the day, under the cover of darkness, and under the influence of a few too many glasses of vin rouge! It was not an easy task at first because several bags had already been stored, and they had to be rearranged so that they could be numbered at the top, next to the tie, and looking forward. These bags were much heavier than I could handle, and Robert Teulier had to come and assist me. I finally managed to mark all of them, and then went about marking the ones waiting to be filled. This was done easily, and I soon could take a break. The men were bent under the heavy loads they were carrying and sweating under the hot August sun. Wheat dust and bran were flying all around, and this made the day seem even hotter. On the table, the bottles of water and the bottles of wine were lined up and replaced as fast as they went empty. Every man and woman had brought their own glass from home, and used only that glass. In the farmhouse, Madame Roussel was cooking up a storm. The fireplace had a hot fire going, the oven was going full blast, and at ten a first break took place, as much to rest the men, as to give the tractor a pause. All types of cold cuts were brought out with the mélées and the tourtes. There was ham, smoked ham, saucisson, bologna, sausage, pâtés of all types, salami, gendarmes (a type of sausage), and in the middle of all this, the most beautiful, golden pâté en croute. Red wine, cider and chilled white wine were served, and it was like a military charge of these men, sweating, already exhausted by six hours of hard work, who were grabbing, cutting bread, pouring wine, laughing, drinking, praising the women who had prepared all of this, and finally sitting down to eat this food they needed so much, simply to be able to go until lunch which would be served at around one thirty in the afternoon. I imitated the men, and rushed to the table, while the women went back to the house to prepare more food for lunch. Aline was also there helping the women carry the dishes back and forth to the kitchen.

Thirty minutes later, the cranking of the tractor engine signaled it was time to get back to work. The men invigorated by the food and the wine were again ready to go, and they worked under the hot midday sun, some taking their jacket off, trying to find a little shade as they traveled along the barn walls. Not one of them spoke now, too focused on accelerating the pace so that they would not have to work until midnight. Tempers were short, and it was the time of day where mistakes were not tolerated. By the time lunch was served, most of them had already worked an eight hour day, and there was another eight to go, if no problem surfaced between now and the end of the day. Le Père Marzet had asked me to take the cows out to pasture at four, and as I left to do so, Aline came with me. We took the cows to La Boissarde and watched them graze while she was talking about Paris, her friends, the car her mother drove—now it was my turn to be impressed as her mother drove a silver 1956 Mercedes-Benz 300 SL Gullwing. I had seen such cars in Monaco in front of the Casino or in the parking spots in front of the Hotel de Paris. And I also knew that the car cost more money than my father earned in five years. And her mother could afford it! Mémé Louise was right, I should marry Aline. I asked her why she came to Limousin. "It's because I have to", she said, "It is in the divorce agreement between my parents. But I won't have to after I am sixteen. That year, I will be free to choose where I can spend my summers, and it will not be here." I quickly calculated that I would be fourteen then, too early to marry, and she was already going to leave me. This was a hopeless love story.

I took the cows back to the stables at six, or so about, let them drink, and then locked them up. I fed them their ration of beets. Then, I when to the chicken yard, and gave the chickens their daily portion of wheat. I reported back to le Père Marzet that everything was in order, and went back to numbering wheat sacks, as the threshing had already produced over two hundred and fifty. At eight, supper was served under the lights which had been set up over the table. The men ate hurriedly, as there was more work to be done. At ten o'clock I left with my grandmother and Robert Teulier who had to work at the sawmill in the morning. He was carrying a sack of wheat that Roussel had agreed to give to everyone who had helped. I fell asleep quickly that night, exhausted by the sun, the dust, and the work, dreaming of my riding around in Aline's mother's Mercedes.

The next day, when I went to the Roussels, there was neither sign of the thresher nor of the activity that had taken place there the day before. It was as if the events had never taken place, the farm had been swallowed again into its torpor. It was only disturbed from time to time by the mooing of a cow or the unconvinced barking of a dog. My grandmother had been enthused by the threshing, she told me the next day. She thought it resembled a country wedding from long ago, with the entire village there, the food, and the wine. Mémé Louise always liked a party, especially when she did not have to prepare anything as had been the case. As for me this day remains in my mind as the day I took care of cows by myself for the first time. Again le Père Marzet had placed great trust in me, and I had been honored that he thought so greatly of me. Whatever else happened that summer it would be hard to top this.

CHAPTER 24
The Belote Champion

The routine of life with Mémé Louise had now been established. I would wake up, have breakfast, and instead of going to feed the cows, I would hop on the bicycle and ride to Ambazac to do the shopping, mainly the daily newspaper (when my grandmother found out I did not know about Le Monde, she made it a point that I should buy it and read it every day, despite the fact that she preferred the lighter toned France-Soir), meat, wine, coffee, and bread. Since my grandmother did not talk to Tata Marie, and did not even acknowledge her existence, I had to keep my visits there a secret. So, I stopped at the épicerie before getting the paper from the bookstore across the street. What was fantastic is that everybody in Ambazac knew that the two women did not talk to each other, and nobody ever made a comment about my visits. Tonton François was probably more upset than most about the situation because he thought the whole thing was impractical. In any case the visits there lasted only a few moments, as I had to ride back and finish my shopping. My grandmother always wanted me to buy the meat first to make sure there were enough of the best pieces left, and therefore, there was an urgency to go back. Sometimes Cousin Hortense who lived on the left at the bottom of the hill coming out of Ambazac would be in her front garden, and I could not but stop to say hello. Of course, she would give me something to drink and a few cookies before she allowed me back on the road to Card. My grandmother had to know that I stopped at Tata Marie's everyday but never commented or asked about it. But Tata Marie also wanted me to go have lunch there and asked me if I could. It was a tough question because

I had to come up with a way to ask. But Tata Marie was smart and she took advantage of one of Robert Teulier's visits to her épicerie to have him serve as a go-between. It was agreed that on the day of Ascension, which is a religious holiday in France, I would be having lunch at Tata Marie's. That day was wonderful. It was so hot that by the time I got to Ambazac I looked like I had raced in one of the stages of the Tour de France. My uncle had gotten up early and had caught some crawfish from the clear waters of the Muret creek, and they were the best I would ever have with the home made mayonnaise of Tata Marie. In the afternoon, we went to the Muret Lake and sat down playing cards under my uncle's fisherman umbrella.

There is a French card game called belote. It is by far the most popular game in France and it is played everywhere: bars, police stations, family reunions, the army, fire stations, and there is not a single Frenchman who does not know the game. It can be played with two, three, or four players and uses a 32 card deck. It is a close relative of Clobyosh, which is played in Jewish communities in many parts of the world, and of the Dutch game Klaverjas. For some reason, Tonton François was practically unbeatable at this game. Whether he cheated, had absolutely stainless steel luck, was gifted for the game, or benefited from a combination of all three, I could never beat him. I understood that I could not beat him when I was eight years old, but as time went by, and I started winning tournaments myself, every time I went back to Ambazac for the summer, Tonton François would pull out the deck, smile, and say "let's see what we can teach you this summer". I remember spending entire afternoons, playing for four or five hours and not winning a single game. My grandfather Lainey was also a fantastic player—he had been a police officer and had played many a game at night in the police station—and I could beat him from time to time. But Tonton François was beyond my reach. My aunt would tell him "but let him win at least once!" To which he would answer "he'll win when he plays well enough to win", as he would beat me again mercilessly. I have since played belote against computers and I can beat the computer more times in one afternoon than I could beat my uncle during his entire life. He would go to the tournaments at the Hotel de France, and would always come out with the prize of farm products that rewarded the winner. If there had been a French championship, Tonton

François would have won it. In our small village of Ambazac he could not even find other people to play against. From time to time, an outsider, or a market vendor would stop by the shop and challenge him to a game. This was immediately a village social event, and the other men would follow the two to the Café, and wait in anticipation to see if the honor of Ambazac would be preserved. It was like one of these scenes in cowboy movies when a desperado comes into town and challenges the retired gun slinger, thinking that he can beat him. The entire village square would gather into the bar, and crowding the card table would witness the dismantling of the poor opponent. First, they had to decide whether the games would be played to a total of five hundred or one thousand points. If the opponent chose five hundred, the entire assembly knew there was the possibility that the tournament would last only a few minutes. This is because Tonton François had the skill to collect almost the entire total in one single hand. Then, they had to decide whether it was best out of three or best out of five. During this time, wine and Pernod would be ordered, served and consumed in large quantities, except by Tonton François who never drank when he played—he wanted to keep his mind clear. If the opponent chose one thousand points and best out of five, my uncle would invariably purposely lose the first round. This gave the opponent a great confidence, which bordered on arrogance and caused him to make more mistakes. If the opponent chose five hundred points and best out of three, he did not have a prayer, and would lose in two games in less then five minutes. In all of the times that I witnessed these shootouts, I never saw one challenger win. One day, one of the challengers accused my uncle of cheating, and the crowd could well see that it was not the case. And accusing the local champion when you are from out of town was not a wise move, even if a gendarme was watching the game. Again, just like in the Far West movies which I loved to watch, the challenger was thrown out of the bar, and told not to come back. My uncle never said a word.

Fights with farmers in Limousin could turn dangerous very quickly. Behind their good nature, these people would not hesitate to make sure their rights were respected. A perfect tool to do that was the Opinel knives they all carried. Opinel knives were created over one hundred years ago by Joseph Opinel in the Savoie region of France. They have a wooden handle and a sturdy design that makes them ideal for farmers. Their blade folds into the handle, and they are made for big hands. Unlike the Swiss Army knife they are very simple and have only one function, to cut. Today the Museum of Modern Art in New York City displays Opinel knives as one of the one hundred most beautiful objects in the world. The original Opinel which the Ambazac farmers carried has a four inch handle and a three inch blade, which remains very sharp even after weeks of use. And these knives were used in fights as well. This may have been one of the reasons why gendarmes had so little work in Ambazac: every man carried his own weapon of dissuasion. My cousin Maxime in Fondanèche spoke one year of the fight that had broken out at the Fête de la Saint-Jean, and how the cousin of Dumas, "you know, the guy who had the farm right outside the village of Saint-Sylvestre on the right as you walk out", had gotten into an argument over the daughter of Boussaraix, "you know her. It's the blonde with the beautiful figure, who works at the Coop" with the son of the mayor. It turned to blows, and the mayor's son was getting his ass kicked. "Dumas's cousin, Albert, is a butcher in Compraignac, and strong as a bull". Well the mayor's son pulled his Opinel and stabbed Albert in the chest. Even with a wound like that, Albert had beaten him silly, and both of them had ended up in the hospital in Limoges. The people in the hospital did not know that these two had just had a fight, so they put them in the same room. Then the gendarmes showed up. Albert told them he had no idea who had stabbed him, and the mayor's son told them he could not remember anything about the fight because of the head injuries he had received. The witnesses had already heard about the scene in the hospital, so when the gendarmes questioned them, none could remember seeing the fight. During that time the two guys in the hospitals were reconciled by the trick they had pulled on the gendarmes, and now they are best friends. Maxime continued "The funniest part is that Boussaraix's daughter could not have cared less about them because she is already the fiancée of La Couleuvre, the one who owns the huge farm at Saint-Yrieix—they have over one hundred fifty cows, so she could not care less about the butcher or the mayor's son." So it was that once again, the gendarmes had been defeated, a conflict solved without them, and that the cunning nature of the Limousin people had outwitted the Gendarmerie.

The problem with the Gendarmerie was that everyone, like the Père Christophe, remembered their role in World War One. And although the

Père Christophe's brother was the sole case in Ambazac of a young man being brought back to be shot by his own army, nobody forgave that. People had had enough of the killing, and this poor guy would not have made any difference in the great scheme of things. But worse, the gendarmes had served the government of Maréchal Pétain in World War Two, and during the Nazi occupation had taken an active role in fighting the Résistance and in helping the occupiers. Many people had been caught by the gendarmes while conducting anti-German operations, had been turned over to the Germans, and had never returned from death camps where they had been sent. And when the Germans had committed atrocities such as Oradour, or Tulle, where they had randomly hanged men from every lamp post in town as a measure of retaliation, the gendarmes had not prevented *that* from happening. And finally, the gendarmes were not from Limousin or Ambazac. They were sent there from other parts of France, did not speak the Limousin language—when they investigated, it was uncanny how many people could not speak French—and did not have the lay of the land. That afternoon, when we were playing cards on the shore of the Etang de Muret, two gendarmes who were checking that no one was fishing without a license, came by our little card game. Tonton François did not seem very pleased with their presence as they walked up. Then one of them inquired "I hope you are not playing for money. It is against the law, especially with a minor". Tata Marie recognized one of the gendarmes was the husband of one her most loyal customers, Madame Maréchal. Fearing the reaction of my uncle, she immediately intervened and stated that of course not, it was a friendly belote game between her husband and her young nephew from Monaco. And she introduced me to the two agents of the law. At the word of Monaco, the gendarmes became interested and wanted to know more. That's when I told them that my grandfather was a police officer and knew Princess Grace, and that my great-grandfather was a retired gendarme who had served in Algeria. These facts duly impressed the gendarmes who decided to take a break, sat down, and asked if they could participate in the belote game while we chatted about Monaco. Tata Marie pulled the white wine bottle out the Etang, where it had been kept cool and because there were not glasses, the bottle made the rounds. Over an hour later, after several rounds of belote which they lost, and with the heavy heat of the day behind us, the gendarmes thanked us for our hospitality and were on their way. Tonton François commented that they were not bad chaps after all, especially since the gendarmes had acknowledged that he was the best belote player they had ever met.

CHAPTER 25
The Trip to Saint-Priest

Mémé Louise had a great sense of family. She was therefore determined that we should visit every member of the family living in Limousin. I had already visited with most of them, and I told her that I had so. She asked me to make a list of all of the ones I knew and we agreed that I got an alibi for these. Unfortunately there were still three names that I had never heard of. First, there was cousin Hortense who lived in Ambazac, then there was Cousin Jean and his wife Louise, who also lived in Ambazac, and finally, there was the cousin of Saint-Priest who was so called because he lived in the village of the same name. Visiting with Hortense and Jean and Louise was relatively easy as they lived in Ambazac and we could walk there from Card. With the shortcut, and even at the slower rate of walking speed of my grandmother, it would take at most forty-five minutes. But Saint-Priest was another matter. The way I saw it, we would have to walk to the railroad station, take the train to Limoges, change trains there, catch the train to Saint-Priest-Taurion, and then walk down to the watermill, where the cousin lived, at the confluent of the Taurion and Vienne rivers. I figured this would take at least two hours to get there and two to get back. Yet, Ambazac and Saint-Priest were only five miles apart as the crow flies, and just less than seven miles on the road, with only one major hill in between. I figured that I could so this in about half an hour on the bicycle—and I was supposed to be gone from Card, from Aline, and le Père Marzet for four hours, just to say hello to a cousin? This did not make any sense. I suggested to Mémé Louise that we should take a taxi. She objected it cost too much money. I reminded her that time is money, and that any time we saved certainly would be worth something to her. She simply responded that it mattered not, as she was on vacation and she was not in a hurry. She obviously did not understand: I had only limited time here, and *I* was in a hurry. I would be bored to tears traveling four fours to go fourteen miles! This was not the nineteenth century: we had cars that could drive fourteen miles in fifteen minutes. I calculated for her that our travel speed would be less than five miles per hour. We could walk as fast! And we had to pay to go that slow? That was outrageous! She finally made a face and agreed that I was right. We needed to go to Plan B. I had a little idea. I had noticed that there was a moped in the barn. It had not been used in years, but I was sure it could be fixed. She objected to that as well saying that she had not used it since Léon's death. I told her I could fix the tires, and Robert Teulier was sure to be able to fix the engine—he was responsible for the maintenance of much bigger engines at the sawmill. It was then reluctantly agreed that if we could get the moped going, we would go to Saint-Priest as a team, my grandmother riding the moped and I the bicycle.

Robert Teulier thought it was hilarious. My grandmother on a moped! He had to see it to believe it! During that time, I pulled it out from the barn, took the wheels off, removed the tires and the tubes and went to the shop by the railroad bridge in Ambazac to get new tubes and tires as Robert Teulier had recommended. The following afternoon, with its brand new set of tires fully inflated—it took me a little while to inflate these big tires with a hand pump—Robert Teulier showed up to start the engine. It took him a few moments as he filled the gas tank cleaned the gas line, changed the spark plug and reset the drive belt. After a few attempts to start, it would not work, and he proceeded with cleaning the contact on the magneto. He pulled the moped on its stand, and three strokes of the pedals later, it was smoking a thick blue smoke as the engine purged itself of the accumulated oil. Then it stalled, and Robert Teulier had to clean the new spark plug. This time it ran perfectly and he took it for a test drive. He came back smiling, telling my grandmother it worked as if brand new. Of course Robert Teulier stayed for dinner that night. He was as jovial as ever, and when my grandmother started on her soapbox about taxes, and how life was so much tougher in the old days, and people today are nothing but whiners, he just kept teasing her, telling her that her political views were so far to the left, he would have to put a sign on the moped to remind her to keep right as she traveled down the road!

It was decided that my grandmother would test the moped for two days going back and forth to Ambazac before the great adventure of going all the way to Saint-Priest, a massive seven miles! Everything went well, and after lunch the day following the road tests, we left Card. I immediately took a significant lead as we went downhill, my grandmother hesitating to open the throttle. Of course, she caught up on the hills, but all in all it was an easy trip, and about forty minutes later, we were in Saint-Priest at the Moulin du Pont (the bridge watermill) where the cousin of Saint-Priest lived but no longer operated the mill. I had never seen a big river from so close. The water was almost at the front door of the sturdy stone house, and the flow of dark green waters mixing in a series of eddies was simply not encouraging. Our cousin was already well advanced in age, and he too was a veteran of World War One. He asked how le Père Marzet was doing. They had been in the same unit, and he wanted to know if le Père Marzet had received his Légion d'Honneur. I was memorized by the proximity of the river and wanted to know if the water ever came in the house. "Oh yes, he said, five years ago the river came in and went almost to the second floor of the house!" "What do you do then", I inquired. "It is simple, you just don't go down to the first floor", he laughed. My grandmother and he started talking and told me I could go outside and play—who was I supposed to play with—with the recommendation to stay away from the water, because even a good swimmer could not fight the current and would drown. After these recommendations, you could be sure I would not even get near the river. But this is when a young boy who appeared older than me approached me. I sensed immediately that the day would end badly, as if I had been in one Sophocles's tragedies. He seemed somewhat slow, as he failed to speak and motioned for me to follow him. He scared me somewhat because he appeared to be a lot stronger than I. I had already figured out from reading Notre Dame de Paris that people who looked like Quasimodo were trouble. So I stayed away from him, ensuring as lion tamers do that he was never positioned between me and safety, and keeping enough distance to be able to outrun him to the door of the house. He seemed to want me to go with him, but the direction he was pointing to led me to believe that he intended to commit some senseless act of danger defiance, like walking on the small wall that retained the wheel of the watermill and overhung the river by several feet. My cousin had said for me to stay away from the water, and I am sure he meant that for anybody else for that matter. I yelled out to him that it was too dangerous, but he laughed. I figured he must have done that a thousand times, and I hesitantly moved forward in the direction of the huge waterwheel. Unfortunately, my action only encouraged him to climb the stone wall, get to the top and start walking like a tight-rope walker on the narrow piece of masonry. I backed off and decided to report these activities to my cousin. As I approached the door to my cousin's house the boy, probably disappointed that I would not pay more attention to him, became even more audacious speaking for the first time and calling to me to join him: "Viens! Viens!" (Come! Come), as he walked all the way to the end of the wall and onto a beam that extended over the water. Below him the turmoil of the water bouncing back from the obstacles in its way and the waves it created were dark green, almost black from the lack of sun, and from the depth. But this did not stop him as he started to demonstrate his skills by jumping up and down. The beam gave way exactly at the same time I was opening the door and telling my cousin that someone was playing on the waterwheel. To my incomprehension, both the boy and the beam disappeared from sight as they hit the water below. The cousin de Saint-Priest simply shook his head and stated matter-of-factly "It was bound to happen one day! It is not your fault!" He told me to go get the gendarmes, and he went down to the river where his flat bottom boat was attached. With an energy I would not have suspected he had, he rowed to the place where the boy had fallen while I ran up the path to get the gendarmes. The gendarmerie was not far. It was up the street and left on the rue des Sagnes, and this is where the fire department was located as well. As soon as I told the gendarmes what had happened, they directed the firemen to the scene. The red trucks rushed down to the river, and the firemen launched their rescue boat. They zoomed down the river as it was obvious that the boy would have been carried far downstream by the current. During that time, the gendarmes interrogated me about the accident. I knew—remember that my grandfather was a policeman—they suspected I could have pushed him in. So, I explained myself very clearly, indicating exactly where I was standing at that time, which was in the house. I pointed to them that I had told the boy not to climb there as my cousin had told me to stay away from the water, and that none of my footprints marked the sandy soil any place near the wall. They were satisfied and thanked me for coming to get them. I was cleared of any wrong doing and I could go. My grandmother wanted to leave, but I wanted to see if the boy had been able to survive. She did not want me to see the body, nor to witness the distress of the boy's mother who by now had been notified. This brought back too many bad memories of senseless deaths in her own family half a century before. So we did not wait for the cousin to come back to shore—he knew the river better than anyone there that day, and guided the fire department efforts. As my grandmother and I made our way up the hill, we saw the boy's mother who was running down to find out what had happened to her son. I only learned the following summer that the poor boy's body had not been recovered for weeks, and that it had finally washed ashore under the Saint-Martial Bridge in Limoges.

This accident dampened our joy on the way back home, but another incident was going to give us an opportunity to laugh. My grandmother had been wearing a light blue summer skirt to Saint-Priest. This was possible despite the fact she was riding a moped because of a network of rubber bands extending from the axle of the rear wheel to the fender in a fan-like manner. These prevented a dress from getting caught in the spokes of the wheel. But the moped had been sitting in the barn for several years, and the rubber suffered from dry-rot. The vibrations of the ride had caused every one of these rubber bands to break on the way to Saint-Priest. The circumstances of our departure distracted us from addressing this small technical problem. As we reached Ambazac, the wind caught my grandmother's skirt which went into the spokes, got tangled up and got torn off my grandmother, exposing her underwear. We stopped as I was laughing so hard from seeing my grandmother in her underwear riding the moped that I could no longer pedal. What was even funnier was that she was unaware of the extent of the damage. We tried to recover as much of the skirt as we could from the spokes, but there was not enough to cover Mémé Louise's derriere. It was a strange accoutrement to see my grandmother rushing home as if in shorts. As soon as we had arrived home, Robert Teulier showed up, having seen us ride up the lane in front of his house. He wanted to know when my grandmother was going to compete in the Tour de France. This certainly took our mind off the previous accident. My grandmother threatened me and Robert Teulier with the worst calamities if we ever talked to anyone else about it. And they both had a glass of vin rouge!

But now that the moped was fixed, I implemented phase two of my plan, which was to get to ride it. My grandmother was adamant I should not—it was against the law, one had to be fourteen to ride a moped. With Robert Teulier's help, I attacked my grandmother's reasoning. First, I went a lot faster on my bicycle that she went with the moped, showing that I could master speed. Second, the law, Robert Teulier emphasized, said it is illegal for someone under fourteen to drive a moped on public roads, and the lane in Card was a private road. With her typical stoicism when she lost an argument, my grandmother agreed, and the following day, I took my first ride on a moped. It was a rush, and I soon mastered this mechanical skill. But I still used the bicycle to go to Ambazac, and preferred the bicycle to ride around the countryside.

CHAPTER 26
The Couty Manor

"In the old days people worked a lot harder than now!" Mémé Louise was now fully engaged in a political argument with Robert Teulier. "If you borrow something, the least you could do is return it! No, it is too simple to just take stuff from other people and keep it. That's stealing. It is like my brother, when he started working he thought he was entitled to everything. Staying with me for free, taking his girlfriend up to the apartment for dinner, dirtying my sheets, and eating all my food. Well, on his first day at work, he had to carry four corpses! On his first day! Can you imagine that? He had to carry four patients who had died, from their hospital bed to the morgue. Oh, he was not so proud that evening when he got home! That was his first day of work when he was eighteen! That taught him a lesson. When I think he ate all my butter and drank all my milk, with his floozies. Because there was more than one! And it was I, who had worked all day, who had to climb down and back up seven flights of stairs to get the milk and the butter. He would never have thought of replacing them. And the day he broke my chair! He had the gall of telling me that my chairs were cheap garbage, but when I went to replace it cost me thirty thousand francs! Well, thirty thousand old francs, so in today's money it is three hundred francs. Anyhow, they were not that cheap. If I went to visit him today, and I broke one of his chairs, I'd like to see what he would say! Now it is quite different, he has to pay for his chairs, so it is not the same thing! Oh no! Communists like that! Oh no! Socialists like that, if you prefer! Everything that is yours is mine. This is their slogan! But you'd better not think that they are going to give you a piece of saucisson for free! I'd like to see you try, and see how they react! With their philosophy of everything that is yours is also mine, they are nothing but a bunch of socialists. You might as well call them communists if you prefer! It's not like it was at my house when I was growing up! When my father came home from work, after twelve or fourteen hours spent on scaffolds, I guarantee you that dinner had better be ready! Oh, no, if it had not been, my mother would have caught hell! But, now you see all these women in short skirts, showing their legs to everybody, when it is not something else... And I pay taxes so that they can go around showing their rear end to everybody!" Robert Teulier and I were more amused than anything else, and we all burst out laughing when he said "From what I saw, you were parading your butt the other day as well!"

The point is that my grandmother was never a believer in ideologies. One day she would be a Gaullist, the next day she would be a socialist, but more important she was contradictory. Whatever opinion her interlocutor had, she defended the opposite. "They are all out to exploit us", she would comment, "It is not with an honest salary that you can have properties all over France, ride in Cadillacs, or eat every day at the Ritz! If it weren't for the unseen advantages and the bribes, nobody would run for senator or representative! It is like living under the Ancien Régime!" By Ancien Régime my grandmother was referring to the king's monarchy, which all of our ancestors had fought so hard to get rid of. She would comment about the Revolution: "It served no purpose! If we guillotined all of them, how come there are so many new aristocrats? I am asking you!" Dinners or lunches would invariably turn to this type of entertaining argument. Mémé Louise confused many things, but she was sure to tell you that corruption was universal, and that nothing good could ever come out of associating with politicians. This was especially true of the people who had purchased the Couty Manor. There was only one family named Couty in Card, and the name remains relatively rare in Limousin. What my grandmother never knew is that the name comes from Languedoc, a province of southern France, and finds its origin in the Latin costa or hill. So, it can be assumed that my grandmother's early relatives lived in Southern France and were associated with a place on a hill. The Couty Manor was a sore point with my grandmother. She imagined that she had some type of right on this property because it bore her mother's name. But now, she was clearly incensed by the fact that the Manor had been sold not only to people who were not for Limousin, but to people who were not even from France.

It appeared that the Manor had been sold to a Dutch businessman who had promptly turned it into an armed camp. The new owner had rebuilt all of the walls surrounding the property (as Mémé Louise commented "I don't know where he found all of that money, but it cannot be from working a regular job!") so that the entire property was now again fully protected by ten feet high stone walls. The drive through gate, which had been in a state of disrepair, was now an ornate forged-iron work of art, and barb wire had been strung on top of the surrounding wall, to discourage potential intruders. But what clearly got people gossiping were the guards who now patrolled the estate. It was understood that whoever purchased the place was a rich and important person from Holland—his name did not appear on any of the public records—and had enough money to pay a "company of guards", in the words of le Père Marzet, guards who patrolled the estate with dogs and were apparently armed. Whoever this person was, he wanted to preserve his privacy. From time to time the gate would open and an official-looking Mercedes sedan licensed in Holland would either drive in or drive out. The place now had a permanent staff to cook and take care of the grounds, and the food ingredients were delivered in a food delivery truck directly from Limoges as was indicated on the side panels. When the truck arrived, the gate closed behind it, and the guards would inspect the truck and its contents before letting it proceed down the tree lined alley to the Manor. This raised suspicions that the owner was a celebrated gangster who needed a lot of security to ensure his safety. Further gossip developed, and raised the level of dislike for the new owner, when people realized the guards spoke German. People were outraged and loudly complained that it was like the Occupation all over again. That we had not fought so hard simply for "them" to buy the best piece of property and come back to haunt us on the site of their crimes (they referred to Oradour). And indeed, the guards, when they were seen through the gates could have been the same people who had operated in Oradour. They wore khaki uniforms "like the Afrika Korps" said Robert Teulier, and were for the most part young and blond-haired. Robert Teulier concluded philosophically that "as long as they don't give me any reason to complain, I won't!" Regardless, the arrival of le

Hollandais (the Dutchman), as he was dubbed, certainly upset Card and in particular my grandmother. "And how do we know he is Dutch?" she would ask, as if it really made any difference, "He could be a war criminal, hiding right under our noses!" And Madame Roussel, who was the closest neighbor, would add with assurance that "he does not even live here, I heard" and other people would not question where she heard, "that he has only spent two days here since he bought the place." And this added more outrage, fanning the flames of hostility toward someone who could purchase such a praised piece of property and not even live there. My grandmother as daring as ever had decided to get to the bottom of things, and she had walked to the gate determined to find out what was going on, as if it had been her business to disturb the privacy of a person who took such great care to protect it. She was politely and firmly rebuked by one of the guards, who far from being German spoke perfect French and simply told her that this was private property and that it would be appreciated if she respected that fact. This is when my grandmother became convinced of collusion between the Hollandais and the local politicians. To be allowed to purchase this piece of property the Hollandais must clearly have dipped deep in the kitty and paid off the mayor, the local assemblyman, and even the senator. This opinion fueled the gossip mill for weeks, and people were absolutely certain they had seen the mayor's car drive in at night—the night when there was this big dinner, and you could see the gleam of the lights through the trees—and drive out at past midnight. Soon, it was the senator who had participated in the dinner party, and shortly thereafter the community was convinced the Hollandais was connected at the highest level of government and was a friend of the Prime Minister, Michel Debré himself. And people to conclude "It is not you or me who could have done that", that remaining undefined, and lending itself to multiple hypothesis—purchase of the place, having private guards, or bribing politicians. In any case, the occupation of the Manor was seen with hostility, and would never be satisfactorily sorted out until much later, date at which most of the people who had been so disoriented about the event would no longer be around to learn the truth about the Hollandais.

In the meantime, life had to go on, and the presence or non-presence of the Hollandais did not change anything to the fact that fields needed to be ploughed under. Les "labours" as we call ploughing in French were a particularly demanding and precise task, which required a well trained team of cows, since in Card with the exception of Lemaunier who had tractors to do that, les labours relied heavily on animal labor. For the Marzet family, les labours were done as a team between le Père Marzet and his son Robert. Le Père Marzet would lead the team of cows, ensuring the furrows were as straight as possible, and Robert would sit on the plough itself adding its weight to it and identifying any potential problem, while the cows stubbornly pulled forward, overturning the rich ground and moving tons of it in apparent effortless determination. At the end of each furrow, Robert would lift the plough's blade while le Père Marzet maneuvered the team to align it with the next furrow in the opposite direction. It was essential that the blade of the plough not be damaged in any manner, and both men's task was to avoid rocks that may surface. It was always surprising to me that rocks could still be found in these fields that had been cultivated for at least two centuries if not more—I would have thought that every rock had long been removed. But every year le Père Marzet and Robert would unavoidably hit one or more rocks. Depending on its size or the angle, the ploughshare would demand attention. The team was unhitched and returned for a well deserved drink at the water trough while Robert would use an anvil and a hammer which had been prepositioned by the field to straighten out the blade and repair the damage. The furrows were always straight but I was amazed by how shallow they were compared to those made by the Lemaunier's tractors. I had seen those when Aline and I had ridden to the field he was ploughing to deliver him lunch. It was one of the only times when Aline had delivered lunch to her father. This is when I saw mechanical farming in action. The tractor went so much faster than the cows... The neophyte that I was knew there was no hope for a Marzet-type farm to survive. The field was far larger, extending a mile out, the tractor turned on a dime at the end of the furrows, instead of needing several minutes to realign the cows, and Monsieur Lemaunier did not seem concerned about the rocks at all, his machine plowing forward as if indestructible. The comparison was not even fair. Like my grandmother said, in the old days people worked a lot harder! It would be one of the rare times when Monsieur Lemaunier spoke to me about farming. He did not hesitate to tell me that despite all of the respect he had for farmers like le Père Marzet he did not see them surviving past this generation. Animals could not be used both to pull heavy burdens and produce milk or calves. This was nonsense. The day was gone when you could farm a few acres and raise two cows. The future belonged to those who had big farms, used automation, and benefited from tractors to do the heavy work required to keep the cows fed. He even invited me to visit his farm for the first time, and see the milking process in operations, and asked Aline to give me the tour, as he relied on workers to do this work. In the years following this short conversation, it would become eminently obvious how right Monsieur Lemaunier was. When I reported the content of my conversation to Mémé Louise she simply commented that this did not concern her, "it has been many years since we ran a farm in our family!" But she was really not happy that the little village was working itself into complete and absolute insignificance. There was no room for individuality and places as small as Card could no longer make a contribution. The republic did not need as many farmers as before, and it did not have a war to fight. "Because who was it but the farmers dying without complaining who had saved France in the Great War? It was not people from Monaco!" I pointed out to her that people from Monaco were not even French, why should they fight for France?

As always, conversations with my grandmother took a tangent, and after a while, I had a hard time figuring out how we had managed to go from the disappearance of small farmers to World War One, which so often came back in her conversations. It was one of the most enraging things with her, and from the moment I was old enough to talk to her, I really never understood how her mind worked. During these discussions, she would be full of energy, and even in later years, when she was in her eighties, seeing how she got excited about a topic or another, you would have thought her indestructible, like Monsieur Lemaunier's plough.

CHAPTER 27
Noëlle

Les Loges is no more that a sprinkling of houses along the Route Départementale 56 (D56) between Ambazac and Saint-Martin-Terressus. As you enter what the locals call a village, you find the old post office on the right, just before the VC that goes to Le Bosc, an even smaller locality. The post office operated until the Second World War. It closed in 1939, never reopened, and is now a regular house. Across the street, is the old café. You can tell it is a café because you can still see the outline of the sign that was at one time painted over the door. Alice had told me to watch myself as I rode my bicycle back and forth to Les Loges and in front of the old café. She had warned me that the lady living there did not have all of her faculties—which was a nice way to say she was crazy. There was a lady like that in Monaco as well. I had to walk past her house on the way home from school, and sometimes nothing would happen, but sometimes she would come out with a stick or a broom and run after us children as if we were the devil, while shouting evil incantations in Monégasque. Of course, there would always be older children who would unceasingly tease "a matta"—the crazy woman, as people called her—by ringing her doorbell, throwing pebbles at her windows or lighting up roman candles and throwing them in her front yard. They then scampered as the old lady, white with rage, would come out running after them with whatever weapon she had within reach, which one day included a fourteen-inch kitchen knife. This incident caused the police to intervene. "A matta" was given a medical evaluation. Word was that she had been sent to the psychiatric ward at the Sainte-Anne Hospital in Nice. I was glad not to have ever harassed her. When she came back to her house, a police officer was guarding it every time school let out. This lasted a few weeks, and the day he was removed the teasing started anew, causing the poor lady to be taken away yet again, and this time she did not come back. Based on this sad experience, I was determined to avoid the old café in Les Loges and pedaled even faster as I rode by. Further down D56 was the sawmill where Robert Teulier worked. It was set about one hundred feet away from the road so that you could almost miss it if you were driving. On my bicycle I could distinctly hear the shrieking of the big saws as they worked through all types of trees. Then up on the right was an estate with the white fences that are telltale of horse farms. The horses were usually grazing on pastures that seemed of a lot higher quality than the ones I took the cows to. But this estate had a fantastic bird, a peacock, and I was always hoping to see him fan its tail feathers, which were the most amazing feathers I had ever seen. This bird was not very obliging, and I would rarely see him in all of his splendor. I was also keen on finding one of his feathers, but le Père Marzet told me that peacocks never lost their tail feathers. He thought the bird to be completely useless because it was not good to eat. Then as you rode out of town, there were a couple more houses, and the sign indicated that you had just left Les Loges, as if you had ever noticed in the first place that you had actually entered a village!

As I rode on every road, Chemin Vicinal, and path of the neighboring region, it would be unavoidable that I would have a flat tire one day. To this end, I always carried a repair kit which my father had taught me to use. And of course, the day I had my first flat tire was right in front of the old café, and not on the opposite side of the road, right in front of it. I was scared that the old lady—maybe it was the same one as in Monaco—would come out after me with a knife, and decided to push the bicycle away to repair the puncture in a more appropriate setting. I froze in my tracks as I heard the heavy wooden door to the old café open. I dropped the bicycle—I could always get it later—and started running out of the village. As I had expected, the old lady ran after me, but instead of incantations in a violent language, I heard a young woman's voice calling to me not to be afraid. I stopped and turned, and saw a beautiful girl in a light summer dress with thick long undulating black hair telling me it was

OK, that she had seen me get a flat, and that she could help me if I wanted to. Well, I was not born yesterday, I had seen Snow White at the movies, and I knew witches could turn into anything they wanted, and they could lie and could deceit even the hunters. She must have read my mind, as she stated that her mother was inside, and everything was fine. Her name was Marie, and she was ever more beautiful when you saw her blue eyes which contrasted her dark hair. She was old, at least twenty-one, and I knew enough about women to know that she was really, really attractive. I could see her body was nicely formed under the light printed fabric of her dress. We walked back to my bicycle, and she helped me unscrew the wheel (I did not have quick releases on my axle), and she brought a basin with water so that I could tell where the hole was in the tube. She knew everything about bicycles because her boyfriend was an amateur racer who hoped to make it into the pros. He had raced in the Ambazac July Fourteen races the past two years and had finished second this year, missing the victory by ten seconds. I was impressed, and I thought it was good to have met her. But my amazement was renewed when her sister came out to see what was going on. She looked very much like Marie, except her hair, which was also long but curlier, was red. It was the brightest hair I had seen on any one, and she did not hide it at all, displaying it instead in all its glorious splendor. I was as if under a spell. I did not move for several moments as I watched her come down the stairs of the café toward me. This amazingly pretty creature was actually going to talk to *me*? It was as if the pages of a fairy tale book had opened and I was in the middle of it. She asked me my name, and she told me hers was Noëlle because she had been born on Christmas Day. I did not doubt it for one second. She asked me where I came from, and when she found out I was from Monaco, she decided she wanted to hear about it. But first, seeing my fascination with her hair, she told me it was real, and that I could touch it. I was transported in a third dimension as I put my hand through the gorgeous heavy and fragrant hair. She then made me sit down on the stairs and tell her about Monaco.

    She and her sister lived in the old café with their mother and their grandmother. I found out their name was Demadrid and their father had died from a car accident shortly after Noëlle was born. Marie was the oldest and was born in 1946, and Noëlle was born on Christmas Day in

1950. That's when their mother still had her senses. But one day, the gendarmes showed up at her house with the bad news that her husband had died in a car accident. She had already suffered through five years of anguish while her husband had been a prisoner of war, losing the small café business at the same time because the customers had simply gone. Her pain threshold had been reached, and she had gone into reclusion, abandoning her two daughters to the care of their grandmother. Noëlle said that without their grandmother they would have starved to death, as their mother had not come out of her bedroom for weeks, refusing to eat, and when she had finally agreed to taking any food, she was so weak she could not walk any longer. She had never recovered, and while her mind had retained some consciousness for a while, she started hallucinating that gendarmes were at her front door to tell her that her husband was dead. She confused the uniform of the mailman with that of gendarmes, and she thought her husband was still a prisoner of war in Germany. She cursed the war and the Germans, and the Maréchal, who by that time was long dead. This is why if anyone came near the house she would rush out and run them out of her property. So, instead of a mad woman, her daughters told me, she was a woman who was in pain, and lived in a constant nightmare. She was now under a sedative medical treatment, but it simply caused her to go into a vegetative drowsy state that hopefully brought her some relief. Noëlle was crying silently as she told me her mother's story, and I felt a great compassion toward her. I wanted to know how come I had not seen them before, and they laughed, telling me they had seen me almost every day but that I pedaled like the devil trying to get out of a church, and they never had had the opportunity to talk to me. They said that the entire community had cast them aside, and outside of the mailman, the traveling baker and the Coop truck driver they talked to no one. Everybody was scared of them as if the pain of their mother could be passed on to other people. They stated that the entire community thought they were witches who could bring a curse on people, especially Noëlle who had red hair, a sure sign that she had connections to obscure forces, and that she had supernatural powers. Well, she did have supernatural powers: she could have asked me anything and I would have done it. I was entirely under the spell of her beauty, and completely and hopelessly at her mercy. As noon time approached, I told them I had to get back to Card, otherwise my grandmother would worry. They understood. We fixed my flat—it had been neglected for all that time—and they made me promise to come back. I did so, and I was so much under Noëlle's spell, I compared myself to Odysseus on the island of Aeaea where he becomes friend and lover to the enchantress Circe. Odysseus is so much under her spell that he even forgets he has a home, and when his men remind him of that fact, Circe tells him he has to travel through Hades to find his way. I was definitely Odysseus.

When I got home I told my grandmother—not that I had been to the old café in Les Loges, I was not that stupid—but that I had found out the story about the old lady who lived there. She asked me who had told me, and of course I lied, and told her that the Italians had related it me. As I described the chain of events that Noëlle had told me, my grandmother plainly stated that it was ridiculous and hardly believable especially since the Italians had told me. "You know how they like to dramatize everything!" My grandmother's mother had had two of her sons die under her eyes, her daughter die in surgery, her other two sons captured a prisoners of war, and she had not lost her mind. With a name like Demadrid, they had to be from Spain, and these people from the South are just weaklings! I was so cross with her I almost yelled back at her, but I simply paraphrased Descartes "reason is, of all things among men, the most equally distributed; for every one thinks himself so abundantly provided with it, that those even who are the most difficult to satisfy in everything else, do not usually desire a larger measure of this quality than they already possess". *That* shut her up. She went pensive for a moment, and asked "You know Descartes? This is "incroyable!" And you are not even ten!" I proceeded to tell her that I was so fascinated with Descartes's book, I knew it almost by heart, and recited the first chapter of The Discourse on the Method. She decided that this called for celebration, and that I was definitely material for Louis-le-Grand in Paris. Tomorrow, we would go to the restaurant in Ambazac. Right now, she said, let's have a glass of panaché! Panaché is a drink made of half and half beer and Seven Up— or as we call it in France "limonade". My friends and I drank panaché at the end of every soccer practice and every soccer game. And while we were drinking, Mémé Louise continued "Of course, Pierre was not that bad off in captivity…but for Adrien, it was something else!"

As the Second World War started, both my grandmother's brothers had been called back into the infantry where they had served during their two year conscription. Adrien was sent to the regular infantry and Pierre to the Maginot Line infantry. Nothing much happened between the time France declared war on Germany, and the time the Germans decided to do something about in. So, until the day the Germans attacked, French soldiers enjoyed leaves, trips to Paris, and various amusements, like watching bicycle races. When the Germans launched the offensive, again, nothing happened on the Maginot Line. For Adrien, however, things were quite different, and combat was fierce particularly as Colonel de Gaulle tried to actually fight the Germans. Eventually, Adrien was taken prisoner. The Germans, according to him, had promised that anyone surrendering would be simply disarmed and sent home as a paroled prisoner. There was not much to be done at that point, and Adrien and his fellow infantrymen put down their weapons. Soldiers rejoiced as they were packed into cattle cars for the trip home. But Adrien, who was a loudmouth and liked to fight, was soon yelling at them that they were a bunch of cretins and that the train was not going south to Paris, and was instead eastbound toward Germany. The following five years were a calvary for Adrien. First assigned to a Stalag (prisoner camp for soldiers and NCOs), he was put to work in a factory by the Germans. True to himself, Adrien refused to work, and got that point across by having a fight with the German work detail supervisor. He was put in solitary confinement and then shipped off to a disciplinary camp in East Prussia, where he spent the next four winters trying to survive the brutality of the camp commander, the sparse rations, and the bitter cold in the rags that the uniforms had become after several years of daily wear. That he survived was a testimony to his determination and character—after all he was a Desjouannets—as he related that many had simply given up, not able to endure the suffering and giving in to the despair of not knowing when, and if their ordeal would end. Finally, as the Russians were starting their conquest of East Prussia, once the shooting got within ear range, the prisoners organized a rebellion of which Adrien was a leader. They fought the guards, killing many in the process, and caught the camp commander, an SS officer. They tried him in the manner of the Committee for Public Safety of the French Revolution. He had been found guilty of murdering tens of French and other nationalities prisoners and had been executed. Then they had left the camp, not wanting to fall into Russian hands, and several weeks later, on a July morning, after walking from East Prussia to France, Adrien had showed up at his mother's front door.

    Pierre had had quite a different experience, and unlike Adrien would talk about it. Unlike Adrien who absolutely hated the Germans, Pierre simply had a profound dislike for what they had done. His prisoner years started when the Germans bypassed the Maginot Line, and simply drove up to the rear of the French positions. The French could not defend themselves because the guns of the Maginot Line could only be pointed toward Germany and could not be traversed to point toward France. Pierre's entire unit surrendered without even firing a shot. The prisoners were then organized in columns and marched to Germany. On the way there several soldiers pretended to be sick or have bad legs that prevented them from marching any further. One particular individual sat down, and told the Germans he could not walk and required medical attention. Whether it was true or whether he was malingering, nobody will ever know. The Germans stopped the column, brought the prisoner forward and an officer stated in French "This soldier can no longer walk", and pulling his nine-millimeter Browning side-arm, continued "this is the way we take care of prisoners who cannot walk". And as he was finishing the sentence, he shot the poor guy dead in the head, leaving him in the middle of the road for all to see. Pierre said that at that moment any thought of escape or pretending to be sick abandoned him and that not a single prisoner dropped out of the column as they reached a processing camp in Germany. There, every piece of each soldier's uniform was marked with two huge letters "KG" in white paint. "KG" means Kriegsgefangen (prisoner of war), and Pierre would wear these two letters for most of the following four years. Each prisoner was then asked what his civilian job was. Pierre stated that he was a farmer, and he was sent to another part of the camp with a bunch of his comrades. The soldiers were then subdivided into groups, put in trucks and were driven away without a single word of explanation. What was going on is that Hitler's madness was catching up with him. While millions of German soldiers were involved in conquering Europe, there was not enough manpower left to run either the factories or the farms. And in complete contradiction to his own edicts, Hitler brought in foreigners by the millions to replace Germans who were no longer in Germany. Once they got to Munich, my uncle Pierre and the others in the truck were finally told that each one would be put in a farm to serve as farm hands. The farmers had strict instructions to report any escape, and if they escaped, when they were caught, they would be executed on the spot. Knowing what he knew of the Germans, Pierre had no doubt they would make good on the promise. He was the last one to be dropped off, in a place he had never heard of, up the hill from the Munich main highway to Garmisch in the small village of Oberammergau. I have since visited Oberammergau many times, and apparently the farm was at the place where the spa is now located, not far from the cable car terminal. It was night time when he arrived. He was dropped off at the entrance of the farm, with no further instructions, and no introduction to the farmer. Pierre was not exactly ready for what had happened next. He had been expecting an older woman, or a couple of elderly Germans, like he was used to see in Limousin. Instead, he was welcome by a very attractive blond-haired Bavarian woman who was in her early thirties. Neither of the two spoke each other's language, but as the days went by, he found out she lived there alone on the outskirts of the village with the herd of cows and the responsibility to take care of her husband's farm while he was gone. Pierre was assigned to sleep with the cows. This proved to be a benefit when winter arrived because stables are never cold. Soon, Pierre had learned enough German to converse with the woman. Magda, it was her name, had last seen her husband before the invasion of Poland in June 1939. By the time Pierre had reached the farm, it was over a year since her husband had been home.

Pierre soon proved to be a great farmer. He took care of the animals as if they were his, and he displayed great sensitivity in their management, staying up with the cows ready to give birth, running up the mountain to find a stray calf, insuring hay was cut and stored for the long and cold Bavarian winter, and making sure that enough wood was harvested to keep the little farmhouse warm. In addition, Pierre started a vegetable garden and raised a pig the second year he was there, so that if they were snowed in there would be enough food for the both of them. After two years of this existence, Magda had moved Pierre into the house, and it had not been long before Pierre and Magda behaved as husband and wife. The real husband was far away on the front, busy invading Russia. Then one day, Magda received a letter that her husband would be visiting for a one week furlough. Immediately she asked Pierre to move back to the stable, and swore him to secrecy, which he obviously agreed to. They spent the following week ensuring there was no trace of his presence and that none of his personal effects were accidentally left in the house. When the husband showed up, after two and a half years of absence—his was part of the Christmas leaves that actually took place before Christmas—he immediately became angry at seeing a Frenchman take care of the farm, and he became even angrier when he saw how well the farm was taken care of—much better than he had taken care of it himself. He suspected that Pierre and Magda had an affair and went into a rage beating his wife while Pierre was hunkered in the stable, unable to help and not about to intervene in a domestic dispute since he was a prisoner of war with no rights. He came out only after he heard the husband leave the house. He found Magda unconscious on the floor of the kitchen, and over the following weeks he nursed her back to health. And Pierre and Magda resumed their lives as before. There was another scary day in my uncle's life, when Hitler came to attend the Oberammergau Passion Play of 1942. The SS scoured the countryside to collect all prisoners so that there would be no possibility of anything going wrong. Magda had the presence of mind to send Pierre to the mountains with the cows and the SS did not pursue the matter any further. Yet, my uncle hid for an extra week before coming back down.

In early 1944 the news came that Magda's husband had died on the front and it was more a relief to her than anything else, because she had already decided to leave him when he came back. Now she hoped that once the war was over Pierre would stay and she and he could get married. Pierre told me they discussed it many times, but he was longing for France and for his family left behind. He had not seen them in four years by then, and he simply wanted to get home. At the end of April 1945, with the US troops in Oberammergau, my uncle Pierre said tearful goodbyes to Magda and left on foot on his way to Munich first, and then to Limoges, with the promise of coming back within a few months, but certainly before Christmas. Finding that going on foot was too slow, Pierre had commandeered a fire truck that he had found abandoned on the side of the road and this is how he reached Paris, leaving the vehicle at the Porte de Bagnolet, where he had jumped on the subway and had gone to my grandmother's apartment.

In the weeks that followed as he visited with his family and tried to figure out what to do next, he also found out how the Germans had behaved during the war, he found out about extermination, about death camps, about Oradour-sur-Glane, so close to his own family, and all of the atrocities that they had committed came rushing at him who had been entirely sheltered from all outside news in Oberammergau. He had lived in a cocoon and he was thoroughly overwhelmed. He also realized that as a prisoner of war he had lived better than most Frenchmen had in occupied France. And when his brother told him he would never speak to him again if he married a German woman, he decided he could never go back to Magda. He still regretted it years later, even after meeting another woman with whom he opened a store in the Rue de Rivoli in Paris. I could tell that his true love had been Magda. I promised myself that I would never do the same thing my uncle had done. So, as soon as we were done eating, after finishing my daily page of vacation homework, I climbed on my bicycle and returned to Circe.

CHAPTER 28
Descartes Gets Me in the Paper

I now had a dilemma. I had been spending my afternoons with Aline ever since her father had bought her a bicycle so that she could ride with me. Her father knew me from the threshing day and had decided he liked his daughter to have my company, especially that I now knew the surroundings like a native. Usually around four because it was way too hot before that, and my grandmother enforced the vacation homework rule, Aline and I would go on endless bicycle rides, stopping at given spots I knew so that we could enjoy blackberries or pick green apples from the Roussel's apple trees north of Les Loges. And after these breathtaking rides, we would end up in the little creek. But now, I wanted to go back and visit with Noëlle and I knew that if I went there I would never be able to leave in time and go riding with Aline. What was even worse is that Aline's father would not allow her to go riding alone, and if I did not show up, she would not be able to ride her bicycle which she loved to do so much. I could not find counsel from anybody, because if anybody I knew found out I had gone to the old café, my grandmother would know in an instant, and I would be forbidden to go ever again—interdiction I had already decided to fully disregard. Furthermore, if Aline came looking for me, she would alert my grandmother that I had disappeared, which was bound to raise the question of where I had been, and so on and so on. Aline was fun and she knew a lot about Paris, but I could not resist the attraction I felt toward Noëlle. She was truly Circe. What would Ulysses have done? I had read his adventures, yet I could not fathom the answer he would have given to this. I simply did not have the maturity to make the right choice, or any choice for that matter.

So, I went back to my Circe. She was sitting on the steps at the back of the house, barefoot on the granite steps, her eyes closed enjoying the heat of the sun. She had rolled up her dress on her thighs and had unbuttoned the top so that she could slide it over her shoulders. She was practically naked, and I could tell that she was not wearing a bra, since she did not have straps, and her nipples were clearly visible through the material of her light dress. Her gorgeous red hair was fanned being her on the worn down rock of the top step. We started again our conversation, and I found out that she had not gone much to school, that people around hated her, and that when she went out, everybody talked about her behind her back. I told her I could not stay long. She looked at me and she said "You have a girlfriend don't you?" I stuttered that I didn't, that she was a friend and we went riding. She answered "It's OK, you don't have to make excuses; you can see her anytime you want, just sit here for a while and tell me more stories about Monaco". She wanted to know about the beach, about bathing suits, about bikinis, and she wanted to know about the boats and what it was like to swim in the sea. She wished she could go there. I told her how easy it was to go there, but she quickly answered it was impossible. She had to take care of her mother with her sister, and now their grandmother was not doing well either. Since she had raised both of them it was their turn to watch after her now, as she grew older. She said that her sister would likely marry and when she did, Noëlle would be left to take care of both women alone. As the sun was baking us on the back steps, I told her it was as hot as in Monaco, she got up, took my hand and we walked to an arbor that was at the end of far end of the garden. I could not believe that this beautiful girl who could surely have had a date with anyone she picked in Monaco was taking my hand and spending time in the arbor with poor little me. I was supposed to leave at about three thirty to go riding with Aline, and that pleasure which a few hours sooner had seemed the paramount of life seemed rather blend now, as I sat next to Noëlle. On top of this, I was leaving on the last day of August and it was already the eighteenth—there were not many days left to enjoy Noëlle's company. The days seemed far away when I played with miniature cars on the kitchen floor of our apartment in Monaco, when I was consumed by which new model Dinky Toys had come out within the past month, and whether I could maneuver a Kronenbourg beer tractor-trailer in the streets of my living-room. And to think that I had cursed my father for taking me away from Monaco and forcing me to come to what I considered the most wretched of all places. I was taken out of my reverie by Noëlle who recommended that I should not talk to anyone about our meetings. These were to remain our secret. I thought to myself that this was the third one I had to keep. I became very good at keeping secrets.

When I caught up with Aline, she could tell my heart was not with riding. Nor was it with anything else. I had been absolutely mesmerized, and it is only when Noëlle's sister had called her to help her with chores that I had been able to leave. Noëlle kissed me goodbye, and I was gone. But I also had a task, which was to pick up medicine for her mother the next morning when I went to Ambazac. She had given me the money and the prescription. This plan almost derailed when my grandmother found the money in my pocket as I went to bed that night. She looked surprised, even alarmed "where did you find this money?" probably thinking that I could have stolen it from her. I told her the truth that I had told an old lady I knew in Les Loges that I was going to Ambazac every day, and that she had asked me to pick up her prescription for her. To my discharge I showed her the prescription and the green insurance form. Of course my grandmother wanted to know who it was and since the name was on the form I told her it was Demadrid. She went on a soliloquy how people from the south always needed others to do their work, but at the end of it, she admitted that I had impressed her for the second time that day, and she gave me a ten franc banknote as a reward for my good action.

So it is that the next day I went to the pharmacy at the corner of the church square. The store smelled of eucalyptus, and behind its big bay windows, it was another world completely insulated from the noise of the street. Jars containing various products made a multicolor mosaic on the shelves behind the counter. Everything was more deliberate. I gave the pharmacist the forms, and when she saw it was for the older Demadrid, she asked "How is she doing these days? The poor woman is really not well at all". I had no idea how she was doing, so I told the pharmacist that I did not know, that I was simply picking up the medicine for her. The pharmacist too was impressed, and offered me a couple of sweets that she kept in a special jar. This was great. The most beautiful creature on earth had asked me to fill a prescription, and when I told the story everybody rewarded me for my good deed. The problem was that I was not really doing it as a good deed for the old woman…And when I went to visit with Tata Marie as I did everyday, she too asked me about the pharmacy. One of her customers had seen me go in, and now Tata Marie was concerned that I should be sick. I told her my story, and she thought it was grand that I should pick up medicine for an old lady. She said that she hoped I would do the same thing for her when she got older, and I assured her I would. She picked up a tablet of Tobler chocolate and gave it to me for my good behavior. Now, the story of my good deed was going around the village. My aunt told one of the customers who told her friend, and before I even got to the butcher's, Madame Bonneau knew that I was helping an old lady. I found it doubly ironic that all of these people were the ones who had outcast the family, and were avoiding them like the plague for fear of a curse, or worse, from fear of catching the spirits. My sudden fame scared me. Someone was bound to remember the two daughters…On the other hand, these people thought that the redhead was ugly and that she was cursed for having been born a few days before her father had died. I stopped by the house in Card to drop off the groceries, and went to deliver the medicine. My grandmother reminded me not to be late because we were going to the Hotel de France for lunch. She had asked Alice to reserve the taxi for us, and it was coming to pick us up at a quarter of twelve.

    I rode to the back door of the house, and Noëlle was waiting for me—and more importantly for the medicine—as she said her grandmother was not doing well without it. I gave it to her and she disappeared inside. I had not yet been invited to go inside and had really no desire to do so. When Noëlle sat down with me on the steps a few moments later, she was not the same girl as the day before. I could tell she was sad and concerned by her grandmother. To cheer her up I told her that Ferrari had a racing car they called the redhead just like her sister called her. That took her mind off her grandmother, and her curiosity took over. She wanted to know more. Did I go to races? Could I tell her what it was like? I could have entertained her through lunch with all my experiences in Monaco on race day. But I wanted to make sure I would not be late for the taxi. I had never taken a taxi before. We kissed on the cheeks, as people do in France with friends and relatives, and I was on my way to Card and to the Hotel de France. The taxi was a Citroën DS19. Now that was a comfortable car, not like the Renault. It zoomed us to Ambazac as the clock was striking twelve noon at the church tower, and Mémé Louise was pretty sure it was the first time she had ever been on time for anything (Mémé Louise was always late for everything) . As we drank our aperitif—she had a Pernod, and I had a panaché—I had to tell her more about Descartes. She was again absolutely amazed that I could understand the famous Discourse of the Method. She asked me if I knew Chapter Two and the four rules of problem solving, and I told I did. I first recited them to her and them summarized them: rule one, never accept what other people tell you is true without checking it yourself; rule two, divide the problem in as many parts as possible; rule three, solve each part in turn commencing with the easiest one; and rule four, make sure you don't forget anything and review your solution. By that time, I had amazed my audience. My grandmother, the restaurant owner, and the other customers, to include one of the school teachers of Ambazac, who simply stated "this kid is a genius", stopped what they were doing to listen to me. The Hotel de France offered me dessert for free—a nice slice of apricot tart in crème pâtissière served on flaky pastry. My grandmother announced proudly to my audience that I would be going to the Lycée Louis-le-Grand in Paris, and that I was already two years ahead in my studies. The teacher agreed with the assembly that no one was surprised by that. He went on to say that his students in twelfth grade could not understand Descartes, and here was a ten year old who not only knew it by heart but could also explain it. It was worthy of an article in the newspaper. And on top of this my grandmother added, he does errands for the old people of the neighborhood! Well, only this morning he got her medicine for an old lady living in Les Loges!

While we were still at the lunch table, the local reporter for the Ambazac portion of the Limoges was called, and he took notes and a picture of me as I explained how Descartes had affirmed his own existence through the thought process, showing that man existed only because he could think. The audience applauded, and my head was spinning. This was fun. I was a hero in Ambazac, and even Tata Marie had sneaked into the restaurant, despite the presence of my grandmother to be a witness to the event. A few days later, the article appeared in the Echo du Centre about this child-genius from Ambazac who could recite

Descartes. No mention was made of my true hometown, Monaco. I was rather proud of myself, and le Père Marzet got me to sign his copy of the paper. As we drove back in the taxi, my grandmother said that I should make sure not to sleep on my laurels, and that I should study even more. While I had been delighting in my moment of glory, she had gone to the bookstore next doors and had purchased the Essays of Montaigne for me to read. I thanked my grandmother for lunch and for the book, changed from my Sunday clothes into my regular clothes and was on my way to see Noëlle. I told her about my lunch, but she did not know about Descartes, or even who he was, and in a sense I was not surprised since she had basically dropped out of school when she was twelve, only going there occasionally afterwards. She was impressed, but I could also tell that she really did not understand the scope of what had happened that day. She was also jealous, and I started to realize that however pretty she was, we already lived in two different worlds that were far apart one from the other. She has plenty of reasons to be jealous: I knew a lot of things she did not know, I lived in Monaco, I could go to school, I did not have a deranged mother, I actually had a father, and I did not have to take care of two generations of sick relatives. Using Descartes' method, I showed her she had a lot more going for her that she gave herself credit. As we sat under the arbor, she told me she was interested in listening to more stories of the rich people. She too had never heard of a Rolls-Royce or a Ferrari (until that morning when I had told her about Redheads). I had always assumed that these names were universal, and that everyone but a village idiot would know about them. I now had to revise my opinion—I had changed greatly since my first day in Limousin. This was also the major difference between Aline and me. She positively despised everything about Limousin, and I suspected that I only made things bearable for her. So I told Noëlle about the Ferraris, and the Coopers and the Maseratis. It was my turn to have her under my spell. Before I left, her sister Marie gave me a new prescription and money, so that I could get medicine for their mother this time.

CHAPTER 29
Jam Making

One of the great events of Card summers was the making of jam. This had all started with Alice Marzet who had introduced both my mother and my grandmother to this art. The reason we knew Alice was making jam is that she did that outside, in the middle of our "chemin", the lane that was Card's main street. She had to do it there because as everyone knows who has made jam, there are two ways to make jam: unpasteurized, if you have a refrigerator to keep it from spoiling, and pasteurized if you want to keep it for a long time without having to have a refrigerator. Thanks to Louis Pasteur, the people of Card were able to make jam, and keep it for a whole year without it spoiling. The problem with this method is that you need to boil everything for ten minutes. Everything means the glass jars, the rubber seals used to close the jar which came with a glass lid—the jars were the "L'Idéale" brand—and of course, the entire jar filled with jam and sealed once the jars are actually full. This required boiling large quantities of water in large containers, and there was no better way than to do it outside, rather than carrying all of this mess inside. So, on a beautiful Saturday morning, after the cows were back in the stable, and chewing the curd, Alice brought out wood, paper, small sticks, and built a temporary cooking area outside her front door, smack in the middle of the chemin! After that, she collected hot ambers from the fireplace, and within a few minutes she had a fire going on. Then, she took two tripods, placed them in the middle of the fire and carried her two lessiveuses. The first one was for the preparation of the fruit, and the second one to pasteurize the jars. In the previous two days, after work, Alice had been collecting fruit: the wild fruit growing along side our country lanes and cow paths, such as blackberries or wild strawberries, the semi-wild fruit growing in the hedges of cultivated fields, such as red current or raspberries, and the cultivated berries of her garden. She had washed them, and now, she was pouring them into the washbasin—which had been fully cleaned, scrubbed, disinfected, rinsed, and pasteurized as well—and she started cooking the mixed berries while adding sugar and pectin, which had been purchased in powder form from the pharmacy in Ambazac. I was amazed by the entire preparation. In Monaco if I wanted jam, I simply went with my grandmother Lainey to the local Printania store (Printania was a French supermarket chain), picked the jam flavor I wanted, paid two Francs fifty, and we went home and ate it. I did not even know how to make jam, had never imagined such a complicated process, and certainly never thought anyone but the Bonne Maman factory could ever be successful in making such fragrant products.

While the fruit was cooking she prepared the jam containers and lined them up on an improvised clean area made of L'Echo du Centre newspaper laid out in the middle of our chemin. Then she placed the containers on it, and once they were pasteurized, she put them on the other side on another set of newspapers. The jam containers were not the standard supermarket type. These were half a quart jars, with an attached and hinged lid that closed over a pink rubber seal with a clasp. Once they were filled and pasteurized, it required pulling on the tab of the rubber seal which would be broken. This allowed using and re-using the jars, while simply replacing the rubber seal. The whole operation required handling boiling hot containers with tongues and filling them up with jam while they were still hot, before bacteria could colonize them. Alice had a fancy jam thermometer to judge whether the jam was ready or not, but in the end she preferred the proven and familiar method of simply dropping a drop of jam in a glass of water. If the drop disintegrated before hitting the bottom of the glass, the jam required more cooking. But if the drop remained intact, the jam was ready to be poured into the jars. This was done with great celerity, the jars were sealed closed, and put once again in the boiling water to pasteurize their content. After about two hours, Alice had twenty or so jars ready to be stored, and a big mess to clean up. The boiling water was used to dissolve the jam that was stuck in the other washbasin, and this was accomplished with the help of a long handled brush. The entire mess was then simply poured onto the chemin, and it trickled down toward the manure pile. Immediately butterflies and wasps were drinking from the spill. Finally, Alice had to clean up the fire which was still hot. She took a shovel, and brought the remaining ambers back into the house, adding them to the fire going on in the fireplace. By evening any trace of the jam factory had completely disappeared. As le Père Marzet would say, "this is how you fool the Boches!"

There was some incredible efficiency in making jam this way. And my grandmother decided that we too should go into the jam making business. It was so simple, she remarked. Her mother had done it in her time, and there was no reason she, Mémé Louise, could not do it! I pointed out to her how easy it was for me to pedal to her favorite grocery store in Ambazac and bring back any quantity of jam she wanted. But there was no moving her on this one. She was determined to make jam. Especially since we had so many plumbs on the trees in the front yard that the branches were ready to snap at any time. We would have so much fun doing this together, she said! I could hardly wait! The plumb picking proved an ordeal: wasps had claimed the airspace above and under the trees and had clear air superiority. Picking the plumbs was an extreme challenge to the wasps' territorial control and Mémé Louise ended up getting stung more than once. She pretended it did not hurt. I knew a lot better than that. A couple of years back a wasp had stung me when I was shopping for grapes with my Mémé Louise, and I was not fooled by my grandmother's sudden tolerance to pain. Once we had several buckets full of the fruit, Mémé Louise proceeded exactly like she had seen Alice do. I regretfully pointed out to my grandmother that I had observed the proceedings from very close range, and according to my expertise in the jam making process she had a situation on her hands. Alice's fruit were berries which did not require peeling or filtering, but we had plumbs which had both a thick skin, and a pit. How were we going to overcome that? "Oh, yes," my grandmother admitted "we need to do something about it". Before she had the time to formulate an answer, I was out of the house and riding away on my bicycle. And when I got home in time for dinner, my grandmother was still in the process of pitting the last plumbs by hand, which I had correctly figured out could be the only solution. I knew that because I pitted the olives for my grandmother Lainey, when we made pissaladière. My grandmother was not happy that I had escaped, and she said that if I wanted dinner I should make my own. That was not a problem at all. I reviewed quickly how many dinner invitations I had: Tata Marie, Alice, and Monsieur Lemaunier. I had just left the Lemaunier farm, and it would have been awkward to go back. Tata Marie was OK but I would have had to ride in the dark, and none of the roads had any street lights passed the railroad bridge. So, I went to Alice. I said that my grandmother was not feeling well—that was the truth: how can anybody feel well after pitting four pails of plumbs—and I was promptly treated to dinner. When I got back, my grandmother asked me if I wanted to eat. I told her no, and that I had cooked my own dinner. She was not happy about that because she *had* cooked dinner. I made her feel better by telling her I really liked Montaigne, and reciting a paragraph of his Essays. But my grandmother made it clear that I had to help her the next day, since I had observed Alice make the jam, and my memory of it was fresher than my grandmother's who had last done it about forty years before.

So it is that the next day, my grandmother with my help as a consultant set up exactly the same operation as Alice had done a few days sooner. I guided my grandmother through the process, explaining and demonstrating how things were done. Alice stopped by and immediately determined that I had learned quickly and was giving the correct advice. My grandmother should actually have listened to me on two accounts. First, she should have filtered the jam to remove the skins, and second she should have kept better track of which jars were pasteurized and which ones were not. Since we did not subscribe to the paper, Mémé Louise did not have a way to properly organize the process, and soon she lost track of which jars had been pasteurized, and which had not. The problems resulting from such elementary confusion were not readily apparent. We did succeed in making jam, and although it was difficult to eat with the skins getting in the way of spreading it on the bread, I had to admit that it was good. Mémé Louise had done a good job, and I had had the chance to put my knowledge into practice. However, the following year when we came back to Card, the consequence of the lack of proper pasteurization was at once obvious and surprising. Left to their own volition for ten months, the bacteria had grown in some of the jars and had expended to the point of even breaking a couple of them which had exploded under the pressure. Mémé Louise was not there to see the disaster because my mother had to clean it up long before she arrived for her August stay.

After this first year experience of spending the month of August with Mémé Louise, it became a tradition that I would stay an extra month and keep Mémé Louise company while she was in Card. My grandmother genuinely enjoyed my company, and she was fun to have around as well, except when she decided to make jam, and send me to fight squadrons of wasps under the plumb trees. I must confess that I had a great time with her. She could always be convinced to try something new, and she was a truly adventurous person who, despite her at times obsessive criticism of the people from the South, was a great companion. The evenings we spent together with Robert Teulier were evenings when we simply had a good time. We did not need anything to be happy except the opportunity to talk and joke—and a couple of bottles of wine. There was no pretense, and Robert Teulier shared some of his country wisdom with me. He was a humble man who was well aware of his shortcomings. He did not make excuses, he did not invent melodramatic stories to justify his drinking and simply admitted that he was powerless over alcohol. My grandmother tried many times to convince him to drink less, "not to stop drinking" like she said. But Robert Teulier would say that it was not who he was. He knew that he was taking tens of years off his life, and he would quote the French anti-alcoholism slogan "Alcohol kills you slowly", to which he would add his own response "It's OK, I am not in a hurry!" And we would laugh and laugh at his joke. Every time he came over, we had a game to make him say it as many times as possible. He soon figured it out and would not say it again, jokingly complaining that we had no respect for him, and that we were taking advantage of him when he was drunk. Robert Teulier was always willing to help, and he was a great person to have around when I faced challenges that were too difficult for my age. That was the big difference between le Père Marzet and Robert Teulier. My grandmother was a lot closer to Robert Teulier and did not hesitate to ask him help when she needed it. One year when we came back to Card, I found out that Robert Teulier had sold all of his cows and had stopped farming, with the exception of the vegetable garden which he maintained until the year he died. I was flabbergasted. I had never imagined that I would ever witness the prophecies of Lemaunier. I had thought, yes, Lemaunier is right, but I could never imagine that it would happen so quickly to Card. Somehow I thought our little community would remain unaffected. Robert Teulier told us that it simply was too much work, and that he did not make any money at it. He had taken the government incentive and had sold the cows. My grandmother of course complained that she paid taxes to make people like him lazy. That day Robert Teulier was not really in a mood to put up with her comments, and he left before dinner. It was plain how sad he was and how hard it had been for him to have given up his cows. Later, sitting on the little step in front of his well, he told me about that day when the butcher had come with two trucks to pick them up. Tears rolled down his cheeks as he told me that he had not been able to stay and see his poor cows being taken away like that. He had helped with the first one, but after that he could bear it no more. He had locked the house, told the butcher to proceed and lock the stables. The butcher had not been surprised, and had been understanding. He was getting used to farmers closing down, and the emotion of the loss was too much for most. Robert Teulier had cried that day, and he cried then as he told me the story again, regretting not having had the strength to say goodbye to his cows. It was the third time I had seen a grown man cry, and he explained it was OK, we could not keep everything bundled up inside. Several years later, he would tell me how sad he still was and how much he still missed them. I did not know then how strong a feeling sadness is, and how it stays with you for ever, like an unwanted visitor. The real problem with Robert Teulier was that outside of the month my grandmother spent in Card, he really had nobody to talk to. He did not have any friends and did not wish to have any. He did not like the Parisian ways of her sister, and after two years, I never saw her or Frédéric again—they probably went on vacation in Monaco or on the French Riviera—and that left him with no family outside of my grandmother.

The day following Robert Teulier's premature departure from dinner, my grandmother sent me to his house to invite him for dinner. And he came. Mémé Louise apologized for her comments saying she had not meant it that way, and that whatever she said did not apply to him. "A la bonne heure!" he exclaimed as we all clinked glasses, had a drink, and the whole thing was forgotten. I thought it was an excellent way to resolve conflicts.

CHAPTER 30
Aline Crashes and a Snake Bites

Mémé Louise was anxious to see me read Montaigne. But Montaigne's work addressed an entirely different problem. As he tries to instill humility in man, he states that "there is a plague on Man, and this is his opinion that he knows something." I was not so familiar with the idea of skepticism, and the relationship with Christianity was of no reference to me since I had never even been to church. But there was one thing I wholeheartedly agreed with Montaigne on, and this was the idea that man is not superior to animals, and that in many respects, it is animals that are better than man. So, we established a routine that every night while Mémé Louise was washing dishes, I would read one or two essays of Montaigne. Our month went on quite well and she was delighted to have such a gifted grandchild, as she told Robert Teulier. Robert Teulier was there often, joking, eating, smoking and drinking wine. I had to buy two bottles of wine every day when I went to Ambazac simply to keep up with his consumption. But he paled in comparison to the old Romanet fellow who came to build the retaining wall for our garden. Romanet, like le Père Marzet was a World War One veteran. They had actually been drafted into the same unit. Romanet—I always wondered why I did not have to call him Monsieur Romanet—was eighty by the time I met him at the far end of our garden, building the famous retaining wall. A few days before, mortar and stones had been delivered by truck and put by the construction site. Romanet, at the age of eighty, rode his bicycle from Ambazac and was at work at eight in the morning. In order to mix the mortar, he had to pull the water from the well, using a crank mounted on a tree trunk on which the chain slowly wrapped itself. It was hard work. Then he had to carry the pails of water to the far-end of the garden. Romanet did not use any commercial measuring devices. He only used a string with knots. I imagined that the Egyptians must have used the same method of measurement. But I would never know since Romanet refused to share with me how he did it. When I went down to see what he was doing, and asked him how he measured things, he smiled and said that this was for him to know, and for me to figure out. I did not succeed in this task. However, what I figured out is how much wine he was drinking. He was proud to tell me that he drank one bottle of wine per hour of work—eight bottles a day. Even Robert Teulier could not top that. Romanet rode the mile and a half from Ambazac with his eight bottles of wine, his lunch and his tools strapped to his bicycle. He worked eight hours, until four thirty, rode back, and before going home stopped by the wine depot and filled his bottles for the next day. The results were amazing. The wall was absolutely straight, and forty-six years later, it is still retaining the dirt of the garden and preventing it from sliding into the path below it. This not withstanding, at least I did not have to go buy his wine every day!

Robert Teulier usually drank a few glasses before he even came to our house for dinner. Thus it was that one night as my grandmother was preparing dinner in the kitchen, Robert Teulier sat next to me and in his sly manner asked "How do you like the Demadrid girls?" after which he sniggered. Seeing my embarrassment and my concern that my grandmother would hear, he quickly added "Don't worry, your secret is safe with me". Then with his hands he drew in the air the shape of a woman, and added "They are bloody hot!" He asked me which one I preferred and I had to tell him the Redhead, and he agreed that the other one was too old for me. Robert Teulier in his rough and unpolished manner was also probably a lot more accepting of people's shortcomings that most. He knew he drank too much, and that eventually it would catch up with him. And as my grandmother re-entered the room, he added out loud "You see, Patrick, I am an alcoholic. I like wine way too much. I like it better than women. That's why I am not married, and live alone all year long, with nobody to talk to. Don't follow my example!"

I was not about to. I was the opposite. I was ten, and had not one, but two girlfriends. There was absolutely no chance I would prefer wine to women, ever. Meanwhile, my deliveries of medicine continued as the patients needed them. Noëlle was ever more enchanting every day, and I could hardly sleep from thinking about her. I had completely abandoned playing with toy cars. I only had occasional exchanges with le Père Marzet, and since the day I had had my flat tire, I had not gone to watch the cows because Aline wanted to go riding at the same time. Aline seeing that my interest in her was waning decided that she had to make things more interesting. One day she decided that we should race, and if I won I would have the right to kiss her. We had set a course between La Boissarde and the last curve before getting to Card on the dirt paths. She took an early lead on the slight incline going to the main path, but as soon as we got on the more sandy part, she chose the sandy side, and I rode on the grass, thus getting better traction and passing her. As the path went downhill, I accelerated, my entire bicycle and I shaking from the stones and the bumps. Like a professional cyclist in the Paris-Roubaix race, I could barely hold on to the handlebar and stay on the bicycle. The race was still pretty even. As I slowed down to take the last ninety degree turn, I was on the outside, ready to take advantage of the dirt banking, when suddenly Aline passed me on the right. She was going way too fast, she would never be able to make the turn. At the same time, I had started to turn right, and brake as I may, I could not avoid clipping her rear wheel. As I had thought, she could not make the turn, and my clipping of her rear wheel certainly did not prove of any assistance to her. She hit the embankment straight on, flying into the air, head first into a bunch of about forty small hazelnut trees in a clamor of scraped metal. At the same time, I was sent off balance by the collision with her rear wheel, and fell on the path, my fall being dampened by the grass that grew in the center of the path, where the wheels of tractors and farm carts never treaded. I got up, shaken up but not injured, and rushed to her as I knew from experience—I had had my own encounters with hazelnut trees—that such falls have a tendency to hurt. Aline was sprawled out in the middle of the trees, crying and holding her head. I had seen in cowboy movies how to take care of a girl in distress, and I did the same. She had several cuts on her hands and knees, and one gash on her forehead. She grabbed me by the neck as I lifted her and carried her out of the trees. I laid her on the soft grass on the side of the path, and tended to her cuts with my handkerchief.

But I soon realized that this was beyond my skills. So I carried her as best I could to the house where Mémé Louise applied mercurochrome and band aids. Aline worried about the bicycles as her father may drive his tractor by and see her bicycle in the bushes and mine in the middle of the path. Before my grandmother could take care of my cuts, I went and retrieved both bicycles, which had not suffered much except for off centered handlebars—an easy repair. While my grandmother went to get a pail of water to clean my knees and hands, Aline said "you were so nice to me" and wincing as she jumped off her chair, she kissed me on the lips, like in the movies. Aline had difficulty walking as I accompanied her back to her father's farm. We both had agreed that it would be a bad idea to talk about any race, and especially to tell why we were racing. After we crossed the Départementale, Aline had said, "You know, we don't need to race to kiss, you can kiss me anytime". I was in heaven. We found her father and I told him that we were riding side by side when I had lost my balance because of a rock in the middle of the path, and we had both fallen, with the results he presently saw. He was not cross with Aline, but it also was obvious from the shape of her knees that it would be a couple of days before she could ride again. He told me to come and meet with her at the house and we could go for a walk until she got better. He recommended we be more careful in the future, and he went to milk the cows. As I left the house, Aline kissed me again. I guess this is how Aline became my girlfriend!

As for me, band aids or not, I had to go to Ambazac the next day, and I had to ride to Les Loges to visit with Noëlle. I pretended I was in the Tour de France, an injured rider, determined not to let pain and adversity get the better of me. It was in the climb to the Tourmalet, the yellow jersey was within reach, and I had to surpass the pain to conquer it. I passed Bahamontes in the last meters, and...I was in Ambazac. The return trip was a bit more painful. Like Aline, I should have been off the bicycle, but in the tradition of the best Tour de France champions, I was not going to let a small injury get in the way of victory. I was in the process of giving an interview to the radio when the ambulance passed me.

I dropped off my load in Card. My grandmother insisted to wash my wounds as she called them, and with new band aids on my knees and elbow I rode to Les Loges. I had never imagined that the ambulance was going there, but when I arrived Noëlle's grandmother was being loaded in the ambulance. The doctor had visited in the morning and had decided that she could not be taken care of in her house. Upon returning to his office, he had called the ambulance to carry the woman to the hospital in Limoges. The lady was refusing to go, saying that she would rather die right there and then than go to Limoges. But the truth was that she no longer had the energy to fight. The reason the transfer to the ambulance was taking so long is that the ambulance crew and Marie were in the middle of a heated argument about what to do. Marie wanted her grandmother to stay because she would surely die in the hospital, and she would be away from her loved ones as they had no means to get to Limoges. The ambulance driver stated that if she stayed at home she would surely die and he had orders from the doctor. The old lady found the force to yell "Screw the doctor!" The ambulance crew gave up and carted her back into the house. This was the first time I was invited in. It was dark and sad, with the girls' mother sitting in an armchair, prostate, and oblivious to what was going on. The grandmother was brought back to her bed upstairs through the narrow staircase. Once the crew had left, and she was re-arranged on her bed, she called for me. I hesitantly went upstairs and entered the bedroom on the left. She was lying in the middle of a big French country bed made of cherry tree wood, on fresh white linen, exhausted from the incident. She could hardly keep her breathing under control. She started in a low voice, which I had to lean over to hear: "The girls tell me that you have been getting my medicine for me. I want to thank you. I don't have much to live, and people have not been very nice to us here. I want you to stay friends with Noëlle: she is going to need a friend when I die. You look like a fine boy. Go now!" I left her room. In the kitchen below, the mother had not moved, and Noëlle was outside waiting for me. We walked to the arbor, and that's when she noticed that my right knee was bleeding yet again. She could not believe that I had ridden to Ambazac for the medicine, even after I was hurt. She hugged me and kissed me. She was so delighted to have me as a friend.

That afternoon I went for a walk with Aline, and told her what the old lady had told me. Now it was my turn to experience my eyes fill with tears. Try as I may, I could not keep from crying. It was the first time I had actually seen someone who was about to die. Aline took me in her arms and wiped my tears with her blouse. She said that she had seen her grandmother die, and it was not a big deal, except that you are really really sad afterwards. We both still had to truly figure out about death. She told me that people who die go to heaven, and I told her that sounded nice, although I did not believe that this could help people with their sadness.

    I had another discovery to make in these closing days of August. Hunting season was upon us, and I wanted to participate. Le Père Marzet had told me he would take me with him, but that was back in early July when I had spent most of my time with him. Now that I had neglected him to be with Aline and Noëlle, I was wondering whether he would take me with him still. I approached him the next morning, and he said he had to get the dog, Fidèle, trained, taking him to the woods and getting him used again to walking around the woods without getting spooked at every thing that lay on the forest floor. He said this would happen later that afternoon at the same time he took the cows to pasture, and I was welcome to join him. I asked him if Aline could join us, since she still could not ride, and he reluctantly agreed, yet telling me that hunting was not a woman's job. I listened to him, but I had to silently disagree. In my history classes I had learned about the famous French women who had saved France, and I could not fathom how shooting a rabbit was beyond their capabilities. I had learned that Joan of Arc had single-handedly led France to victory against England when the big moron of a king was too stupid and cowardly to do so; I had read how Jeanne Laisné had led the women of Beauvais in repulsing the attack of the Burgundian troops in 1472, and how this had saved France from becoming a province of Burgundy; and I had been mesmerized by the story of Charlotte Cordet who had brought the years of the Terror to an end during the French Revolution by assassinating the tyrant Marat. I was not going to argue my points with le Père Marzet, but I did know I was right. We gathered the cows and the dog and went on our way with Aline. We had almost reached the pasture, actually le Père Marzet was opening the gates to let the cows in, when we heard the yapping and the barking of the dog. He came running to us, almost knocking over le Père Marzet. The dog had been exploring the chestnut tree woods, and le Père Marzet dismissed him at first, thinking he had been spooked, while taking care of the cows. But as the dog whined and laid on the ground he noticed that his snout was swelling. As he looked closer, he saw the two teeth bite mark of a viper. Le Père Marzet had to do something immediately or the dog would die. Now, he was happy that Aline had come. We left Aline to watch the cows, while he instructed me to run back to Card with two sets of instructions: if Alice was not home, I had to go to the closet in the cellar staircase, and on the first shelf by the door, find the anti-venom serum and ride my bicycle back with it (he gave me the key to the house); if Alice was home I had to do the same thing, except I had to ask her to prepare the injection, since le Père Marzet had never done it. In the meantime, he would pick up the dog and carry him back as fast as he could, as time was of the essence. When I reached Card, the Marzet house was open and I knew Alice was home. I rushed in out of breath and told her Fidèle had been bitten by a viper. She went to the cellar closet, and fetched the anti-venom kit. Instead of letting me ride back with it, she decided to run back with me to meet up with le Père Marzet. We found him about halfway home, and Alice administered the serum. She then had to get the vet to come and examine the dog—since no one had a car, the dog could not be carried there. She jumped on her moped and she was gone to Ambazac, hoping she would find the vet in his office (no one had a telephone either). I then returned to the pasture and watched over the cows with Aline until it was time to lead them back home. By that time the vet had come, had looked at the dog, had decided that the serum had worked properly, and had told le Père Marzet he should not let his dog roam around the woods at this time of year as vipers tried to eat as much as possible before going into hibernation, and were even more aggressive than usual.

CHAPTER 31
The Trip to Auvergne

That July there had been a lot of discussions with my parents about visiting our cousins Nicole and Baptiste in Auvergne. Auvergne is the province of France immediately to the east of Limousin, and the province of the famous volcanoes of Auvergne, those that had created real concern when I had first heard of Limousin. Nicole and Baptiste were our closest cousins in Monaco where they also lived. We were related through Nicole whose father Eugène Spinetta was my grandmother Lainey's brother. Baptiste was a cabinet maker of some renown, and they had two daughters, Chantal and Elise whom I called my cousins as well. Nicole and Baptiste had a hotel in the spa town of La Bourboule in the département of the Puy de Dome, and they ran this hotel during the summer months. La Bourboule benefits from sitting next to the volcano known as Puy de Sancy, and because of the chemical qualities of the underground water has become a thermal and spa town specializing in treating lung and respiratory ailments. By French standards, it is a brand new town without the ancient history one would expect in a province the shield of which is a Roman ensign. It was built in the nineteenth century, and had only one purpose, propose thermal treatment. However Nicole and Baptiste got the hotel they operated I don't know, but they had invited us to go visit and stay with them. I was still concerned by the volcanoes. I did not really understand them and my father had provided absolutely no logical explanation as to why they would not erupt again, and why they would not erupt on the precise day of 17 July 1964 when we were in Auvergne, walking up and down inside their craters.

It was not exactly comforting to hear in the same sentence that the volcanoes were extinct, but that they were active into the last ice age, which was only 14,000 years ago. What was known to pre-historic men had been lost to modern men until the eighteenth century when French people realized that these mountains were indeed volcanoes and not the Alps of Central France, as they called them at that time. Modern technology has established that the Auvergne volcanoes were in fact still active until 8,500 years ago, or may be even 6,500 years for the Pavin volcano, which is now a crater lake. In preparation for this visit, my father had purchased the green Michelin Guide of Auvergne, and each evening, before we left, I had to read about Auvergne, its history and its cities. This guide clearly stated that all of the Auvergne volcanoes were extinct. That was very good news, but even today, activity takes place on a regular basis along the Auvergne fault lines in the form of earthquakes. Recent earthquakes in the region have measured up to a 7 magnitude on the Richter scale, and it is clear as well that the Auvergne mantel is not cooling down. Why so many volcanoes exist in this very spot (France has the largest number of volcanoes in continental Europe) has never been determined satisfactorily, and three theories are considered, none really convincing any of the experts: the first theory advances the existence of a hot spot deep under Auvergne; the second theory believes that the formation of the neighboring Alps weakened the mantle and created the volcanoes; and the third one relies on a model directly related to classic plate tectonics movement. Of all these theories, the second one is more conventionally regarded as the cause of the existence of the Auvergne volcanoes.

In any case, the trip to Auvergne was to be a short drive from Ambazac (barely one hundred miles), but as always, my father made the planning look like we were going to participate in the annual Paris-Dakar automobile race. Since I was older, I was included in the preparations which entailed setting the roof rack on top of the Dauphine, checking the oil, the tire pressure, ensuring the spare tire was in good order, and listening to the engine idle to make sure there was no unusual noise (I was highly qualified to detect unusual noises in an engine, sine the previous year Grand Prix of Monaco, when I had correctly predicted that the number sixteen Ferrari engine was not going to last the entire race). The jack set was tested, in case this simple (and in the case of the Dauphine, primitive) instrument decided not to work, and put back in place, and the tools were inventoried to ascertain we had all of the wrench sizes that could possibly be used in the repair of any Dauphine. I was wondering what my father could fix on the Dauphine, since I had never seen him work on any mechanical device. These pre-road trip checks would have made an Air France pilot look like an amateur. We loaded the trunk, in front of the passenger compartment as you may recall, put a couple suitcases on the roof rack, packed snacks inside the car, and we were on our way! Except that when my father turned the ignition key nothing happened! My father who was not inclined to swear profusely came out with some good ones that morning "Merde de bordel de putain de merde! Quelle connerie de bagnole de merde!" which is basically a non-sensical litany of juxtaposed swear words. Fortunately the car was a standard shift car, and it could be push-started by popping the clutch, a new maneuver for my father, and I was certain a maneuver bound to fail on the first attempt. Of course, he sat in the car while my mother and I got out and pushed the car. Before we could gather enough speed, my father popped the clutch effectively stopping the car and sending him almost flying into the windshield (remember there were still no seatbelts on that car). "Bordel de merde de con!" he yelled as we went for a second round of pushing. Robert Teulier, seeing the scene from his farmhouse, and laughing at the scene of our predicament, came to the rescue, pushing as well, as my father failed to start a third time, and a fourth time. We were running critically short of chemin before we would be on the Départementale. By this point it was Robert Teulier's turn to swear "Putain de merde!" he said in Limousin (I understood these very useful and succinct words), and he told my father to get out and push while he took his seat. On the first attempt the car started, and we were on our way to the Renault Garage in Ambazac instead of the Volcanoes of Auvergne! The garage was on the rue Basse, so we went to visit with Tata Marie while the car was being repaired. It turned out the alternator had gone bad and the battery had been discharged. We had lunch at Tata Marie's and like the drivers in the Le Mans race now had to make up for the time lost in the pits! My father smoked even more than usual as he valiantly tried to catch the competitors ahead of us on the road, and my mother, my brother and I hanged on for our life in our respective seats (my sister was strapped tightly in her baby seat). There was no talking. We did not want to de-focus our driver who was passing Peugeots, Citroëns, Panhards, Simcas and all types of other cars and trucks as if they were standing still. We were certainly making up for lost time. My father had just established the best lap record, passing the Aston-Martin of Salvadori when the race officials flagged him down! I could not believe that we were slowing down and pulling over, but the officials were there on the side of the road in the blue and black uniforms of the Gendarmerie Nationale! "Merde!" this was succinct and to the point. My mother immediately added: "I told you not to drive like a madman!" There was no arguing with the fact that my mother had a much higher regard for gendarmes than anybody else I knew, since her grandfather had been one. It turned out that in his bid to regain the lead of the race, my father had disregarded the existence of a portion of the double yellow line, "biting it slightly as he finished his passing maneuver. And there was no car coming the other way," as he explained to the gendarmes. This did not impress them at all. With a hefty ticket added to his wallet, my father commented "Bande de cons", as he drove away. This comment had the double effect of expressing my father's displeasure with a bunch of morons who refused to see his justification in driving slightly over the yellow lines, and triggering the immediate volcanic reaction of my mother "I only see one moron, and it is you for driving that fast! We have three children in the back! If you don't slow down, I am getting out of this car", and she opened the door to step out, ordering me to do the same. This was definitely not a good start. My father had now to simply make sure he finished the race, and he drove conservatively—I guess to save his engine as I had seen the Formula One drivers do in Monaco—and when we finally made it to the finish line in La Bourboule, my parents were still not talking.

My cousin Nicole immediately noticed the problem: "From what I see, I guess the trip was not a success!" My mother kissed her and answered "It would have been a success if we had planned to get a three hundred Francs ticket!" Baptiste commiserated with my father that wives never fully support their husbands when they need it the most. And yes, gendarmes were all morons who blindly applied rules instead of using common sense when the infraction did not endanger anyone's life. By the time the evening was over, Nicole and Baptiste were no longer talking either. But I was having a good time with my cousin Chantal.

The next day my parents were talking to each other again—this was a miracle to me, and it was long before I would find out about make-up sex. With this settled, we could be in route to see the various volcanoes. We started with the Puy de Sancy, since it was the closest volcano to where we were staying. I was impressed by the size of the mountain which is actually the core of the old volcano. I tried to imagine how big it was when it had been active, and realized how lucky we were to live in the quaternary age. The Puy de Sancy would always remain a special place: the first volcano I ever climbed, and even in the dead of summer, it was a cold and windy place. I would go back to the Puy de Sancy a few years later, and would be engulfed in a sudden rise of fog and clouds that would remove all visibility and force me to sit down on the path and wait for hours before the clouds lifted again and it was safe to return to La Bourboule. But this volcano did not show the typical cone shape that I had seen on postcards and on travel brochures and these were the volcanoes I wanted to see. I picked up a couple of rocks, which I called lava, and found out later had the scientific name of trachyte. As we went back to the hotel that evening, I realized with stupefaction that my cousin Chantal was not in the least interested in volcanoes and did not even know that all of Auvergne was nothing but volcanoes. We had a fun time with our cousins. Nicole was always ready to party and to organize fantastic meals out of nothing. She would say "If there is enough food for six people, there is enough food for seven!" In that, she was the first sophist I ever met, making seemingly logical statements that were anything but. She would continue, "And if there is enough food for seven, there is enough for eight!" I pointed out to her that this could not possibly be true, but she had Baptiste explain to me that it was absolutely and undeniably correct. It made as little sense as Zeno of Elea's paradox according to which a fast runner cannot catch up with and pass a slow turtle because the runner must first reach the point from where the turtle started, so that the slower turtle will always hold a lead. Nicole had another paradox that would have thrilled my friend Zeno. When she did not spend money on something she might have bought, she would say: "Two hundred francs I did not spend, plus two hundred francs I saved, I made four hundred francs not buying that dress." It made no sense to me, but I knew that Aristotle might have argued she was right. To me, she just talked silly, and it was truly entertaining to see her argue her point to skeptical listeners, including some of her customers staying at the hotel.

Based on her reasoning, her inviting us to stay at the Pension was costing her a fortune, and I figured her welcome was even more generous than I had thought when I realized that we were occupying two rooms for five nights at two hundred and fifty francs a night. As she would have said "Two thousand five hundred francs I did not make and two thousand five hundred francs I did not save", our stay was costing her five thousand francs! Our trip continued with he climb of the Puy de Dome, the road of which is famous for having been included in the Tour de France on multiple occasions, and from its summit, I could distinctly see the Puy Pariou, the most beautiful of all Auvergne volcanoes, with its perfect conical shape, and its slopes covered with a dark green grass. We also discovered the Lac Pavin inside the crater of the same name, and reflected that this was the youngest volcano of the chain. The most captivating part of the trip came when my father decided to challenge a bull that was standing in the middle of the path as we were walking down from the Puy Pariou. The bull was grazing clearly intending not to give way and immediately looked menacingly at my father who was wearing a red sweater. My mother and I had led my sister and my brother on a short detour around the animal, and my father had ridiculed us, telling us that this was only a bull and that he should move from the path. Again, I had been around cows for four summers by then, and I had never seen my father pet one, even less a bull. I knew trouble was around the corner. As he bravely advanced, the bull turned around, and without warning charged my intrepid father. He realized his mistake and started running—unfortunately uphill. The bull, like in the run of the bulls in Pamplona, lowered his head and when he lifted it again, my father was literally sitting on it. Projected in the air, my father fell back on the down slope of the volcano, and rolled down several tens of feet before he could stop. That had all of us folded in half in laughter, to include some other tourists, except my mother, who did not think this was funny at all. She simply turned around, humiliated by the scene, and pretended not to know my father who limped back to the car, as best he could. He announced proudly that "You see, I made him move out of the way!" The return trip to Card was a lot less eventful than the trip to Auvergne. I would have surmised from the way my father drove that he had retired from racing, and he was a lot more careful with and respectful of the yellow lines.

CHAPTER 32
Tonton Gilbert Comes to Card

My mother had family in the North of France. This came as a complete surprise—just like the discovery that I had family in Limousin. One day I heard her speak about her uncle Gilbert and her aunt Emilienne, and the next day they were sitting in our living room in Monaco. And they lived as far north in France as you can get. Five more miles from their house, and it was Belgium! Tonton Gilbert was my grandfather Lainey's brother. With their other brother Jean, they were the three Lainey brothers. Jean Lainey owned the famous pastry shop "Le Gateau des Rois" in Hénin-Liétard, a few miles away from where Tonton Gilbert lived. Tonton Gilbert had been borderline juvenile delinquent in his younger days. His father the gendarme had found a job for him in the city of Nice, through a business owner whom he knew. So, every morning, Gilbert (who lived with his parents) would leave home to go to work at the patisserie this person owned. A few months later my great-grandfather had met the owner in the street, and had asked him how his son was doing. The owner had been completely taken by surprise by the question "You son? Gilbert? He never even showed up for the first day of work!" Now it was my great-grandfather to be taken by surprise. It turned out that Gilbert had pretended to go to work every morning for at least three months but had preferred to go for drinks with his friends. Where he got the money that he brought home for three months, Gilbert would never say. After all, his father was a gendarme! During the Second World War, Gilbert was drafted by the Germans in the STO. The STO, or Service du Travail Obligatoire, was a German program of French workers deportation to support the war effort of Germany. With the complicity of the French Vichy government, Germany requisitioned 650,000 workers who lived in work camps in Germany. The Germans also conned young men to join the STO under the false pretense that their doing so would secure the liberation of a French prisoner of war who might be their father or older brother. Gilbert did not have much say in being drafted into the STO. The French police, which had been renamed "Milice" or militia, showed up at his house one early morning, gave him thirty minutes to get ready, and he was en route to the Ruhr industrial area. That day, he also left behind his fiancée, Thérèse. Upon his release from Germany, instead of going home, Gilbert took the first train he could find for Marseille, and went to the Fort Saint-Jean to join the French Foreign Legion. This was a tradition in the Lainey family. The family was from Lorraine, a province whose ownership was constantly disputed between France and Germany. And several relatives had joined the Foreign Legion rather than be drafted in the German Army. On a wintry day of early 1945, Gilbert Lainey became Légionnaire Lambert, hometown Montigny-lez-Lens, Belgium, making himself a Belgian citizen so that he could get the enlistment bonus (French citizens did not get an enlistment bonus at that time, because they were expected to serve in the Army regardless). Seven years later, after being wounded in Indochina, Légionnaire Lainey came home. He had been gone for a full ten years and had never written a letter home. During that time, his brother Jean who had been one of the evacuees at Dunkerque had worked with the London Free French and had taken part in the liberation of France. He had returned home, found Thérèse attractive and no longer tied up by any promises. She had been his brother's fiancée, but when Gilbert had failed to show up with the last prisoners coming back from Germany, she had accepted Jean's marriage proposal. When Gilbert saw that his brother had married Thérèse, he had no problem with that. He knew her sister, Emilienne and the two became a couple, living together but never marrying.

Emilienne as well her sisters (she had a two more sisters) were tough girls from Northern France, a country of coal mines which reeked of coal smell, and a place that was permanently enveloped in a coal dust cloud. She ran a vegetable stand on the public markets, getting up a four in the morning to buy her vegetables and fruits from the wholesalers in Lille, driving her dark green Hotchkiss truck all over the countryside, setting up her stand, selling all morning, packing up, parking the truck in the garage not far from her house, and starting over the next day, while Gilbert worked in a chemical plant in Lens, thanks to the skills he had acquired in Germany. So, one day they showed up at the Maison Risani, where we lived. I have no independent recollection of this visit. It must have been a lot of fun, because I am in pictures with all of the guests and hosts smiling and laughing. This was not a Faure family reunion, and there was a distinct difference between Faure and Lainey family reunions: the Laineys did not end up in a pugilistic contest. The pictures bear the date August 1955, that's the only reason I cannot dispute meeting Tonton Gilbert and Emilienne (since she was not married to Gilbert, we never gave her the official title of Tata) before they came to Limousin to visit with us. My mother liked her uncle Gilbert a lot. Therefore once the work on the Card house was done (electricity, toilet, and general upkeep of the house) it was logical that Tonton Gilbert be invited. We sent them the instructions on how to get to Ambazac and from Ambazac to Card—there was no Internet, Mapquest, or Google Earth at that time for people to find where you lived. We were expecting Tonton Gilbert and Emilienne on a Tuesday night for supper. So we waited for the Citroën 2CV driven by Emilienne (Gilbert did not drive) to show up at any time. We waited till supper, and no one showed up. Finally we ate, and no one showed up. And we went to bed, and no one had showed up. The next day was an absolutely glorious sunny summer day. Since I knew everybody, and every path and road in the region, my mother asked me to get on my bicycle and ride around to see if I saw a Citroën 2CV parked someplace in the neighborhood. My mother concluded that they had gotten lost, but that their car would be easy to spot because it had the famous two identifying digits on their license plate, and theirs was 62, while every car around was 87. I rode to Ambazac, and the first car I saw when I reached the church square was a 2CV with a 62 license plate. I went straight to the café, and there were Tonton Gilbert, Emilienne and her sister Jeanne having breakfast! They had spent the night at the Hotel de France, incapable of finding Card. They had asked people and no one knew of the Faure family. By that time Tata Marie's épicerie had been closed a while (she had retired) and they could not find her new house either.

Leading the way on my bicycle, I rode in front of the 2CV like Anquetil in front of his team car during the Tour de France time trials. I had to put in the performance of my life. I zoomed down the downhills as fast as I could pedal, climbed the hills standing on the pedals off the seat, knowing that my imaginary team manager was behind me, encouraging me, and ready to give me a new bicycle if I had a flat. In record time, I turned onto our chemin, past Robert Teulier's house and reached our front door. Tonton Gilbert could not believe it. He said "We were here last night! The guy at the first house was in his front yard [he was talking about Robert Teulier] and we asked if this is where the Faures lived. He told us he had never heard of the Faures!" My father laughed, and told Gilbert "Not only does he know our family, he is our cousin!" "Ah le con!" was all Gilbert could answer. He wanted to go and confront Robert Teulier on the spot. It took all of my mother's persuasion to avoid this one-sided confrontation. At over six feet, and with years of experience in the Legion, Gilbert was a formidable man. He was especially upset that they had to stay in a hotel, and a lousy one at that, when they had been within a hundred fifty feet of our house. That evening we had Robert Teulier over for a drink—he could not remember Gilbert, the 2CV, or being asked for instructions. After he left, my father commented that it was the beginning of the end, that Robert Teulier could not resist a bottle of red wine. That was gossip, because Robert Teulier told me later that he remembered perfectly the incident. He was simply protecting us and our privacy. He said "I had never seen this guy before. He drives up with a plate that's not from around here, I would not tell him anything." And looking at me straight in the eyes, he added "I would expect you to do the same thing fro me!" Tonton Gilbert, unlike le Père Marzet, did not like to speak about the war, his years in the Legion, or Indochina, where he had spent his entire tour of duty. Emilienne was a strong lady, with a piercing voice, a heart of gold, who spoke Chtimi, the patois of northern France, which was absolutely impossible to understand. When she spoke it with her sister and Gilbert, the people from Limousin were amazed that they were actually French. During her stay Emilienne wanted to visit the public markets to see how the stands were set up and if she could get some ideas to improve hers. We first stopped in Ambazac, but then drove to Limoges to the Marché Couvert (the indoor public market). There, Emilienne and our group went around evaluating and rating the fruit and vegetable displays. But the best treat was lunch, when my father treated us all to the Limousin Crêpes at the restaurant inside the Marché. They were made of buckwheat and were served with cheese, ham, eggs, or boudin (blood pudding). They were the best my father said, and I had to agree with him, especially when I got my dessert crêpe stuffed with chestnut jam and crème fraiche!

CHAPTER 33
Noëlle Vanishes

Rain was always a hindrance to my activities and to my social visits at Card. For some reason my mother thought rain was dangerous to my health and I was supposed to stay indoors or play in the disaffected stable the moment it started raining. My mother had thereby instituted another rule that Mémé Louise was supposed to enforce, and that was to keep me inside when it rained. This was not going to happen. Since it was fine for me to get drenched to get the groceries in the morning, I reasoned it should be fine for me to get drenched to do whatever I wanted to do the rest of the day. Monsieur Lemaunier did not have such a rule for Aline, and I for sure was not going to embarrass myself by revealing the existence of such puerile thinking at my house. I went about my routine, riding to Ambazac, getting the groceries—I was riding faster and faster—and going to Les Loges to visit Noëlle. By the time I got there I was completely soaked, and she had me go in the house and sit in front of the fire. I removed my shirt and she gave me a towel so that I dry myself. She went to her room and got one of her shirts for me to wear and we sat by the hot fire. Her mother was in the room, but it made little difference since the woman had not addressed me or given any indication that she knew I was in the room. I entertained her with stories of Monaco, making it sound even more exciting than it was. I told her how the race cars would go back to the garages around town after the practice sessions. One day, as I was going home, the mechanics had decided to take a break and have a drink at a local café. They had parked the four Ferrari racers in front of the café, by the curb, as if they had been regular cars...Noëlle had been kept inside all of her life, like me on a rainy day. The difference was that it was a lot easier for me to disregard the rules than for her to have a regular life. I was sad for her, and I wondered if I should not paint such a beautiful picture of Monaco, of things outside her house. She was already a tormented person, simply because she came from the Café at Les Loges. When she had attended the school in Ambazac, she had had to go on foot (there were no school buses in France), and when she got there other kids would torment her, pull her hair, throw things at her, spill the dark purple ink used on every desk on her hair, and beat her up. She had given up going at all. I could not believe that this had happened. She told me I was the first person whom she had met and who actually like her hair, who had touched it in wonderment rather than to pull it out of her head. She would not venture away from the house any longer, and she had no opportunity to learn because they had no interface with anyone. This is when I proposed to be her teacher. There were ten days left in my vacation, and I would be her teacher. We dug up paper and pencil, and I started by asking her what she wanted to study. She wanted to make sure she could read properly. There was not a single book in the house. This is when my grandmother's demand that I should learn the Fables de la Fontaine came in handy. I wrote down the Crow and the Fox, and had her read it. She was amazed that I could remember so much. It turned out her reading was hesitant, so we spent the following days improving that. I collected books from the house in Card, from Aline, and from Tata Marie, so that before I left for Monaco, Noëlle would have a small collection of about thirty books to read during the winter. This is when I asked her if she knew how to ride a bicycle, and she said she didn't. I held her up as she hesitantly got on mine in her backyard and learned how to ride. Next on the list of things to learn was arithmetic. I also noticed that Marie was slowly integrating our learning sessions, and I decided that maybe I should become a teacher.

The following day was the opening day of hunting season, and in the evening le Père Marzet taught me how to disassemble, clean and oil a shot gun, as he and Robert were busy cleaning their weapons. They had promised to take me hunting with them, but when I asked them if Aline could come with me, they absolutely refused saying that this was not a woman's activity. At five in the morning the next day we were on our way, and we made for La Châtaignerée, this expanse of chestnut tree woods that formed the largest parcel of woods in Card and regrouped the land owned by my grandmother, Roussel, and le Père Marzet. The dog was let go to find the rabbits, but we were ready in case he raised a sanglier instead. We did not see much wildlife that morning and I was rather disappointed to only see a small rabbit scamper out, which neither le Père Marzet nor Robert judged worthy of a shot. If this was hunting, it certainly was not for me. When I reported our failure to Tonton François, he laughed, declaring "They don't know where to go! They should go to the Camp de César! Of course, most of the land there belongs to Lemaunier and he does not want anybody to hunt on his land..." So it was that I understood why le Père Marzet had not wanted Aline to join us on any expedition. Tata Marie had given me a package to deliver to cousin Hortense on the way back, and I had to stop there. Cousin Hortense lived alone in a small but well proportioned stone house a little off the street. This allowed her to have a courtyard in the middle of which grew a big horse chestnut tree. But cousin Hortense's house was not very exciting. It smelled of moth balls, and sometimes the smell was strong enough to make me cough. I never knew how Hortense was related to us, but her house was a bit overwhelming. In addition, cousin Hortense liked to touch me, and I was not too keen on that. She never did anything inappropriate, but she just liked to hold me, to take care of me, to give me drinks, and she and I did not have anything to talk about. I found her to be an utterly annoying person. She always insisted on giving me a little glass of Marie-Brizard, a sweet anise liquor, that she enjoyed drinking. I tried to avoid by any means the glass of the nauseating liquid, but I simply could not outsmart Hortense, and I was stuck drinking the infamous liquor. That morning was no exception, as I delivered the package from Tata Marie to Hortense. Hortense, of course, wanted to give me flowers for the house in Card. She was indeed a remarkable gardener and she tended to a beautiful garden, which unlike all of the other gardens I had visited thus far, was purely dedicated to flowers. In these closing days of August, she had an explosion of dahlias in her garden: white water-lily dahlias, purple single-flowered ones, decorative and ball dahlias of all colors, white, mauve and bright-yellow pompon dahlias, red and pink cactus dahlias, and all colors of the fine fimbriated or carnation dahlias. She cut the flowers with over long stems and I was soon buried under them. Once this was done, we went to the kitchen, she made a huge bunch of them, selecting only the best ones, and I was on my way to the house with the dahlias tied up on my bicycle carrier. I never had such a big load, and there was no way I could take the shortcut because I would have lost the flowers. When I finally got to the house, Mémé Louise was delighted by the gift of flowers from cousin Hortense, so I had the honor of going back to Ambazac with a thank you gift that my grandmother had kept for an occasion just like that. It was a bottle of wax sealed wine, a limited artisan production of Burgundy wine that bore the mark of the winemaker and unlike the regular production was hand sealed with wax. I was given two instructions: one, do not break the bottle; two, if you are invited stay there for lunch. Stay there for lunch? You must be kidding. I could not possibly eat there. I rode with care, making sure the bottle arrived in one piece. To my great relief, cousin Hortense did not invite me for lunch, which meant I could now rush to Les Loges and see Noëlle. I could stay there over lunch and my grandmother would not be concerned that I had not shown up for lunch. I rode with great anticipation. But when I got there, the house was locked up, there was nobody to talk to or to inquire about the whereabouts of its occupants. I figured that the grandmother had been taken to the hospital and that everybody had gone with her to Limoges. Since Limoges was a big trip at the time, I did not expect them to come back before the evening. I rode there just before dinner, after dropping off Aline, and there were no lights, or any sign of life. The house was still locked, just as it had been at noon time, and through the window I could see one of the books I had given Noëlle, lying on the table. The next day, it was the same, and the day after, and the day after. I only rode out to the house once a day now, and I lost hope that I would see Noëlle again before I left for Monaco. I was devastated. It was Ulysses reversed. Circe had left, and Ulysses was dumbfounded. The day I had to take the train to return to Monaco, I picked up a bunch of flowers, put them in a vase and rode to Les Loges with the vase in my hand. I knocked at the door a last time. But there was no answer that day either and I could see through the window that nobody had been in the house, because not a single object had been moved. I set the vase on the back step by the door, then I went to the arbor, and I simply sobbed until I could not stay any longer because I had to get back, get in the taxi and leave. It turned out that the day I taught Noëlle how to ride a bicycle was also the last day I would ever see her. She and her family had simply vanished, and I would never find out why or where she had gone. The following year when I went back to Les Loges, I found the remnants of the vase, broken at the bottom corner of the stairs, probably toppled over by the winter winds. This told me that they had not been back. Over the following years the house would fall into disrepair, the windows broken, the roof caving in, and trees starting to grow from inside the house. For years, every time I rode by, my heart ached, for Noëlle had been the first improbable passion of my young life.

To add to my misery, it was also time to say goodbye to Aline, who was going back to Paris a few days before me. Vacation was over, and Card which had been a magic place suddenly became the empty shell of a remote hamlet where I could find only sadness, melancholy, and the painful memory of the good times Aline and I had enjoyed. I rode my bicycle to all of the places where Aline and I had had so much fun, including the corner where we had both crashed. She had cried when I had said goodbye, and I had as well. She had given me a last kiss, and had ridden home without finding the courage to look back and wave. I had ridden into the woods and hid until I could stop crying. That evening my grandmother tried to lift my spirits, but the only thing I could do was watch my tears roll down my cheeks and fall in my soup. I could not eat, and I went to bed where I cried myself to sleep. And this was only the beginning because within two days time I would have to say goodbye to Tata Marie and Tonton François, and then it would be Robert Teulier and finally le Père Marzet. Life was unfair that I should have to be torn apart from all these people and return to horrid Monaco. Even the thought of my grandmother Lainey was not enough to console me, and the scrutiny under which I lived in Monaco compared to the freedom I enjoyed here in Limousin was a major factor of my distress at having to leave.

CHAPTER 34
What Happened to All of Them

Over the course of the forty-five years since I visited Card for the first time, many changes have occurred: the telephone was brought in, running water was installed in all the houses, the chemin was paved, and central heating was installed in most houses. The landscape remains basically unchanged, but fields that had been pastures are now new forests, and the cow path to La Boissarde has been completely overgrown by bramble, heather and blackberry bushes; it is impassable. But time has taken its greatest toll on the many actors who influenced my life so much in these formative years.

Aline Lemaunier—Over the following three or four years after the events of this book, Aline Lemaunier and I spent almost all of our days in Card together. But one year, before I went back to Card for the summer with the anticipation of seeing her again, she wrote and told me that her father had sold the farm, and that she would not go back to Limousin. Aline and I exchanged almost daily letters after that, and we saw each other every time I went to Paris on vacation for Christmas or Easter. We were planning to meet in Monaco in the summer of 1968, as I had convinced my parents I should stay in Monaco and work. This meeting was not to take place as Aline and her mother had a car accident when her mother lost control of her Ford Mustang, not far from Monaco. Neither of them survived. Aline was eighteen.

Mémé Louise retired from the French Post Office and spent her time between Card and Paris. She learned how to drive, and purchased a

Citroën 2CV traveling all over France with it. We visited her many times in Card and in Paris. She continued to climb the seven flights of stairs to her apartment, but moved permanently to Limousin in 1986. She had become a Southerner! One day she suffered a mild stroke while driving her 2CV and crashed. She was hospitalized and had to move to assisted living in a small retirement house called "Les Platanes" in Saint-Martin-Terressus where she stayed until another stroke forced her hospitalization. She died in Limoges in 1989. She was eighty-six.

Tata Marie and Tonton François soon retired to a house they had built in Ambazac on the Route de la Crouzille—this house now belongs to my father. Of their épicerie and wooden clog shop, nothing remains, as the building was leveled to make room for a street. It is sad that there is not a single trace remaining of the place where we had shared so many happy moments. Tonton François died in 1969 at the age of seventy-eight, and Tata Marie in 1984 at the age of eighty-eight. They are buried side by side in the little cemetery in Ambazac.

Tonton Emile of Fondanèche lived on his farm until he died in 1983 at the age of ninety. Tata Marie of Fondanèche broke her leg when she was ninety-five and died the same year in the house where she had been born. The farm was transferred to her grandson Raymond Faure, who modernized it, sold all of the animals except for the cows, and runs one of the most modern farms in Limousin today. Tonton Emile's three children are still alive: Maxime, who is seventy-eight, lives in Ambazac a few hundred feet from the house of Tata Marie. Gustave, who is now seventy-three, lives with his wife Yvette not far from Fondanèche, but has lost much of his mobility, the consequence of a treatment to fight endemic tumors in the back of his eyes. Marcelle lives in Saint-Pardoux in her house, and is now eighty-four.

Marcelle lost her husband André in 2002, when he was eighty-six. Their two sons live in the area. Petit-Louis became a roofer. Unfortunately he fell off a roof, becoming paralyzed on his right side. He never recovered because of the extent of the brain injuries he suffered. Raymond retired from the French postal service, and sadly his wife died of a brain tumor when I was writing this book. She was only fifty-seven.

The Marzets still live in their house in Card. Le Père Marzet died in 1981 at the age of eighty-seven. But his memory is still cherished by Alice and Robert who are both retired. I cannot but think of the days when I knew this World War One hero, when we went walking together in the fields to check if the wheat was ready to be gathered, when we shared an apple under the leaning apple tree, and when we went mushroom hunting. Le Père Marzet taught me everything I know about vegetable gardening, he showed how to take care of animals, but most importantly he shared his values with me. It is these values that I cherish most and which have allowed me to be successful in life. He taught me not to be afraid, to be true to oneself, and to love work. Whatever I became, I owe a great deal to my good friend, le Père Marzet.

The House in Card is still in our family, and is now the property of my brother Philippe.

Robert Teulier died an early death, passing on in 1988 at the young age of sixty-two. His sister Carole now owns the house, but rarely comes to Card. Her husband is also gone, having died in 1988 at the age of sixty-three. I have no idea what happened to Frédéric.

What happened to the other people who were not related, I can only speculate, since I lost track of them, and I never had a chance to see them again. The Roussels retired from farming and moved on. I hope they are still alive, someplace in Limousin. The Père Christophe and Mother Milk are also long gone, having died before the 1960s were over.

I have no idea what happened to the Martins. I know their grandson went on to be a mining engineer, maybe inspired by that visit to the dolmen in La Jonchère.

Only two houses are permanently occupied in Card: the Marzets' and the house of the Père Christophe which is now the property of a Portuguese couple. There is no longer any concern about the wells going dry since town water connection was made a few years back.

Le Camp de César has been completely disfigured. Sometime in the early 1980s, the trees were cut for lumber, baring the land, and new fir-tree saplings were planted. There are no longer any chestnut trees, no mushrooms will ever grow there again in my lifetime (chanterelles and porcini do not grow under conifers), and the little creek with its sandy bottom is a muddy mess in the full blast of the sun, and actively participates in the erosion of the mountain. There is no swimming in it these days.

Tonton Gilbert and Emilienne retired and lived in their little house in Montigny-les-Lens until Emilienne died in 1991. Gilbert remained there for a few years, but then decided to move south as well, to the city of Menton, near the French-Italian border. Aware that he was losing his short term memory, he placed himself in a retirement home where he is living, the last of the three Lainey brothers. He is eighty-five years old.

Cousins Baptiste and Nicole eventually sold the Pension and built an absolutely gorgeous house overlooking Monaco, where we had many a dinner party during our visits with them. I lost track of my two cousins Chantal and Elise. Baptiste suffered a severe stroke in 2005 and he was reduced to spending the rest of his life in a wheelchair. He also died as I was writing this book at the age of seventy-five.

The Deschamps family disappeared from our life—I have no idea what happened to them.

The house in Les Loges was somehow sold, probably at a public auction, and has been repaired to make it usable.

The Alsacienne cookies brand disappeared in 1994, and the Tobler chocolate brand only survives through Toblerone.

There are no longer any Panhard or Simca cars, and my uncle Adrien mourned the passing of Panhard, swearing never to buy another brand and to drive his to the end. And he kept his word.

Our family in Limousin is no longer as big as it used to. Many of the cousins did not have any children, and every year as we arrived for out vacation there were less and less visits to be made. My father was an only child, so I had no uncles or aunts, and no cousins. Soon I was spending my summers in England or Germany as I was perfecting my language skills, or simply stayed in Monaco to enjoy summer with my friends, and I lost more contacts with the Limousin family. When I was staying in Card as a child, I dreaded these family visits, especially the visits to the Quatre-Vents, but know that they are all gone, I look back and wish they were all still there so that I could visit and feel the same sense of belonging to this beautiful land, Limousin.

To find out more, visit http://www.asummerinlimousin.com/

Printed in the United Kingdom
by Lightning Source UK Ltd.
125092UK00001B/265/A